"Malone is a macho jerk!"

Cleo told her neighbor. "But if he wasn't a cop, and if he didn't think I'd pushed my ex-husband off a tall building, I might think he was…relatively handsome." Gorgeous, actually, if only his dark eyes hadn't been so tired. "But the man has a serious testosterone problem," she added defensively.

"Okay, on the Barney Fife–Bruce Willis scale of masculinity, where does this cop fit?"

Cleo sighed but didn't hesitate. "Fifteen."

* * *

Praise from *New York Times* bestselling author Linda Howard

"Damn, this book is good! I loved it. I fell so in love with Luther, it's ridiculous."

Dear Reader,

They say that March comes in like a lion, and we've got six fabulous books to help you start this month off with a bang. Ruth Langan's popular series, THE LASSITER LAW, continues with *Banning's Woman*. This time it's the Banning sister, a freshman congresswoman, whose life is in danger. And to the rescue… handsome police officer Christopher Banning, who's vowed to get Mary Bren out of a stalker's clutches—and *into* his arms.

ROMANCING THE CROWN continues with Marie Ferrarella's *The Disenchanted Duke,* in which a handsome private investigator—with a strangely royal bearing—engages in a spirited battle with a beautiful bounty hunter to locate the missing crown prince. And in Linda Winstead Jones's *Capturing Cleo,* a wary detective investigating a murder decides to close in on the prime suspect—the dead man's sultry and seductive ex-wife—by pursuing her romantically. Only problem is, where does the investigation end and romance begin? Beverly Bird continues our LONE STAR COUNTRY CLUB series with *In the Line of Fire*, in which a policewoman investigating the country club explosion must team up with an ex-mobster who makes her pulse race in more ways than one.You won't want to miss RaeAnne Thayne's second book in her OUTLAW HARTES miniseries, *Taming Jesse James,* in which reformed bad-boy-turned-sheriff Jesse James Harte puts his life—not to mention his heart—on the line for lovely schoolteacher Sarah MacKenzie. And finally, in *Keeping Caroline* by Vickie Taylor, a tragedy pushes a man back toward the wife he'd left behind—and the child he never knew he had.

Enjoy all of them! And don't forget to come back next month when the excitement continues in Silhouette Intimate Moments.

Yours,

Leslie J. Wainger
Executive Senior Editor

Please address questions and book requests to:
Silhouette Reader Service
U.S.: 3010 Walden Ave., P.O. Box 1325, Buffalo, NY 14269
Canadian: P.O. Box 609, Fort Erie, Ont. L2A 5X3

Capturing Cleo

LINDA WINSTEAD JONES

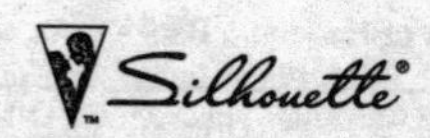

INTIMATE MOMENTS™

Published by Silhouette Books

America's Publisher of Contemporary Romance

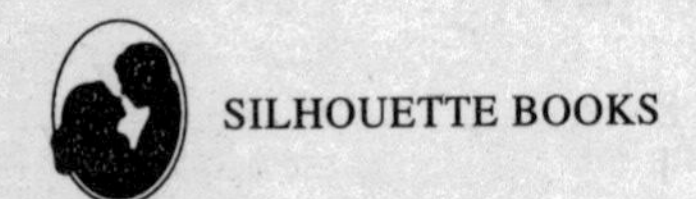

ISBN 0-373-27207-3

CAPTURING CLEO

This edition published by arrangement with Harlequin Books S.A.

Visit Silhouette at www.eHarlequin.com

Printed in U.S.A.

Books by Linda Winstead Jones

Silhouette Intimate Moments

Bridger's Last Stand #924
Every Little Thing #1007
Madigan's Wife #1068
Hot on His Trail #1097
Capturing Cleo #1137

LINDA WINSTEAD JONES

would rather write than do anything else. Since she cannot cook, gave up ironing many years ago and finds cleaning the house a complete waste of time, she has plenty of time to devote to her obsession for writing. Occasionally she's tried to expand her horizons by taking classes. In the past she's taken instruction on yoga, French (a dismal failure), Chinese cooking, cake decorating (food-related classes are always a good choice, even for someone who can't cook), belly dancing (trust me, this was a long time ago) and, of course, creative writing.

She lives in Huntsville, Alabama, with her husband of more years than she's willing to admit and the youngest of their three sons.

She can be reached via www.eharlequin.com or her own Web site www.lindawinsteadjones.com.

Chapter 1

He'd known when the phone started ringing well before sunup that it was going to be a long, bad day. He'd been right. On occasion, he really hated being right. Here it was seventeen hours later, and the day dragged on.

One last stop, and he could call it a night. Luther stepped from his car onto the downtown sidewalk. At this point in his career—in his *life*—nothing should surprise him. Little did. Except the worst and nasty surprises were few and far between. Luther stared at the building before him, wishing someone else had gotten that early morning phone call. He didn't need this. He had a gut-deep feeling this weird case could be full of nasty little surprises.

He was due for a vacation. In fact, he was past due. He had the trip planned, in his head, he just hadn't gotten around to requesting the time off. Two weeks in Florida, sleeping all day and walking the beach at night. The sound of the surf, seafood and bikini-clad women. What else did a man need?

But, no. Instead of those temptingly beautiful things, he

had one dead body, heartburn from a too-quick, too-late barbecue supper, and a craving for a cigarette like he hadn't had in months. He played with the cellophane-wrapped candy in his coat pocket, running a few pieces through his fingers. The candy had helped him quit smoking, but sometimes he felt like he'd traded one addiction for another. The February night air cut through his coat jacket, damp and chilling, making him long for Florida once again.

Detective Luther Malone quit fiddling with the candy in his pocket and stood perfectly still on the sidewalk while he glared at the blue neon sign over the single, shuttered window of the redbrick nightclub in downtown Huntsville: Cleo's. Muted piano music and a woman's voice singing something old and bluesy drifted to his ears. It was the kind of music that would be very easy to go to sleep to, and since he'd been up since 4:00 a.m. he was momentarily tempted. It was now past nine at night, and this really could wait until tomorrow morning. He'd already spent all day filling out paperwork, combing the scene for clues and talking to the victim's hysterical girlfriend and his neighbors. And now this. Yeah, tomorrow would work just fine.

But why put off until tomorrow what you could screw up today? Besides, since this Cleo Tanner was a nightclub owner, the best time to catch her was likely at night. She probably wasn't any more of a morning person than he was.

He threw open the door and stepped inside. The club was small. *Cozy* was a kinder word, and it suited the warm and welcoming place. A long bar stretched along the wall to the left, and a number of small, randomly scattered tables and chairs, half filled even though this was a Monday night, were arranged in a haphazard kind of symmetry. At the rear of the room a small stage rose above the dimly lit crowd. A woman perched on a stool there and sang. He recognized the song now: "I Got It Bad and That Ain't Good." A piano and a piano player shared the stage with the singer, but as he watched and listened, the instrument and the longhaired musician faded into the background, necessary but insignificant.

Luther stared, over heads and past hanging silk ferns, at the singer whose warm, husky voice had captivated the crowd. And him. It wasn't just the voice that fascinated him, it was the whole, luscious package. Damn. Now, *this* was a woman. Grace was always trying to set him up with one sweet thing or another, certain he was not yet past saving, sure that he, too, could be as disgustingly happy as she and Ray were. But she'd never offered up anything like this woman.

Long, wildly curling black hair fell past the singer's shoulders; her lips were red and lush; her eyes slightly slanted and rimmed with dark lashes, giving her an exotic air. She perched on that stool, back straight and yet perfectly relaxed, shapely legs crossed at the knee. The body beneath her slinky black dress was rounded and curved, soft in all the right places and begging to be…

Luther shook off his daze and headed for the bar and the bartender. It really had been a long day.

The surly bartender was an older man—late fifties, early sixties, Luther guessed. He was built like a fireplug, short and solid, and had a thick head of silver-gray hair and a flat face only a mother could love. And he was offended that a potential customer took his attention from the woman on stage. He looked Luther up and down, scowled, and asked what he wanted to drink, in a gruff voice that matched his craggy face.

"Nothing," Luther said. "I need to speak to the owner. Cleo Tanner."

"I know who owns the place," the bartender snapped. "Wait around. She's kinda busy right now. You can talk to her in about twenty minutes."

Annoyed, Luther lifted his jacket to show the fireplug his badge, and to offer a glimpse of the snub-nosed revolver he carried in a shoulder holster. "Tell her Detective Malone from HPD is here and has a few questions for her,'' he said.

The bartender didn't budge. ''I tell you what. You go up on stage and flash that badge and gun at her. Maybe, and I ain't promising anything, that'll get her to end her set early.''

Luther cut his eyes toward the stage. ''That's Cleo Tanner?'' *Surprise.*

''Yep.''

He should've known. Cleo Tanner was a singer, he already knew that. Her one recorded hit, popular almost eight years ago, had been the sappy country love song, ''Come Morning.'' He glanced around the club, taking it all in while he waited. The small crowd was mesmerized, as he had been when he'd first seen her. They ate and drank, and smiled serenely. If she pulled in a good crowd like this on a Monday, the weekends were probably really busy. She was doing all right.

But from what he'd learned today, Cleo Tanner could make a real killing in the business if she went back to using her married name and sang country music. She could pack a much larger place than this and make a small fortune. Hearing her now, watching her, he knew she had the talent and the presence to make something like that work.

Luther took a deep breath. ''Coffee,'' he said, taking a stool and leaning on the bar. ''Black.'' He stared at the singer, but she was as oblivious to his presence as she was to everyone else's. She didn't look at the crowd, she didn't sing to a lover at a table close to the stage. She sang with her eyes fixed above the crowd, a satisfied smile on her face, an evident contentment in her eyes.

She finished the song to enthusiastic applause, and after flashing a small smile she almost immediately went into the next number: ''Someone To Watch Over Me.''

Cleo Tanner was gifted, beautiful and incredibly sexy, but like it or not she was still suspect number one. His day wasn't getting any better.

* * *

Cleo left the stage with a smile on her face. No matter what happened during the day, when she sang everything got better.

"Good set," Eric said, coming up behind her. "How about a late dinner to celebrate?"

Cleo smiled over her shoulder. Eric was a great piano player, he was cute and he was extremely talented, but he was too young for her, and besides...she didn't need any man looking at her this way, with adoring and hopeful eyes and a wicked come-hither smile. Not now. Maybe not ever. "No, thanks."

"One day you'll say yes," he said, shaking a long finger.

"Don't hold your breath, piano man." Their banter was lighthearted, without passion or vigor. But she did wish he would quit asking her out and find a nice girl close to his own age. With his thick, pale brown hair, blue eyes and that baby face, he should have no problem finding willing women. And yet he persisted in asking her out. Seven years wasn't a huge difference, but Eric was such a kid and she was such a jaded old woman. Too jaded for thirty-two, maybe—but there was no going back.

Sometimes she wondered if Eric was the secret admirer who'd been sending her flowers and romantic notes over the past four months. She'd considered it, but really didn't think it was Eric's style. He'd be more likely to show up with flowers in hand, get down on bended knee and expect his due appreciation for the gesture.

She planned to head to her office to catch up on a little paperwork before going home, but Edgar lifted his hand and waved her over to the bar. He looked none too happy, and the tall, dark-haired man leaning against the bar wasn't exactly a ray of sunshine, either.

The man in the black suit was trouble, and she knew it at first glance. He was too tall and stood with his spine too rigid, even as he went for that casual pose against the bar. But it was the way his eyes bored into hers that said *trou-*

ble, the way his mouth thinned. Heavens, he had a hard face. No softness muted the cut of his jaw, the sharpness of his cheekbones and the line of his nose. Sharp or not, he was a very nice-looking man. He was definitely too good-looking to be so openly sour. Men who looked like this, with nicely even features and unbroken noses, solid bodies and killer eyes, smiled and got what they wanted. They didn't do glum the way this guy did.

Another glance, and she knew who he was. *What* he was, anyway. A cop. A tired, cynical, overworked cop, and he was here to see her.

Somehow this was Jack's fault, she knew it. Her ex would do anything in his power to make her life more difficult.

"What's up, Edgar?" she asked, purposely ignoring the cop.

"This detective wants to talk to you," Edgar said, with an apologetic nod of his gray head.

"Malone," the cop said, offering his hand. "Detective Luther Malone."

Cleo ignored the offered hand, and eventually he dropped it. She looked him over, her eyes raking up and down the rumpled black suit, the white shirt, the slightly loosened gray tie. Either Detective Malone had had a very bad day, or he slept in his clothes.

"What can I do for you, Malone?" She imagined, in a split second, a hundred different kinds of grief Jack might've planned for her this time. False charges, wild stories, out-and-out lies. She wondered if she should offer her hands for the cuffs the cop no doubt carried under that suit jacket of his.

The cop leaned slightly toward her, turning those broad shoulders in her direction and bending in and over her. Eyes so dark brown and deep they looked almost black scrutinized her. "Jack Tempest," he said, those eyes locked to hers as if he were waiting for a reaction.

He got one. She surely couldn't hide the fury the mention of her ex-husband's name roused within her. She felt the heat rise in her cheeks, the increase of her heartbeat, the flare of her nostrils. "What has he accused me of this time? Something's missing and I must have it. I've been harassing him, I threatened him, I threatened his latest bimbo." She kept her voice low, but Eric and Edgar were both listening intently. Cleo offered her hands, wrists together and palms up. "So arrest me, Detective Malone. Take me in, lock me up."

Malone didn't make a move for his cuffs. In fact, his only reaction was a slight lift of his finely shaped dark eyebrows. "Maybe we should discuss this in private," he said in a low, calm voice.

"Maybe we should discuss this right here."

He stared at her offered hands, his gaze lingering on her wrists in a way that made her heart beat too fast once again. "Tempest is dead," he said softly, his gaze rising to meet hers as he awaited her reaction.

Cleo dropped her hands, and her knees unexpectedly went weak. "Dead?" she whispered. "How? When?"

The cop glanced around, obviously not comfortable with having this conversation here and now. Edgar and Eric listened in, not even trying to hide their interest, and Lizzy, the regular cocktail waitress who was here six nights a week, was doing her best to sidle closer.

"Late last night," Malone said simply. "And it looks like a homicide."

Eric placed a steady hand on Cleo's shoulder. "That's too bad," he said. "And to think, we were here so late last night, we were probably right here when it happened."

Malone glared over her shoulder, and Eric dropped his hand. "Is that a fact? You were here on a Sunday night? I thought the club was closed on Sunday."

"We were rehearsing," Eric said, and his voice only wavered a little. "Until the sun came up."

Cleo opened her mouth to tell Eric not to lie for her! She understood immediately what he was doing. Everyone who knew her knew how much she hated Jack. She was bound to be a suspect, and he was making sure she had an alibi. But lying would only get him in trouble. Before she could say a word, Edgar spoke up, his gruff voice cutting her off.

"Yep. I was here myself, cleaning and going over the liquor order at first, and then just listening." He gave her a smile that didn't quite work on his wrinkled, bulldog face. "I do dearly love to listen to Cleo sing. She has a voice that will—"

The detective raised a silencing hand. "Now can we talk in private?" he asked, his voice rumbling.

Cleo nodded and turned toward the narrow hall that led to the rest rooms and her office. Her head swam, and she was suddenly and inexplicably dizzy. Dead. Jack was dead. A moment later the cop was there, taking her arm as she led the way. His hand was steady, strong and warm, and she liked it. Annoying as he was, this was the kind of man a woman could lean on. After a moment that lasted just a little too long, she shook his hand off. She didn't lean on anyone anymore.

"I don't need your help to make it down the hallway," she snapped.

"Coulda fooled me," he mumbled.

Dead, she thought again as she opened the door to her office. Somehow she just couldn't picture Jack as being gone. Permanently.

The tiny, square room was dominated by a desk piled high with bills and correspondence, a phone and fax machine, and a couple of old coffee mugs. The chair behind the desk was fat and comfortable and swiveled with a loud *squeak.* The only other place in the room to sit was a battered avocado-green love seat Eric's mother had donated last year when she'd gotten new furniture.

Cleo rounded the desk and plopped into her chair, leaving the cop the sagging love seat. Instead of taking the uncomfortable seat, he propped himself against the edge of her desk and looked down at her. Sitting that way, his jacket gaped open, and she saw the badge on his belt and the shoulder holster housing a snub-nosed revolver.

"I just have a few questions," he said, taking a small notebook from his pocket and snapping it open. "When was the last time you saw Mr. Tempest?"

She hated tilting her head back to look him in the eye, so she stared at his chest, instead. It was a nice, broad chest in a white shirt. Still feeling fuzzy headed, she concentrated on the plain gray tie. "He was in the club last week with his bimbo of the moment," she said, trying to keep her voice sharp.

"A Miss..." He consulted his notebook as if he didn't remember, but she had a feeling this guy never forgot anything. "Rayner. Randi Rayner."

"Randi with an *i,*" Cleo snapped, annoyed that Malone would play games with her. "Bleached hair, implants and the IQ of a chipmunk. Virtually indistinguishable from Jack's never-ending string of women."

Malone flipped his book shut and returned it to his pocket. "She tells me you threatened Jack last week, when they were here."

Cleo's head shot up, and when her eyes met the cold, cynical cop's eyes she shot to her feet so she could look at Malone dead-on. "I did not threaten him. Dammit, the jerk is dead and he's still trying to cause me grief." She laughed, the sound coming out short and harsh. Momentarily, she considered telling him that Eric and Edgar had both lied, that she had been home all night. Alone, unless you counted one overly friendly mutt and a neighbor who had gone home long before Jack must have been killed. She didn't. Such a confession would only get Eric and Edgar in trouble, and she didn't think either of them could handle this guy. She could, though. She could handle anything.

"You haven't told me how Jack died."

"We'll get to that," Malone said calmly.

"Well, when you've finished grilling me, don't forget to

check with a few of his bimbos' husbands, the long list of musicians he cheated, and...and..."

"A lot of people wanted him dead?" Malone asked, again in a voice so calm she wanted to scream.

"Just about everybody he met," she said, trying for the same aura of tranquillity the detective possessed, but falling far short. "I'm surprised he didn't get a bullet in the back a long time ago." Her knees went weak again, so she sank into the chair. It swiveled slightly and squeaked.

"About this threat..." Malone began.

"I didn't threaten him," Cleo said through clenched teeth.

"Something to do with a grapefruit," he said.

Cleo felt her face turn cool and most likely white as a ghost. "That wasn't a threat," she said. "It was a joke."

"A joke?"

"A joke I told on stage," she clarified. "Jack had shown up, stirring up trouble as usual, and...and I was angry. Sometimes I talk to the audience for a few minutes before I start to sing, so when I went on stage I told this joke."

"Share it with me?" Malone asked. It wasn't a question, though, it was an order.

Cleo lifted her eyes and bravely met his dark, intense stare. "If you drop my ex-husband and a grapefruit from the top of the tallest building in Huntsville, which one will hit the ground first?" She paused for effect. "Who cares?"

Malone nodded wisely. She did *not* like that nod.

"I see," he mumbled.

"How did Jack die?" she asked again, a terrible feeling creeping slowly through her body.

"We'll get to that—"

"Tell me," she interrupted.

She knew he was waiting for her reaction. He was judging her, weighing her. "About two o'clock this morning, give or take an hour, your ex-husband went off the roof of the First Heritage Bank building that's under construction four blocks from here."

Cleo felt suddenly dizzy, but she fought the weakness back. What a horrible way to die. Even for Jack.

"It's unclear at this time if he jumped, fell or was pushed, but since the death is suspicious, it's under investigation as a homicide until something comes to light to prove otherwise."

"Jack would never commit suicide," Cleo said softly. "He loved himself too much."

Malone nodded, as if he'd already come to this conclusion.

"But I didn't..." she began. "I hated his guts, that's no secret, but I would never—" She shuddered. "But it is quite a coincidence, that I told that joke and then a few days later..." She hugged her arms, suddenly cold.

"It was no coincidence, Ms. Tanner," Malone said confidently. He stared at her thoughtfully. "You see, Mr. Tempest didn't fall alone."

"What do you mean?" She held her breath. Was someone else she knew dead? Who else had gone off the roof of the tallest building in Huntsville?

"A grapefruit was found beside the body," he said, very matter-of-factly. "That detail has not been made public, so I'd appreciate it if you'd keep it to yourself, for the time being."

"A grapefruit," Cleo said softly.

Malone caught and held her gaze. "A grapefruit."

Chapter 2

Cleo Tanner was no longer suspect number one, which left Luther nowhere. He positively hated being left nowhere. Her alibi was iffy, at best, but it was an alibi with two witnesses.

The shaky alibi wasn't the reason he thought she was innocent. He trusted his instincts, and his hunches were almost always right. Cleo had hated her ex-husband, and once the shock wore off she would not be sorry he was dead. But right now she was shaken. She tried to hide it, but her knees wobbled and her face had gone pale. She had expected something, some kind of trouble, when she'd seen him and recognized him as a cop, but she had not expected the news that her ex-husband was dead. There had been no tears in her fascinating amber eyes, but she hadn't been able to disguise the shaking that had worked its way through her body. Unless she was a damn good actress....

"I don't want you to drive me home," she protested, snatching her arm from his hand.

"I can't let you go off like this," he said sensibly.

"I'm fine," she snapped, walking down the sidewalk and briskly away from him, reaching into her purse for her keys.

For a moment he forgot that she was part of a murder investigation and just...watched. Cleo Tanner was not a slender woman. She had ample hips and breasts that were practically poured into that black dress, and wonderfully shaped long legs beneath the too-short hem. Those legs ended in high-heeled shoes that no human being should be able to walk gracefully in. She definitely shouldn't be able to stalk away from him so confidently, that gentle sway of her hips tantalizing and teasing him this way.

"Fine." He surrendered. "I'll follow you home and make sure you get there all right."

"You will *not* follow me home," she said, glancing over her shoulder with an angry toss of her long black curls.

She turned down a narrow alleyway that led to a small private parking lot. There were just four cars there—hers, Edgar's, Eric's and the barmaid's, he imagined. Keys in hand, she headed for the ruby-red Corvette that was parked beneath a street lamp. It was several years old, but was in excellent shape...and it was, after all, a Corvette.

"Nice car," he said to her back.

"Thanks," she said tersely. "It was Jack's, and it was the only thing I got out of our marriage that had any value to speak of. He hated me for leaving him, but he hated me more for getting custody of the car."

"It'll be all right here overnight. I'll have a patrol car drive by—"

"Thank you, but it's not going to be here overnight," she insisted.

He was tempted to toss the obstinate woman over his shoulder and carry her home that way, but he didn't think she'd stand for it. Still, she was in no condition to drive herself home.

Her hands trembled as she attempted to fit the key into the car door lock. She tried, but it wasn't quite working for her. As the key finally slid into the slot, Luther reached around and placed his hand over hers. She jumped as if she'd been shocked, but he didn't remove his hand. His fingers brushed the veins at her wrist; his body pressed close to hers kept her in place.

"I need to ask you a few more questions, anyway," he said softly. The last thing he wanted to do was scare her. "I'll drive you home, then in the morning I'll pick you up, take you to the station to answer a few questions and then bring you back to your car." This close, he could feel her deep tremble. And more. The softness of her body, the fascinating curves that fit him, somehow. "You're in no shape to drive, Ms. Tanner. It's not safe."

"I'll be fine," she said again.

He slipped his fingers into her palm and confiscated the keys, snaking them easily into his own grasp and lifting them away.

"Hey!" she shouted, spinning on him as he took a step back. "Give me those keys!"

"I'll give them to you when we get to your house," he said, turning his back on her and heading for the alley that would lead to the street and his car. He didn't have to turn to see that she followed. He heard the tempting *click* of her high heels against the asphalt.

"You have no right," she began breathlessly.

"So call a cop," he mumbled, just loud enough for her to hear.

She mumbled herself, something obscene and just short of threatening. Luther smiled. "I'll drop you off, then pick you up in the morning at nine to take you to the station to complete my questioning." Yeah, he still had plenty of questions about Jack Tempest and Cleo Tanner.

Cleo stayed a distance behind him but kept pace, her step

clacking on the walk in a rhythmic way that made him want to turn and watch. He didn't. He led the way to his car and opened the passenger door for her, facing her at last. Man, she was pissed, big time.

But she did slide into the passenger seat, giving him one last glimpse of those terrific legs in the light of a street lamp, as she pulled them in behind her.

He wondered if she'd bolt before he reached his seat and started the car, but she barely moved. As he pulled out of his parking space, she turned to glare at him.

"Ten," she said softly but insistently. "I'm not a morning person."

Cleo slammed the door of her duplex. Slammed it hard enough for that irritating cop to hear from where he sat, calmly watching from the car that idled at the curb.

She tossed the keys he'd taken from her onto the couch, threw her purse to land beside it and kicked off her shoes. How dare he? How *dare* he!

Rambo padded into the living room to welcome her, and Cleo bent to rub the dog's soft head. "Hi, girl," she said. "Did you miss me?"

Rambo, a golden-colored mutt of uncertain origin that was about the size of a bird dog, answered with a low *woof* that sounded suspiciously like a yes.

Cleo was heading for the bedroom to change clothes, when the soft knock sounded on the door.

"What now?" she snapped, spinning around and heading for the front door, Rambo at her heels. "Am I now incapable of finding my way to bed alone?" The very idea of Malone insisting on coming in and helping with that chore made her heart lurch.

She threw open the door, only after putting an unyielding expression of distaste and disgust on her face.

''Jeez,'' a tinny voice said softly. ''What happened to you?''

Syd Wade lived in the other half of the duplex. Cleo considered herself short, at almost five foot four, but Syd barely topped an even five feet. She had a neat head of medium-length very red hair and an almost girlish shape and face. An artist, Syd made her living with a small picture-frame shop, and painted portraits on the side.

''Sorry,'' Cleo said, opening the door wide and shedding the tough expression. She glanced quickly to the street, and saw that Malone was gone. ''I thought you were someone else.''

''Obviously,'' Syd said as she stepped inside and closed the door behind her. ''You're home early, your car's not in the driveway and you're really mad at somebody. Gotta be a man.''

In spite of the disastrous evening, Cleo managed to smile. ''You're so astute.''

Syd knew her way around Cleo's place, and not only because it was a mirror image of her own home. Syd and Cleo had stuck together through thick and thin. They'd shared holidays when neither cared to make the trip home to celebrate with their dysfunctional families: Cleo to Montgomery and Syd to Knoxville. They went to movies together, and commiserated when things went wrong. Cleo couldn't paint and Syd couldn't sing, but they were both artists. They understood one another.

And they talked about men. Cleo had given up. Three years of marriage to Jack was enough to ruin any woman. But Syd, who was a few years younger and had not yet been badly burned, still held out hope for finding that perfect man.

Syd made her way to the kitchen and took two tumblers from the cabinet. She poured juice in each glass and handed one to Cleo as she left the kitchen and made her way to her favorite chair in the living room. "Okay," she said, plopping down and tucking her feet beneath her. "Tell all."

Cleo sat on the couch and leaned back, Rambo at her feet. Her smile was long gone. "Jack's dead."

Syd's eyes got wide, and she leaned forward in her chair. "What happened?"

"He either jumped or fell or was...pushed, from the First Heritage Bank building this morning."

Syd's mouth dropped open. "I heard about that! They didn't give the victim's name, but I saw it on the news when I got home, and there was a small article on the front page of the evening paper. Oh my God, that was Jack?"

Cleo nodded. She got cold again, and shivered. "I hated him," she said. "I really, really hated him. But I used to love him. I was young and stupid," she added, "but..."

"I know." Syd rose from her chair, set her juice on the coffee table and sat beside Cleo, placing a comforting arm around her shoulder. "You probably don't know whether to be mad or sad or happy, and I can't blame you. Jack really did a number on you."

Cleo shook her head. "It's a shock, that's all. I didn't love Jack anymore, hadn't for a very long time, but...but hearing he was dead made me remember a lot of old stuff." She could still remember loving him, or, rather, loving the man she'd thought him to be. That first rush of what she'd thought was love had been so powerful, so beautiful. So false.

She had defied her family for Jack, had run away with him with her head and her heart filled with dreams and hope and love. Within three years he'd managed to kill them all. Heaven help her, she didn't dare to dream anymore.

"No wonder you slammed the door when you got home," Syd said, giving her a friendly squeeze. "Shoot, I thought I'd find the thing off its hinges when I came over to see what was wrong."

"I didn't slam the door on account of Jack," Cleo said, her sadness quickly being replaced with anger. "This…this cop showed up tonight to give me the news, and I swear, I'm pretty sure he thinks I killed Jack."

Syd snorted as she left the couch and returned to her chair, snatching up her juice along the way. "Moron. If he knew you at all—"

"And I am not finished with this guy," Cleo interrupted. "He's coming by tomorrow at ten to take me to the station to finish his interrogation."

"Want me to come with you?" Syd asked, wide-eyed. "I can close the shop for a few hours."

"No thanks. I can handle Malone." *I think.*

"So, this Malone is the man who made you slam your door?"

"He wouldn't let me drive home," Cleo said, looking for confirmation that she'd been right in being incensed. "He said I was too upset and it wasn't safe, and then he took my keys right out of my hand and insisted on bringing me home."

"Oh," Syd crooned, "that actually sounds kind of sweet."

"Sweet?" Cleo took a swig of her own juice. "Malone is not sweet, not at all. He's a…he's a macho jerk."

"Good-looking?"

"Syd!" Cleo shook her head in dismay. "What does that have to do with anything?"

"That's a yes," Syd said, with a small smile.

Cleo shook her head. "All right, if he wasn't a cop, and if he didn't think I'd pushed my ex-husband off a tall building, I might think he was…relatively handsome." *Gorgeous, actually, if only his dark eyes hadn't been so tired.*

"But the man has a serious testosterone problem," she added defensively.

"Too much or not enough?" Syd teased.

"Too much," she muttered.

Syd leaned forward, hands spread wide. "All right. On the Barney Fife-Bruce Willis scale of masculinity, with Barney being one and Bruce being ten, where does this cop fit?"

Cleo sighed but didn't hesitate. "Fifteen."

Syd fell into peals of laughter, and Cleo couldn't help but smile.

"I've got to meet this cop," Syd said as she fell back.

"You do not."

"A fifteen! I'm impressed. I need to judge for myself."

"This from a woman who's looking for a man who will slide along the scale to fit her every whim."

Syd straightened her spine defensively. They'd had this discussion before. "What's wrong with looking for a man who will rub your feet and cook dinner when you need a four, and be a warrior when you want a ten? Or a fifteen," she said, with a waggle of her red eyebrows.

"Nothing," Cleo said, "except that such a man does not exist."

"Of course he does."

Syd was so optimistic, and Cleo had given up on winning this argument long ago. Some things a woman has to learn for herself.

But Cleo would do anything to keep Syd from learning the lesson the way she had.

Last night it had been too dark to see much of anything, but by morning's light Luther got a good look at Cleo Tanner's place. She lived in a neat duplex in an old neighborhood, with tall, ancient oak trees by the curb and bushes growing wildly around the front porch. Those bushes would flower in the spring, he was almost certain. The yard was neat but not precise. There were spots of green in the dormant grass.

It was two minutes after nine when he left his car and made his way to Cleo's front door. He could hope otherwise, but he didn't expect she'd be happy to see him.

Too bad.

He knocked once, then rang the bell. Someone inside the place shuffled, then shouted "Just a minute" in a sleepy, huskily sexy voice that made his innards tighten. Luther smiled, but made sure the smile was gone before the door swung open.

Last night Cleo Tanner had been all vixen: slinky black dress, high heels, red lipstick. This morning she was straight from the bed. Curling black hair going everywhere, lips au naturel, though still lush and enticing. And instead of a slinky black dress she wore a T-shirt that hung to her knees. The T-shirt was purple and had a grinning spread-eagled cat in the middle of it: a paw rested over each breast.

She was yawning, but when she stopped yawning and realized who had awakened her, her golden eyes went wide and she slammed the door in his face.

"You're not supposed to be here until ten!" she shouted through the closed door.

"I said nine," Luther said, leaning against the closed door.

"I said ten!" she said, and then he heard her stomp away.

The door next to Cleo's opened, and a petite redhead wearing jeans and a too-large denim shirt stepped out. She looked him over suspiciously.

"Detective Malone," he said, lifting his jacket to flash his badge.

She was not intimidated. "I figured as much." She mumbled something as she reached tentatively past him to try

Cleo's front door, finding it locked. "Fifteen, huh?" she muttered.

"Fifteen what?"

"Nothing." She circled around him to the mailbox, which hung on the wall not two feet from the front door. In a few of these old neighborhoods, the mailman still came right to the door. The redhead reached behind the mailbox to grab a small magnetic box on the underside. She opened the container and took out a key, using it to unlock Cleo's door.

Luther's urge to smile disappeared. Not only did the woman not have a peephole in her front door, or the common sense to ask who was there when someone knocked, but she stored her spare key in such an obvious place that any self-respecting criminal would find it in a matter of seconds.

The redhead flashed him a small smile and slipped inside. A moment later she was back, holding the door open wide and inviting him in.

"Cleo's in the shower," she said, leading him into the living room. "You're early."

"Actually, I was two minutes late," Luther said, glancing around. The place was as neat and plain on the inside as it was on the outside. Very homey, very feminine. The furniture was mismatched and looked comfortable, and a few odds and ends added color. There was even a vase of red roses on an end table. Something from the boyfriend, he imagined with a frown. Whoever that might be.

While he was contemplating possible suspects for the role of Cleo Tanner's love interest, a big dog padded up to him and sniffed uncertainly.

"Be nice, Rambo," the redhead said, then she fixed a calculating smile on Luther. "I'm Syd Wade," she said. "I live next door."

"Luther Malone," he said, offering his hand. She took it and shook, very briefly.

"I have a picture-frame shop in town. I've Been Framed."

"What?"

"I've Been Framed. That's the name of my shop."

Luther nodded, figuring it would not be nice to tell her he'd never heard of the place.

"And I would love to stay until Cleo gets out of the shower, but I have an order to put together before I open at ten. Since you're a cop, I guess it's okay to leave you here unsupervised."

"I'll be fine."

"And for your information, there's no way Cleo killed that moron she used to be married to," she said defensively.

He agreed with her but wasn't ready to say so aloud, so he just nodded an acknowledgment.

"Behave yourself while you're waiting," she said with a smile. "Or Rambo will get you. She's a real tiger under all that hair and those big brown eyes."

Luther looked down at the dog, whose big, friendly eyes and wagging tail did not jibe with the name Rambo.

Syd left, and Luther sat down on Cleo's couch. Rambo joined him, placing her chin on his knee and looking up with eyes that begged shamelessly for love and attention.

"Okay," he said, scratching behind the dog's ears. He was almost certain Rambo sighed in delight.

No, he didn't think Cleo killed Jack Tempest, but she was definitely involved. The grapefruit was no accident. In fact, it was downright creepy. If he'd thought Tempest had any reason to kill himself, he'd think the man had jumped with the grapefruit in his hand, just to point the finger at Cleo. From what little he'd learned, Tempest had done his very best to make Cleo's life difficult since the divorce.

Stealing the publishing rights to the song she'd written and recorded years ago had only been the beginning. He hadn't exactly let her go after the divorce. He kept turning up, like the proverbial bad penny, wherever she went. She moved, and a few months later he was right behind her. He managed a few unsuccessful musical acts, and a couple that had done fairly well. Surely his business had suffered when he'd given harassing Cleo so much time and attention, but he'd managed to do okay.

He'd tried to ruin her credit by listing her name on his old unpaid debts, causing her all kinds of grief. Whenever she seemed to be doing well, Tempest turned up to throw in a monkey wrench, somehow. He'd gotten her fired from countless singing jobs. He'd harassed her for years, while being very careful not to cross any legal line.

The latest bit was, Tempest was behind a petition to get Cleo's liquor license revoked. Something about being too close to a church, even though the church in question was three blocks away and she'd been in operation there for over two years without a single problem.

Jack Tempest had either loved his ex-wife very much, or hated her beyond all reason. Sometimes it was hard to tell the difference.

"What the hell are you doing here?" she asked, coming into the room and catching him daydreaming with his fingers enmeshed behind Rambo's ears.

Cleo looked too damn good. Hair damp and curly, blue slacks and matching blouse snug, heels high—if not as audaciously high as last night—she was soft, nicely curved and feminine.

"I thought cops were like vampires and had to be *invited* in," she said in a voice that was definitely not soft.

"Your neighbor, Syd, let me in."

Cleo rolled her eyes and mumbled something obscene, and Luther forced back a smile.

"I don't suppose you have any coffee?" he asked.

"No," she said. "I don't drink coffee."

"No wonder you're not a morning person," he said, rising slowly and pushing back the urge to find out if Cleo would growl and sigh if he rubbed behind *her* ears. She'd probably bite his hand off. Changing the subject seemed like a good idea.

"Why didn't you ask who was at the door before you opened it?"

Cleo stared at him, wide-eyed and disbelieving. "I thought you were my neighbor. She often drops by in the morning before she goes to work."

"And why in hell do you keep a key under your mailbox?"

She shook her head. "Sometimes Syd lets Rambo out when I work late, and sometimes I forget my key, and…it's really none of your business where I keep my spare key."

"It's not safe," he argued.

"Who are you," she said. "Keeper of the city? Defender of the weak?"

"Watchdog over the stupid," he added.

Her amber eyes narrowed. "So now I'm stupid."

"No, but keeping your key—"

"I pushed my ex off a tall building *and* I'm stupid." She did as she had last night, offering her hands to him, palms up, wrists together.

His eyes fell to the delicate veins there, to the curve of her wrists and the pale softness of her fingers.

"So cuff me, Malone. Take me in. Arrest me and get this over with."

He leaned in, ever so slightly. Just enough to make Cleo lean back. "Don't tempt me."

Chapter 3

"This is not the police station," Cleo muttered, as Malone pulled his gray sedan to the curb. "As a matter of fact, we're not even close to the police station."

Malone threw open his door and unfolded his long body from the driver's seat, ignoring her statement. He rounded the car and opened her door for her, leaning slightly in. Like it or not, he took her breath away when he moved in close like this.

"The Rocket City Café has better coffee," he said as he offered his hand to assist her from the car. She grudgingly placed her hand in his and stood. "Besides," he added as he released her hand and closed the car door, "you're nervous. The station would just make matters worse."

"I am not nervous," she retorted.

The annoying Detective Malone responded with a brief smile.

The Rocket City Café was a small restaurant with plastic red-and-white checkered tablecloths and a strange collection of patrons. Two old men sat in a corner booth and argued about local politics. A group of elderly women crowded around a table in the center of the room, and from the excited utterances about brownies and bundt cakes, it seemed they were planning a bake sale. A middle-aged waitress in a pink uniform and a white apron leaned against the counter where a No Smoking sign was prominent, and smoked as if she really enjoyed every puff. A very young short-order cook, with his long hair in a hair net, scrubbed the grill behind the counter. He was singing, and not very well.

When the waitress saw Malone she smiled and put her cigarette out in a nearby coffee cup. "Hey, Sugar," she said, with a grin that transformed her face into a mass of wrinkles. "The usual?"

"Yeah, and..." He glanced down at Cleo. "What do you want?"

"Nothing."

"Don't make me eat breakfast in front of you while you sit there and glare at me. Get something to eat. They have really great doughnuts here, and if that doesn't grab you, they have pancakes. Eggs. Cinnamon buns."

She stared at him silently.

He lifted finely shaped eyebrows and pinned those dark eyes on her. "At least get something to drink."

The waitress was waiting. Malone was waiting. And Cleo just wanted to get this over with. "Orange juice," she said, giving in too easily. "And toast."

Malone led her to a booth against the window, where they could watch the people passing on the sidewalk. This position also placed them as far away as possible from the other customers, no doubt so he could interrogate her without having to lower his voice.

Cleo sat, and the old cushion sank.

"So," Malone said, taking his own seat, which didn't seem to sink quite so low. "Tell me about Tempest."

Cleo fixed her eyes to Malone's. He thought she was nervous? She'd show him. She could be fearless when she had to be, and she was not afraid of this cop or anyone else. "Jack was a mean-spirited, unfaithful, unscrupulous snake. Marrying him was the worst mistake of my life, and I am not sorry to know that I won't ever have to see his face again."

The waitress popped into the picture to place a huge mug of coffee before Malone and a tall glass of cold juice before Cleo. Their conversation ceased until she moved away.

"Do you know who killed him?" Malone asked calmly.

"No."

"Would you tell me if you did?"

"Probably not."

Malone took a long swig of coffee. "Fair enough," he said as he set the mug on the table. "I'll need a list of everyone who was in the club last week when you told your little grapefruit joke."

"If I can remember."

"Do you have a gentleman friend, Ms. Tanner?" He didn't look at her as he asked this question, but stared into his cup of coffee. "Someone who might have felt compelled to defend your honor and then leave a grapefruit behind so you'd be sure to know this murder was a...gift?"

"No gentleman friend," she said precisely, her heart clenching at the idea that someone might have thought she'd consider Jack's murder a *gift.*

"Oh," he said. "Then, who sent the roses?"

The temperature of her blood rose a notch. She was not about to tell Malone about her secret admirer. He'd probably find it all very amusing. Besides, secret admirers were harmless. She'd had more than her share. They all turned out to be shy, sweet men suffering from something that was no more intense than a crush, ordinary men too timid to approach her even to say hello.

"None of your business."

"You are going to cooperate, aren't you, Ms. Tanner?"

She didn't like the way he said that, or the way he lifted his eyebrows and planted his eyes on her and asked the question as if it wasn't a question at all, but a demand. No one pushed her around anymore, no one told her what to do. Not even Luther Malone.

Cleo was saved from answering when the waitress appeared again, bearing a tray laden with food. She placed a heavy white plate with four pieces of toast—three more than Cleo would eat—on the table, along with a bowl filled with small containers of butter and strawberry jam.

Malone's plate was huge: scrambled eggs, a mound of bacon, a bowl of grits and one of those doughnuts he'd tried to entice her with. Glazed.

She shook her head and smiled as she reached for the preserves, letting loose a very small laugh.

"What's so funny?" Malone asked defensively.

"Nothing. Just wondering if I'll be a suspect when you keel over with hardened arteries." She glanced at the plate. "Something which is certain to happen any day now, if *that* is your 'usual.'"

"Oh," he said, reaching for the pepper. "I thought you were laughing at the doughnut."

"That's just icing on the..."

"...doughnut?" he finished.

She liked the fact that he ate such a huge and fat-laden breakfast and then finished it off with the cliché of a cop's doughnut. It made him more...human, somehow. Her smile faded. It was bad enough that she'd placed him so high on the Barney-Bruce scale and thought he was inappropriately good-looking; now she actually had to *like* something about him? Bad news. Very bad news.

"And to answer your question," she said, putting on her most severe face. "No, I don't see any reason why I should cooperate with you."

He nodded his head as if he had already figured that out.

Cleo took a bite of her toast, glad that Malone was giving at least some of his attention to his breakfast. He did keep looking at her, though, lifting his head and staring at her hard, as if he might see something different, this time.

He lifted his head, stared at her face and pointed. "You have..." He wiggled that long finger in her direction.

"I have what?" she snapped. "Guilt written all over my face? A suspicious glint in my eye?"

He reached across the table and touched her face, there near her mouth, dragging the tip of his finger slowly and gently down. It was a shock, when he touched her—a literal, heart-jolting shock. His warm finger briefly brushed her lower lip, sending a riot of sensations she did not want or need through her body. Her heart beat too fast, her temperature rose, and she was quite sure he would be able to see the heat she felt in her cheeks.

Malone showed her his finger as it withdrew. "Strawberry jam on your face."

When he licked the jam off his finger, she thought she would swoon.

And Cleo Tanner did not swoon! She took a napkin and rubbed it vigorously against the corner of her mouth, there where he had touched her, doing her best to wipe away any remaining jam as well as the lingering effect of that warm finger on her face and her lip.

Malone seemed unaffected, by the contact and by her reaction to it. "Do you think Tempest would commit suicide?"

"No," she said, while he dug into his breakfast. "I already told you that."

"I know, but...it's the grapefruit that mucks everything

up. Would he jump with a grapefruit just to screw up your life again?''

Again, like Malone knew everything about her and Jack. ''Maybe,'' she admitted softly. ''If Jack was going to kill himself, he'd definitely go out of his way to pin it on me.''

Malone wagged an egg-laden fork in her direction. ''That's what I figured, but still...I don't see suicide.''

He sounded almost disappointed. ''Then, why the hell did you ask?''

''Gotta cover everything.''

''Then, don't forget about Randi with an *i,*'' Cleo said. ''She'd been with Jack long enough to know what he was like, and she didn't like me.''

''Why not?''

''Because Jack wouldn't leave me alone, that's why,'' she said softly.

He nodded, again as if he understood.

''Now will you hurry up and eat that monster breakfast so you can get me back to my car and I can go home? I've had about all the cooperation I can take.''

Luther didn't hurry, but he did quit questioning Cleo and gave his breakfast the attention it deserved, while she played with a piece of toast and sipped at her juice. Cleo Tanner hadn't tossed her ex-husband off the First Heritage Bank building, of that he was ninety-percent sure. But she was at the middle of it, somehow.

He wished she'd eat a little more, maybe get more jam on the corner of her mouth so he could remove it for her. Wiping it off had been bad enough. What he'd really wanted to do, what he still wanted to do, was lick it off.

Stupid idea. Cleo was gorgeous, in an exotic, all-woman kind of way, but she was too stubborn for his taste. She liked to argue, to butt heads. And what a mouth! He liked his women soft and sweet and compliant.

Well, soft, sweet and compliant was great for an hour or two, he admitted grudgingly. After that, most women lost their luster. They wanted too much, they *needed* too much. Cleo Tanner was anything but compliant. She was also anything but sweet. As for soft…

He almost groaned aloud when Russell walked into the diner, smile on his face, not a single golden hair out of place. The kid didn't even dress like a homicide detective. Tan pants, blue shirt, brown jacket, burgundy tie and those damn loafers. The kid looked like he'd just stepped out of *GQ,* right down to the brilliant grin he turned on them.

"I figured I'd find you here," the kid said, and then he laid eyes on Cleo.

The kid was transparent, and he'd just fallen instantly, deeply and annoyingly in love. Well, in lust, anyway. Luther had a feeling that happened a lot to Cleo. She sucked unsuspecting men in like a swirling, dangerous, inescapable black hole. If he wasn't careful, he could be next.

"What do you want?" Luther asked.

"We're supposed to be partners, remember?"

"That doesn't mean we're joined at the hip," Luther grumbled. God, the kid was so damn…enthusiastic.

"My mistake. I thought we were working on the Tempest case today. I didn't know you had a…" He laid adoring eyes on Cleo again. "A breakfast date." Russell actually blushed.

"Michael Russell, this is Cleo Tanner."

The kid's smile faded quickly. He knew the name well. "Oh." Still, he offered his hand, and Cleo took it. "A pleasure, ma'am."

"I wish I could say the same," she said, with a frosty smile that Russell apparently found endearing. He sat beside her, and she scooted toward the window to give him room.

"Cleo Tanner," Russell said, nodding his head knowingly.

Cleo sighed. "Yes, Jack Tempest was my ex-husband," she said in a no-nonsense voice. "Yes, I hated his guts. No, I didn't kill him. You're up to speed, now."

Russell smiled at her, that sweet smile that probably had women falling at his feet. Luther was glad to see that Cleo didn't immediately fall. She looked as wary as ever.

"Glad to hear it," the kid said.

"Robin," Luther said, signaling to the waitress as he took out his wallet and threw a few bills on the table. "Get Mikey here a good breakfast."

Russell bristled at being called Mikey, as he always did, and Robin waited for his order. The kid debated for a minute, until Luther rose to his feet and signaled for the kid to let Cleo out. Russell came quickly to his feet and offered Cleo an assisting hand that she blatantly refused. Good for her.

"No, I'm not hungry," Russell said as he stepped back and let Cleo rise from the booth on her own. "I'll ride with you guys, if that's okay. I can pick up my car later."

Luther growled and took Cleo's arm, and she shook him off with a muttered and sardonic "The more the merrier."

He drove Cleo to the lot where her car was parked, Russell chattering away in the backseat. Luther tuned the kid out, and apparently so did Cleo. Russell was not deterred; he talked about the weather, a movie he saw last night, the traffic. Inane, polite, irritating chatter. He was still talking when Luther pulled into the lot where Cleo's car was parked.

She exited the car quickly, and Luther did the same. When Russell tried to open his door and join them, Luther pushed it in and glared through the window. The kid got the message and settled back with that damnable smile on his pretty face.

Cleo wasted no time. She had her keys in her hand and had inserted one into the door lock, as Luther came up behind her.

"Put a peephole in your door," he ordered.

"Mind your own business."

"And move that damn spare key."

She had the door open. "Screw you, Malone."

Oh, he could only wish... He shook the inappropriate cravings off and grabbed Cleo's arm, preventing her from slipping into her Corvette and out of the parking lot.

"I don't like this," he said.

She stared at the hand on her arm. "Neither do I," she said frostily.

For a second, a long second where nothing moved, Luther wondered if either of them was talking about Jack Tempest, murder or grapefruit.

He didn't release her. Not yet. "I would like to believe that your ex committed suicide, but I don't."

Some of the toughness faded from her face, leaving her looking momentarily vulnerable. "Neither do I," she said again.

"And like it or not, the grapefruit means you're involved."

"I know," she said.

"So put a peephole in your door and move that friggin' key."

She almost smiled. The tension faded for a moment and she was more tempting than ever. For a second he saw the unguarded Cleo, a real warm woman who needed to be scratched behind her ears until she purred. "I'll think about it."

He released her, and she immediately opened her door and dropped into her seat. Before she could close the door, he leaned in, placing his face near hers. He could almost see every muscle in her body tense, and her eyes—golden eyes that had been almost laughing a moment ago—became guarded. She didn't like it when he got too close, he had sensed that from the beginning. Tough.

"Like it or not this is my case, Ms. Tanner, and alibi or no alibi, you haven't seen the last of me."

She said something obscene, and he withheld a smile. "You kiss your mother with that mouth?"

"Not if I can help it," she said, reaching past him to grab the handle and pull the car door closed. He barely had time to jump out of the way.

She jammed the keys into the ignition, then hesitated. After a moment she rolled her window down and lifted softened eyes to him. "I didn't mean that," she said, almost apologetically. "About my mother."

He could not imagine why she was telling him this, but he nodded as if he understood completely.

"True, we get along much better when she's in Montgomery and I'm in Huntsville, but..." Her face fell. "Crap. I'm going to have to call and tell her about Jack. She hated him more than I did, but she will want to send flowers to the funeral." She rolled her eyes in disgust. "It's the right thing to do, you know."

"Do you want me to make the call for you?" he asked.

She laid her strangely golden eyes on him, no longer angry. This Cleo was guarded but honest. She was a little afraid, a little shaken, and she refused to admit to either. Still, the strength that put fire in her eyes and a sassy retort on her lips was there, as much a part of her as her shape, her mouth, that amazing head of hair. And he wanted, more than anything, to kiss her.

"You would do that?" she asked.

"If you want me to."

"No, thanks. I can handle it." She shook her head slightly. "God, Malone, you would have to turn out to be a nice guy."

"You make that sound like a bad thing."

"It is," she said as she began to roll up her window.

Oh, this was a bad idea. Cleo was a suspect in a murder, and even though he had dismissed her as a viable option, she was connected to the investigation. She was off-limits. This was his damn job, and he never mixed business with pleasure. He couldn't start now, no matter how tempted he might be.

Cleo was talking to herself as she drove away. He couldn't hear her, but he saw her mouth move. Maybe she was cursing his name. Then again…

"Now, *that's* a woman," Russell said, and Luther turned around to see that the kid was leaning against the car with an annoyingly jaunty air.

"Too much woman for you," Luther said as he headed for the driver's side.

"But not for you," Russell said, with a smile, hurrying to the passenger seat so he wouldn't be left behind.

"Maybe she is," Luther said, starting the engine. And then he thought about the way she'd looked fresh from bed, in her cat nightshirt with her hair going in every direction; the expression on her face, the fire in her amber eyes when he'd licked the jam off his finger; and the hint of vulnerability that had flashed over her face when she'd agreed that somehow she was involved in her ex-husband's death.

"And then again, maybe she's not."

"Did she do it?" Russell asked, as Luther pulled onto the street. His bright smile faded rapidly as they got back to business.

"No."

"Does she know who did?"

Luther sighed. "I'm not sure. I'm going back to the club tonight. Whoever did this might be there to see Cleo's reaction to the murder. If he's fixated on her, he might be there every night."

"So what are you gonna do, take up hanging around bars as a part of the job? Can I come?"

Luther opened up his very clean ashtray and plucked out a peppermint, unwrapping it expertly and quickly. At times like this, he wanted a cigarette so bad he could almost taste it.

Truth was, another pair of eyes would be a good idea. Russell looked at everything from a different slant, and, like it or not, that made them good partners. What one missed, the other often saw.

"Sure," he said. "And don't forget to bring your ID."

Russell growled, and Luther smiled. The last time they'd gone out for a drink, Mikey had gotten carded.

"Dress casual, and let's go in separately and keep it that way." Yeah, another pair of eyes would be great. "There's a barmaid about your age, pretty girl named Lizzy. You can cozy up to her and pick her brain over the next few days."

Russell nodded. The kid loved undercover work, even something as simple as this. "That's great. What about Cleo? Should I try to pick her brain, too?"

It was true, Luther usually let Russell interrogate the women. They just seemed to crumple when he smiled and asked them questions. A woman who was intimidated by Luther would fold in a heartbeat for Mikey.

But he had a feeling Cleo never folded. Besides, she'd chew the kid up and spit him out before he had a clue he was in trouble. Besides…

"Cleo is mine."

Chapter 4

The last person Cleo needed or wanted to see, as she pushed through the club door, was Malone. The man was a menace. And he stood at the bar talking to Edgar as if he owned the place! Confident, supremely relaxed, he looked like he belonged here as much as she did. And it was *her* place!

He turned to watch her walk toward him, his eyes squinted against the afternoon sun that shone brightly behind her as the door swung slowly shut.

"We're not open yet," she said.

"I know." Malone nodded to Edgar. "He let me in."

First Syd and now Edgar! Her friends were turning against her. Cleo gave Edgar a warning glare, and received a shrug in return. She headed for the office, and heard the annoying clip of Malone's step as he fell in behind her.

"I suppose you're here for a reason," Cleo said, without glancing over her shoulder.

"Maybe I just wanted to say hello."

Cleo snorted softly as she opened her office door. ''You don't strike me as a social butterfly, Malone. I doubt you ever drop by anywhere just to say hello.''

Every nerve in her body went on alert when he shut the office door behind him. She didn't like being this close to him, pinned in, wondering why he was here. She didn't have to wonder long.

''Jack didn't jump,'' Malone said curtly.

Her heart lurched. ''How can you be sure?''

''He was probably unconscious when he went off…when he died. There was a substantial amount of a drug in his blood—not enough to kill him, but more than enough to knock him on his ass for a while.''

Cleo rounded the desk and sat down. Something about Malone and the news he always carried with him made her knees weak. ''Maybe he took it on purpose. Trust me, Jack wasn't above a little recreational—''

''No grown man uses furniture polish for recreational purposes,'' Malone interrupted. ''Even if it is a furniture polish that takes a nasty turn when ingested.''

Cleo tilted her head back and looked up at the detective. Usually she didn't care for this position. She preferred eye-to-eye and nose-to-nose. Not right now. ''So somebody gave Jack something to make him…easy to handle, and then pushed him off the roof?''

Malone stood on the other side of her desk, his eyes on her. Did he still think she might have killed Jack? For the first time, Cleo was really scared. No one had wanted to see Jack dead more than she. If she were investigating the case, she'd definitely suspect her.

''It doesn't make any sense,'' Malone continued. ''There are easier ways to kill an unconscious man than throwing him off a roof. It looks like he was already out of it when he was taken up there. That wasn't easy.''

Cleo swallowed, wanting nothing more than for this man

to leave. Quietly. Without another word. Without another opportunity for argument. "Why are you telling me this?"

Malone placed his hands on the desk and leaned forward, bringing his face close to hers. Eye-to-eye, nose-to-nose. "I don't think you killed him," he said. "But I think you know the man who did."

"How do you know it's a man?"

"Ever tried to drag a body up several flights of stairs, across a roof, and then toss it over the side? There was a four-foot rail. Whoever tossed Jack over had the strength to lift that unconscious body over the rail. You don't have that kind of strength."

She wanted to argue with him. These days she didn't let any man tell her what she could and could not do! But he was right. And she would be a complete fool to argue with him about that particular point.

"Why do you think I know the man who killed Jack?"

Malone shook his head. "If whoever did this just wanted Tempest dead, he could've poured more furniture polish down his throat, or smothered him with a pillow. The job could have been finished in any one of a dozen other ways that were simpler and cleaner than this. That's not what happened. When the killer tossed Jack and the grapefruit over the side of the building, he was sending a message."

"To me?" Cleo whispered.

"To you."

Malone backed away slowly, and withdrew a small notebook from his jacket pocket. A slim pen followed. The way he sat there, half sitting, half leaning against her desk, made his dark jacket gape open. His shoulder holster rested at his side, snug and somehow natural looking against the plain white shirt. The gun housed there was small, a compact.

"I'm going to need the names of everyone you've dated in the past two years."

"I don't date."

Malone latched his dark eyes to hers. ''Come on, Ms. Tanner. You don't expect me to believe that, do you?''

His skepticism stole away her fear and made her angry. Thank goodness. She much preferred anger. ''I have my own business, Detective Malone. It keeps me quite busy.''

''Too busy for...'' He let the question die away.

''Yes,'' she snapped. ''Too busy *for*.''

He closed the notebook and returned it, and the pen, to his pocket. Very smoothly, he traded the implements of his profession for a wrapped candy, a strawberry-shaped sweet he deftly unwrapped and popped into his mouth.

''What's with the candy, anyway?'' she asked sharply. ''You have a sweet tooth or something?''

''I ask the questions here.''

She ignored him. ''Are you determined to buy your dentist a new car?''

He laid his dark eyes on her. ''If you must know, when I quit smoking I relied on candy to help me get by. Now I have to find a way to get rid of the candy.''

Cleo smiled. ''Oral fixation.''

''Excuse me?''

''You just traded one oral fixation for another.'' She rather liked the fact that such a hard, seemingly perfect, man had a weakness. Even if it was for something so ordinary as hard candy.

''Thank you, Dr. Tanner,'' he said dryly. ''But now that we're through analyzing me, let's get back to—''

''So the only way to get rid of the candy,'' she interrupted, ''is to trade it for another oral fix. Back to cigarettes?'' she teased. ''Or maybe you can start sucking your thumb.''

Cleo was so sure she had the upper hand with this latest turn in the conversation, and then Malone threw her for a loop without uttering a single word.

He stared at her mouth.

"I, uh, haven't dated in the past two years, I swear," she said, lowering her voice. "To be honest, it's been a lot longer than two years."

Malone allowed his gaze to drift upward. "There must've been someone."

Cleo shook her head. And felt guilty for not telling Malone the truth when he'd asked about the roses. Knowing what she knew now, she had no choice.

"I have had a secret admirer sending me notes and flowers for the past four months," she said, trying to sound casual. "It's the sort of thing that happens all the time when—"

"A secret admirer?" Malone asked, shooting up off the desk and standing tall, and menacing, before her. "And you just now tell me about it?"

"I didn't think—"

"No, you didn't."

She took a deep breath to calm herself. Malone had every right to be peeved, but there was no reason for him to lose his cool. She was certain the man who had written her those innocent letters couldn't possibly be a murderer. "The letters are very sweet, and he sends me flowers about once a month. That hardly makes him an obsessed madman."

Should she tell him about Eric and her stray thought that he might be the man sending her notes and roses? No. Eric didn't have a violent bone in his body. Turning Malone on him would be downright cruel. And senseless. There was no way Eric could have killed Jack. Oh, but she was going to have to talk to Eric and Edgar about lying for her! Their intentions had been good, she knew, but sooner or later the truth would have to be told. Sooner would be better.

"Tell me you kept the letters," Malone muttered.

Cleo sighed. "Yes. They seemed more like fan letters than any kind of threat." She slid open the bottom drawer of her desk and riffled through the small stack of bills there.

She kept the notes and other fan letters she got on occasion, just beneath the bills. As she searched, a sharp discomfort grew. "They're not here," she said.

"What?" Malone rounded the desk and dropped down to his haunches to search the drawer himself. He pulled out his pen and used it to lift the bills and other papers in the drawer, being careful not to actually touch anything.

"I'm telling you," Cleo said, "they're not here."

"When did you see them last?"

"A few days ago," Cleo said. "Maybe last week."

"Don't touch anything else," he ordered, glancing up at her. "I'm going to have the office dusted for prints."

Cleo grinned. "Do you have any idea how many people are in and out of this place? And I haven't polished this desk in...okay, I've never polished this desk. It's got to be covered with prints."

"It's a long shot, I know," Malone said as he stood. "But right now, it's all we've got." He offered his hand to help Cleo to her feet. "Except you."

For a split second he had thought she was lying. How did a woman who looked like this one go so long without a date? He could see guys lining up to date Cleo, and he could see her going through them the way a normal woman went through tissues. Use one and toss it away. Grab another.

But that thought hadn't lasted long. The man-eater toughness was a part of her act; it was the way she kept men away. Thanks to Jack, he imagined.

Luther sat at a table near the center of the room. From here he could see everything. Lizzy, her long brown ponytail swaying as she leaned against the bar, Edgar barely mouthing the words to the song Cleo was singing, customers scattered about the room with drinks before them and their eyes and attention on the stage.

And Mikey sitting in the corner. Once he'd come in and made himself comfortable, he'd started hitting on Lizzy. And quite successfully, too. In his jeans and denim shirt, and wearing that devil-may-care smile, Russell looked nothing like a cop.

Right this minute, Russell behaved just the way all the other customers did. He stared at Cleo and listened closely. The place was so quiet as she sang. No one so much as whispered. Luther had scanned the room for a potential obsessed secret admirer, for a potential killer, but had seen nothing suspicious. So now he listened like the others.

She sang old forties tunes, mostly, in a resonant voice that filled the room and seeped beneath his skin. Cleo Tanner was a smart-mouthed, tough broad, but when she sang…when she sang there was nothing else. He could see it in her eyes, in her relaxed posture. She didn't care if anyone listened, if the room was full or empty. She sang from the heart.

Of course she had secret admirers. There were probably a dozen men who came to listen to her sing and dreamed of being the one to break through her tough facade to find and claim that heart she sang so beautifully from.

Was one of them a killer? Would one of them kill Cleo's ex-husband because he was a thorn in her side? Or was someone trying to point the finger in her direction to lead Luther away from the real killer? That supposition made just as much sense as anything else.

She was singing a heartrending version of "Do You Know What It Means to Miss New Orleans," when the couple arrived. Cretins, they talked to one another in normal voices and broke the spell that filled the room. Luther turned to watch them walk to the bar, removing their coats as they went, talking loudly even though they received a number of sharp glares.

The woman was tall, reed thin, and had her dark blond

hair cut in a chin-length bob. Her coat was expensive. So were the diamonds in her ears and on her fingers. Money. The big fella who walked beside her carried himself like a man who was accustomed to being waited on. His well-cut suit downplayed his size. The watch on his wrist was gold. More money.

Edgar shushed the noisy couple when they reached the bar, and in turn they both pursed their mouths in disapproval. But they did shut up. The others in the room returned their attention to the stage.

Luther listened to Cleo, but he kept his eyes on the newly arrived couple. They didn't belong here. They were country club people who held themselves stiffly, as if to touch anything in this place would dirty them. Eventually they laid their eyes on Cleo, and he could have sworn the woman sighed and shook her head just slightly.

Cleo was finishing up with "Do Nothin' Till You Hear from Me," when a cell phone rang. The patrons knew where that noise came from, and several turned to glare at the well-dressed man who dug in his jacket pocket to retrieve his phone. One customer, a small, elderly fellow, tossed a balled-up napkin in the couple's direction as the man answered and stepped toward the corner of the room, one hand to his ear so he could hear.

Cleo left the stage to a hearty round of applause. God, half the men in the room were in love with her, Mikey included. And she didn't know it, Luther realized as she left the stage. She had no idea how her voice and her appearance sucked a man in.

If she'd known where his mind had taken him this afternoon when she'd started talking about "oral fixation," she would've kicked him out of her place by now.

Cleo walked to the bar, where Edgar had a glass of water waiting. Luther headed in the same direction, hoping to arrive about the same time she did. The sight of the tall blond waiting at the bar caused Cleo's step to falter.

"Thea," Cleo said as she reached the bar. "What are you doing here?"

The woman Cleo called Thea sighed. It seemed well-practiced. "We heard about Jack, and Palmer and I are here to offer our support."

Cleo's eyes flickered to the man in the corner. He had his back to them and was still talking on the phone. Was that panic he saw in Cleo's eyes? Maybe. It was gone too quickly for him to be sure.

Luther stepped to the bar so he stood behind Cleo and could see everything that happened. He leaned there and nodded to Edgar, asking for another cup of coffee.

"Thank you," Cleo said to the blonde. "But I really don't need any support. I'm fine."

"Cleo, your ex-husband was *murdered,*" Thea said, lowering her voice.

"I know that," Cleo answered. "I appreciate you coming, but there's nothing you can do."

Thea, who had obviously hoped for a warmer welcome, squared her shoulders. "Well, we will at least stay for the funeral. Someone should represent the family. When will it be held?"

Cleo turned slightly and tilted her head back to look at Luther. "Do you know when the funeral is?"

"Friday."

Cleo dropped her eyes and returned her attention to Thea, who leaned to one side to get a glimpse of the man Cleo had spoken to.

"I wish I had a guest room so you could stay with me," Cleo said, not very convincingly.

Thea looked properly horrified. "Oh, we have a suite at the Marriott. We wouldn't think of putting you out." She straightened her spine again. "I'll stay as long as you need me."

"Thank you," Cleo said, her voice turning kinder. "But I'm fine. Really."

Thea held out stiff arms. "Don't you have a hug for your big sister?"

Sister? Luther digested this information while he watched the women engage in a perfunctory embrace.

When they parted, Thea kept her hands on Cleo's shoulders. "I won't leave you to go through this alone," she said in a strict, schoolteacher-like tone.

"I'm not alone," Cleo insisted. "I have Edgar, and Eric and Syd..." she looked over her shoulder and a wicked gleam lit her amber eyes. "And Malone."

Thea cast him a wary glance. "Malone?"

"Detective Luther Malone," Cleo said with a smile. "He's a new...friend."

A woman like Cleo had a way of saying a simple word like *friend* that gave it all sorts of meaning.

Thea paled. The man who had arrived with her, Palmer, ended his conversation and joined them.

One good look at Palmer was enough for Luther. His gut instinct had served him well over the years, and he never ignored it. He did not like Palmer. Most importantly, he didn't like the way Palmer looked at Cleo.

The big man opened his arms and offered Cleo a hug and a smile. Cleo extended one hand, signaling that she'd prefer a shake. Palmer moved in for a hug, anyway, and Luther stepped to her side to get in the way.

Palmer's gaze snapped up. He was no fool. He saw the warning on Luther's face and dropped one hand. The handshake he pressed on Cleo was brief.

"Palmer, darling," Thea said tersely, "this is Detective Luther Malone, Cleo's new *friend*."

"Detective," Palmer muttered, and then he swallowed. Hard.

They had come to their own conclusions, and Cleo was doing nothing to dissuade the notion. Luther figured she must have a reason. So he didn't move. He stayed beside her. He smiled tightly. And then some demon within him forced him to drape his arm around her shoulder.

He looked down at Cleo. She looked up. "This is your sister?"

"Yes," Cleo said, not attempting to move away or toss his arm off her shoulder, as she surely would if they were alone. "And her husband, Palmer."

Luther look back at the couple. "I've heard a lot about you two."

Palmer went a little pale. Oh, Cleo definitely had some explaining to do!

Cleo glanced up at him. "The funeral's Friday?"

"Yes. The coroner has promised to release the body by tomorrow afternoon. He expects to be finished with his tests by then. Miss Rayner has made all the arrangements for the funeral."

"I don't know if I should go or not," Cleo said, not sounding nearly as confident as usual.

"I'll go with you," Luther said. "It'll be okay."

"Wait a minute," Palmer injected. "If you two are friends, surely you're not investigating the case. I mean, Cleo is sure to be a suspect."

Luther gave Palmer his darkest glare. "Why on earth would you say that?"

For a big man, Palmer squirmed too much. "It just seems a little out of the ordinary, that's all. She was the victim's ex-wife."

"Cleo is not a suspect," Luther said. "My involvement in this case might be considered unusual—" and it was getting more unusual by the minute "—but we haven't broken any law." *Yet.*

Luther glanced around the room. No one was paying what might be called an inordinate amount of attention to their conversation. Not even Russell, who was proving to be damn good at undercover work. But if the secret admirer were here, he'd be incensed to see another man with his arm around Cleo, wouldn't he?

Luther shifted his arm and settled his hand at the back of Cleo's neck, beneath a wealth of curling black hair and against her warm skin. She flinched just a little, but not so that anyone would notice her reaction. He *felt* it, but no one would see.

"I'm taking you home," he said, sounding possessive and commanding.

"But..." Cleo began.

"No buts. You can't go back into your office until the crime scene techs are finished, and they won't even get started until morning." Luther glanced at Edgar. "There's crime scene tape across the door to her office. No one goes in." Russell would see to that, up until closing time, and Luther himself would be here in the morning when the crime scene techs arrived. "The door's locked," he added, "and I have the key."

"Why?" Thea asked brightly. "What happened in there?"

Cleo opened her mouth to answer, but Luther was quicker. "We can't discuss that. Sorry."

Again, Cleo looked up at him. Her eyes were so wide, her skin so flawless, her mouth so tempting. He could very easily kiss her, here and now. It would cement this ridiculous charade, and besides...he would never get another chance. God, what a great oral fixation she'd be.

"All right," she said, oddly subservient. "You can take me home."

He smiled, but didn't give in to the urge to kiss her.

''Lunch tomorrow,'' Thea said, as Edgar handed Cleo her purse from under the bar. ''We're at the Marriott. Call me in the morning.''

''Sure,'' Cleo said lifelessly. ''Lunch.'' Edgar handed her coat over the bar. They'd cleared everything she might need out of the office when he'd taped it off, and Cleo had locked the door and handed him the key.

Before Cleo could grab her coat, Luther took it and draped the black wool over her shoulders. He even allowed his hands to linger on her shoulders. She didn't seem to mind. If he didn't know better, he might even think she liked the way he rested his hands there, just for a moment. He might even think that gentle touch calmed her. The trembling she hid from everyone else seemed to subside.

He led Cleo toward the door. Thea and Palmer followed, slipping on their own coats as they went. ''Don't forget lunch,'' Thea said breathlessly.

''We won't forget,'' Luther answered, including himself in the invitation.

Chapter 5

Cleo unlocked her door and stepped inside to be greeted by a prancing Rambo, who was more enthusiastic than usual tonight.

"Hi, sweetheart," Cleo said lowly, leaning down to gently scratch the top of the dog's golden head.

Behind her, Malone closed the door soundly. Rambo, the traitor, loped to Malone and lifted those big brown eyes to beg silently for adoration. The detective obediently scratched behind Rambo's ears.

"Okay," Malone said as he followed Cleo into the living room, Rambo at his heels. "You have some explaining to do."

"I told you in the car—"

"You have nothing to say. I know. Indulge me."

Cleo slipped off her coat and headed for the kitchen. "Would you like something to drink?"

Malone hesitated. "I know you don't have coffee."

"Orange juice, water and flat diet soda."

"I'll pass."

Cleo stepped into the kitchen and poured herself a glass of juice before walking to the living room to join Malone. Like it or not, she would have to explain a thing or two.

Malone stood over the roses her secret admirer had sent. "Where's the card?"

"There was no card this time," Cleo said as she dropped into her favorite chair.

"Is there usually?"

"At first," she said, as Malone crossed the room and sat on the couch, facing her. "They were usually just simple notes. 'Great set last night. I love that red dress.' Stuff like that. Lately they've been delivered without a card. Since it was red roses like before, and came from the same florist, I just assumed they were from the same guy."

"What florist?"

"I can't remember the name, but it's the one in the mall."

Malone nodded his head, apparently satisfied. "I'll get someone on that right away. Always red roses, you say?"

Cleo nodded. "One dozen, delivered to the club. Usually on a Saturday. Friday night is when we have our biggest crowd, so it was impossible for me to come up with a face in the crowd that might fit the notes and the flowers."

Malone leaned forward. "Tell me about Palmer."

Cleo felt her cheeks go cold. "He's my sister's husband. What's to tell?"

"Come on, Cleo. Give me a little credit."

Rambo padded over to Malone and rested her chin on his knee. He didn't seem to mind, but began to absently pat the dog's head.

"She'll shed all over your suit."

"It'll brush off," Malone said tersely. "Palmer."

Might as well tell all. She had a feeling hiding anything

from Luther Malone was hard work. And she didn't have the heart for it at the moment.

"Thea is everything my mother ever wanted in a daughter. Tall, slender, refined. I think she was born with the desire to join the Junior League. She's an interior decorator, and is very choosy about the jobs she takes. Hers is a suitable profession. Mine is not."

"Palmer," Malone said, urging her to move forward.

"I'm getting there." She took a sip of juice, and Malone visibly relaxed. Rambo, sufficiently scratched, laid down at the detective's feet and rested her chin on his shoe. "All my life, I had to deal with the sad fact that I'm not enough like Thea to make my mother happy. I'm short, I am most definitely not thin, and if you made me join the Junior League, I'd probably turn into a serial killer or something." She didn't mention the fact that her mother had been horrified when she'd gotten breasts at an early age. Her mother's people were not voluptuous.

Malone smiled.

"When I decided I wanted to sing, when I realized that I *needed* to sing, my mother was quite distressed. A daughter of hers in a public profession? Making a spectacle of herself on stage?" Cleo studied Malone's hard, expressionless face, and wished, momentarily, for a hint of softness. She didn't get her wish. "In my family, making a spectacle of oneself is the worst possible crime."

When had she started actually trying to make a spectacle of herself? Early on, though she couldn't remember the exact moment. She hadn't been able to win her mother over, so she'd learned to fight the only way she knew how. After her father had passed on, things had only gotten worse.

"So all my life I'm compared to this perfect daughter. I tried for a while, but finally accepted that I could never live up to that standard. I'm not like Thea, and by God, I don't want to be.'' She didn't want to admit, not out loud, that it still hurt. She was too old to be hurt because her mother loved big sister best. ''When Thea married Palmer, it was just icing on the cake. His family has old money *and* a long string of car dealerships, he played football at the University of Alabama, he's a handicap golfer and he runs in all the right circles.''

''The ideal husband.''

''Yeah,'' she said tightly, ''except for the fact that he'll screw any woman who has the misfortune to wander into his line of vision.''

Malone's jaw tensed, his eyes narrowed. For a moment all was silent. Well, she had wished for a show of emotion, hadn't she? Malone was angry.

''Did he hurt you?''

''No,'' Cleo answered quickly. ''He just…makes a pass at me every time we're alone.'' In the kitchen, in the driveway, in the hallway of the family home. The man knew no shame.

''What kind of a pass?'' Malone asked tersely.

''He likes to grab.''

''He likes to grab *what?*''

If she had taken any of her mother's teachings on decorum to heart, she wouldn't answer that question. But so few of her mother's teachings had taken. ''He likes to sneak up on me and grab what my flat-chested sister doesn't have.''

A muscle in Malone's right eye twitched. ''He's plenty strong enough to be our guy. Do you think he'd—''

''No,'' Cleo interrupted. ''To commit murder, you have to care a little bit, right? You have to have some kind of passion to commit a crime of passion.''

''I suppose.''

''Palmer has no true passion. He grabs me and makes passes because I'm not a notch on his belt. If I ever did

get desperate enough to agree to sleep with him, he'd los
interest. That's how he treats all his women.''

Malone shook his head. ''Doesn't anyone else knov
about this guy?''

''They all know,'' she said softly. ''But they look pas
it because he has money and the right social standing, an
he is a real and true football hero. Disgusting, isn't it?''

''Yeah.''

''I'm the bad guy, here. If Palmer makes a pass at m
it's because I've tempted him somehow. It's because I insis
on making a *spectacle* of myself.''

Malone leaned back and relaxed...well, for him thi
might be called relaxing. He was still wound pretty tigh
''This is what we're going to do,'' he said in that voic
that held no room for argument. ''Tomorrow morning, I'l
meet the crime scene techs at your office and let them ir
then Mikey and I will get your car home.''

''Okay.''

''We'll go to lunch with your sister and brother-in-law
and if Palmer even looks at you wrong, I'll make him regre
it.''

She wished for specifics, but got none. Oh, she woul
dearly love to watch Luther Malone make Palmer sweat!

''Then tomorrow night I'm back at the club. Like it c
not, we started something tonight. People will be talking
What do you think your secret admirer would think of yo
having a boyfriend?''

She grinned. ''I'm a little old for a *boyfriend,* Malone.'

''Okay,'' he said, not at all taken aback. ''A lover, ther
And if we're sleeping together, you'd better call me Lu
ther.''

Cleo's smile faded quickly. ''I don't think that's such
good idea.''

''Why not?''

Because no one got that close. Because she already liked Malone too much. "I just...don't."

"Good argument," he muttered dryly.

"If there really is someone out there who's fixated on me, don't you think it might be a little dangerous to pretend to be my..." Oh, she couldn't say it. She absolutely, positively could not look Malone in the eye and say *lover.* "Boyfriend?"

He grinned. "That's the idea, darlin'."

"Please tell me I don't have to call you Sugar or Honey or Pooh Bear."

"Luther will do."

He had met a thousand women like Thea Woodson, in his years on the force. They were innocent bystanders, victims of crime and long-suffering relatives. They were never suspects. They often dabbed at their eyes with starched hankies, if they thought they should, but hysterics were not in their repertoire. Cleo was right: To commit a crime of passion, you had to possess some passion. Thea had none, and neither did her annoying twit of a husband.

Palmer was not completely stupid. He hadn't looked directly at Cleo since they'd met in the restaurant parking lot. He kept his head down, his eyes averted. When he did get brave enough to lay his eyes on anyone other than his wife, it was usually Luther. Palmer was curious. Surprised. And more than a little afraid.

Before Palmer headed back to Mobile, he was going to get a little sermon on the folly of messing with Cleo. He might be playing it safe today, since Cleo was not alone—but what would happen the next time she went to a family gathering and the bastard cornered her somewhere? No, that wouldn't do.

Not looking at Cleo had to be a chore. She was dressed more conservatively than usual, in a navy-blue dress with a high collar and a hem that touched her knees. But nothing could disguise the figure beneath the dress, and the way she walked.... There ought to be a law.

"So," Thea said, laying her eyes on Luther as she played with her salad. "Is law enforcement a family profession?"

"No," he said succinctly.

"Well, you seem to be an intelligent man. I suppose you have plans to study the law. Or run for some kind of political office, or—"

"Luther is a cop, Thea," Cleo said. "He likes being a cop. He will *always* be a cop. Right, honey?"

He cut his eyes to a very amused Cleo. She was always beautiful, but when she smiled she lit up the room. Even when it wasn't real. "That's right, darlin'."

"Well," Thea continued, undeterred. "What does your family do?"

"My mother waited tables, until she died. I was eleven. I never knew my father."

Thea paled, no doubt horrified that her sister had taken up with a man with such a common background. Luther didn't care, not anymore. There had been a time, though, when he had hidden the sad facts of his childhood from everyone.

"Any brothers or sisters?"

"No."

Palmer wagged his fork in Luther's direction. "If you ever want a job selling cars, just give me a call. We're always looking for—"

Luther gave Palmer a glare that silenced him, mid-sentence.

Thea straightened her already rigid spine. "It's just that I know how little police officers make, and it's such a thankless job..."

"You don't have to try to find Luther a new job," Cleo said sharply. "And you don't have to worry about me sul-ying the good family name by marrying a cop. We're not engaged, we're just sleeping together.''

Thea was sufficiently embarrassed, as Cleo had no doubt known she would be. The woman pursed her lips and paled, then blushed. ''I was just being friendly.''

''Besides,'' Cleo said, ''if you ask me, cops are a lot more noble than car salesmen or football players or interior decorators. I can live without those people in my life, but I would hate to live in a world where we didn't have men like Luther watching out for us.''

''There's no need to get defensive,'' Thea said.

''I'm not defensive,'' Cleo said as she set her fork down. ''I'm pissed.''

No wonder Cleo didn't like to go home to her family for the holidays. He suspected she and Thea always butted heads this way.

Luther laid his hand on Cleo's knee, and she jumped and jerked her head around to look at him.

''It's okay,'' he said softly.

''It's not,'' she answered. ''You shouldn't have come. This always happens.''

''Why don't we talk about something else,'' he suggested. ''What about Jack? No one liked him, right? I imagine that's a subject you can all agree on.'' Besides, he would love to hear what Thea and Palmer thought about Jack. Cleo didn't see them as suspects, but Luther did. At this point, anyone and everyone was a suspect.

''I kinda liked Jack,'' Palmer muttered.

''He stole the publishing rights to the songs I wrote!'' Cleo snapped.

''No,'' Thea said. ''You signed them over to him. That's not stealing.''

Luther looked down at his salad. It was going to be a *very* long lunch.

* * *

Thank goodness Thea and Palmer had decided they needed to retire early and would not be coming to the club this evening. A few hours with her sister drained her. An entire day might be lethal.

Cleo took a deep, calming breath. This club was *her* place, where no one made her feel small. Where no one looked down their pointy noses at what she did. She was safe here.

There was already a good-size crowd waiting for her set. They drank and talked and laughed, and one of them kept plugging quarters into the jukebox and calling up old instrumental tunes. Sad piano, mostly. Some poor guy whose heart had been broken.

It had taken a while, but she had finally gathered Eric and Edgar, when Malone was not around. The three of them put their heads together behind the bar.

"I can't believe you guys lied about me being here the night Jack was murdered."

Eric and Edgar exchanged a quick look. "We knew you'd be a suspect," Eric said. "You can't expect that we'd just sit back and not help."

"Yeah," said Edgar. "I didn't like the way that cop looked from the minute he walked in. He's trouble."

"He's just doing his job," Cleo whispered. "I'm going to tell him the truth. Tonight."

"No!" Edgar and Eric said together, one voice gravelly, one almost childlike.

"He knows I didn't do it," she said, reaching out to take Edgar's wrist and Eric's in her hands. "There's no reason not to tell—"

"He's trying to sucker you in," Eric said. "He's… flirting with you so you'll let down your guard and tell him everything, and then once you tell him you don't have an alibi, he'll arrest you. It's always the wife or the ex-wife, you know, when a man is murdered."

"Not always," Cleo said in a soothing voice.

"He's a cop," Edgar reminded her. "Be careful. Think of this alibi as…a little insurance."

She considered going along with them a while longer, but finally she shook her head. "No, I can't. I'm going to tell him the truth."

Cleo was standing at the bar, a bottle of water in her hand, when Luther walked through the door less than an hour later. It was a good thing he thought her earlier defense of his chosen profession was all a show. If he knew she truly believed he was one of the good guys, a modern-day knight, a warrior of the new millennium, he'd think she was such a sap.

Tonight she'd dressed for him. Not consciously, not at first, but as she'd taken this emerald-green dress out of the closet and strapped on the matching shoes, she'd wondered what he'd think. She wasn't blind to the way he looked at her—like he appreciated what he saw even though she wasn't tall or slender.

She didn't notice until Luther had almost reached the bar that he carried a package wrapped in royal-blue paper. There was no ribbon, and no visible card. But it was definitely a gift.

When he reached the bar, he placed the package before her. She studied the crooked tape on the end, the badly bunched paper where it had been sloppily folded. "Don't tell me," she said with a smile. "You taught Rambo how to wrap presents. That's really going to come in handy at Christmastime."

"Very funny," he said, taking a stool beside her. No one stood near, and still he leaned close to her and whispered in her ear. "Open the damn package, and don't get any ideas. It's all for show."

"Of course it is," she whispered back, reaching for the package and carefully picking off the tape. She unwrapped the present slowly, taking her time, peeking at the plain white box beneath the paper, then lifting the lid slowly. What would Luther buy a woman he was supposedly sleeping with? Lingerie, she guessed. Something silk and red and crotchless.

She dropped the box lid to the bar. "Oh," she said, lifting the package inside. "A peephole kit."

"I'll install it this weekend."

Cleo turned the package over and quickly scanned the directions. "I don't have a drill."

"I do."

She started to give him a husky *I just bet you do,* then thought better of it. You could only push a man like Luther so far, she imagined. "It's very…thoughtful. No one's ever given me a peephole before. Thank you."

"You're welcome," he said grudgingly.

She leaned toward him. To anyone watching, the way they whispered to one another might appear to be intimate. Cozy and romantic and sexy.

"I'll pay you back."

He shook his head. "No, it's on me. I'll feel better if you have a peephole in your door."

"Will the department pay for it, since this is part of a job?"

He grinned. "No way."

"Everyone is watching us," she said.

"I know."

Something she didn't expect shimmied through her body. She liked this; Luther sitting close, his scent wrapping itself around her, his shadow enveloping her. It wasn't real, it didn't mean anything…but she didn't want it to end. Not yet.

"Dance with me?" she said, trying to put off the confession that her alibi was false.

He shook his head. "I don't dance."

"If you're going to be my boyfriend, you must dance."

"I don't know how."

"I'll teach you."

He pulled his head back, looked at her and shook his head. She couldn't help but smile. She wouldn't have thought there was anything he couldn't do. Or that he would admit it, if there was.

He killed her smile with a simple sentence. "I heard your song today, 'Come Morning.' Found an old tape at a place that sells used CDs and cassettes."

Cleo scanned the faces in the club, looking for someone, anyone, who might be a murderer. A man who was strong enough to toss Jack off a building. A man who might send her flowers and sweet notes and then do her the favor of killing her ex-husband. She didn't see anyone who fit the bill. She continued to search. *Anything* to take her mind off the life Luther had reminded her of when he mentioned that tape. She'd written a few of the songs and performed some standards in her own style, but only "Come Morning" had been a hit.

"I'm sorry," she said softly.

"Why? It's a great song, and your voice was—"

"It was a stupid, saccharine, naive, heartrending, juvenile pile of—"

"It was nice," he said. "Maybe a little naive, but in a sweet way."

"'Come Morning,'" she said. "I wrote that for Jack right after we were married, and I was so stupid I believed every word." She'd opened her heart for the world to see and hear. How foolish.

"This afternoon you said he stole the rights?"

Ah, that's why he had gone to the trouble to search out an old copy of her song. More motive. "The publishing rights. That's where all the money is."

"What happened?"

"He convinced me to sign the rights over so he could more easily handle all my business. That way I wouldn't have to worry my pretty little head about it." She shook her head, marveling at her own gullibility. "I never dreamed, when I signed, that we wouldn't be married forever. I couldn't imagine that he would betray me, in more ways than one."

"Do you still write?"

"No."

"You should," he said. "It's a talent."

What could she say to that? *Thank you. Bug off. I don't have the heart, anymore, Jack killed it.* "I was just a one-hit wonder."

Edgar brought Luther a cup of fresh coffee, and Luther accepted with what seemed to be genuine appreciation. "You make great coffee, Edgar," he said.

Edgar just grumbled as he moved down the bar. He didn't like Luther much. Neither did Eric. They were both convinced that Malone was still trying to pin Jack's murder on her. How could she blame them for trying so hard to protect her?

She hadn't told them that the courtship was fake, a ruse to smoke out the real killer. She was afraid one or both of them would give the gig away.

"The funeral is day after tomorrow," she said, when Luther turned back to her.

"I know."

He leaned close once again. Something about him smelled so good. Not cologne, not the scent of the peppermint that usually surrounded him, but something more basic than that. He smelled like a man was supposed to smell.

"I'll pick you up and we'll go together. I want you to keep an eye out for anyone who looks familiar. Someone who shouldn't be there."

She brushed her cheek against his and whispered, "Can I wear my red dress?"

"No," he muttered.

Her heart lurched. "I won't pretend to mourn him."

"Fine, but don't dance on his grave, either."

She took a deep breath. She hadn't been this close to a man in years. She usually took great pains not to get too close. But this was nice, so she didn't rush to back away. She wanted to stay here for a while.

"Did the crime techs find anything in my office?"

"They took a bunch of prints. Nothing's come of it yet, but that usually takes a while." His voice was comforting, and she wanted him to whisper in her ear a little more. She didn't care what he said. She just wanted him *here.*

"Do you think they'll find anything?"

"It's a long shot."

His head was close to hers, their bodies barely touching here and there. There was nothing sexual about the way they touched, nothing improper, and still...

She might as well tell him now that her alibi was false. He would understand. He might be angry at first, but he would eventually understand. "Luther—"

"Cleo," Eric said, sneaking up behind her. "Time."

She backed away from Luther slowly and turned her head to smile wanly at her surly piano player. "I'll be right there."

When she faced Luther again, he reached out and cupped her chin in his hand. She could see, in his dark eyes, that he felt something of what she did. Tension. Electricity dancing in the air between them. He moved toward her, slowly, his head tilting, his lips parting. "Just for show," he whispered, right before his mouth touched hers.

She hadn't been kissed in so long, she'd forgotten how powerful it could be. Her eyes drifted closed as Luther's mouth moved gently over hers. Oh, she had never been kissed like this. It wasn't deep, or demanding, or forceful, but was an almost sweet kiss that lasted a moment longer than a sweet kiss should. There was energy here, something beautiful and strangely elusive. It wasn't real, it wouldn't last, and yet she wished this kiss would go on forever. For a moment, after Luther pulled his mouth from hers, she couldn't breathe. She felt that kiss to her very bones.

Oh, no. She couldn't do this. She couldn't let her heart go soft. It would only get broken again, and she couldn't survive a second time. She knew it.

This kiss, the peephole, the way he whispered to her—it was all for show. Luther said so, and she knew it, had known it all along. The kiss felt real, still, but when this was over Luther would walk away and not look back. She was a part of his job. Nothing more.

It had been a long time since her heart had been endangered. She protected it faithfully, guarded it against men like this one. No one hurt her, not anymore. No one made her feel small. She was in control, always.

"Can't dance and can't kiss," she said, with a sassy smile that only hurt a little.

Luther's eyebrows lifted slightly.

"Poor baby." She patted him on the cheek and turned away, her smile fading as soon as her back was to him. *Just a job,* she reminded herself as she walked toward the stage. *Just a part of the job.*

When he got the results of the coroner's tests, maybe he'd have something to go on. Right now, he was grasping for something, anything, that would lead him away from Cleo.

He knew she wasn't involved, for several substantial reasons. But that damn grapefruit... Either Cleo's secret admirer had killed Jack for her, or someone had killed Tempest for a completely unrelated reason, and the grapefruit was just a red herring.

There was no shortage of suspects. He and Russell had carefully gone through the desk drawers of Tempest's modest office, searching for something that would point them in the right direction. A direction that might lead away from Cleo. They'd found plenty of possibilities in business associates Jack had cheated. And his little black book was full—full of women's names and possible motives.

They checked out everything, but so far they were getting nowhere. Police work was often dull as dishwater. By the time homicide got on the job, the crime was over. It was all in the details.

He approached the flower shop in the mall, wishing it could be simple. The man who bought Cleo flowers paid with a credit card, had a record and confessed the moment he was confronted. Luther should be so lucky.

The girl behind the desk was bright, more cheerful than anyone should be. The place was busy, but then Valentine's Day was right around the corner—next Friday, just eight days away. When the clerk was free, she turned her smile on Luther.

He flashed his badge and her smile died. "I'm looking for information on deliveries made to Cleo's, a nightclub downtown."

"How come?" she asked.

"It's confidential," Luther said. "Can you help me out?"

"Maybe. When were the deliveries made?"

"There were several deliveries made over the past four months, all red roses. I don't have the exact dates, but if that's what you need, I could probably get them."

The young girl bit her bottom lip in obvious consternation and flipped her pale blond hair with practiced precision. "The owner's not here, so I don't really know what to do. Don't you need a search warrant or something?"

Luther smiled, trying to borrow some of Mikey's charm. "I don't know, do I?"

The girl returned his smile and went to the computer. "Nah, I trust you. You have an honest face."

"Gee, thanks."

It took her a while, and she had to stop several times, but she finally found three of the deliveries on the computer. Not that what she found was a lot of help. Payment was always made in cash. A different clerk had taken the order every time, which was inconvenient and possible well-planned on the purchaser's part. Since this was one of the busiest florists in town, and there were several part-time employees, all the guy had to do was walk around the mall until he saw a fresh face.

"I don't suppose you took any of these orders," Luther asked, discouraged.

"Nope. Sorry."

He threw his card onto the counter. "If anyone remembers anything about these orders, or if anyone else comes in to place an order for a delivery to Cleo's, call me."

"Sure." The clerk leaned against the counter. "Don't you want to order something for Valentine's Day while you're here?"

Luther held back a groan. "I don't do Valentine's Day," he grumbled. Hearts and flowers, teddy bears and candy. Hopes were up, reality went out the window, and some poor schmuck somewhere was going to be very disappointed. "I don't believe in Valentine's Day."

"That's just kinda sad," the girl said. "You should try it, you know. I *love* Valentine's Day."

Another customer came in, and Luther took the opportunity to escape.

Chapter 6

Cleo stood near the end of the bar, watching the crowd. Luther was beside her, doing the same. They talked, he drank coffee, and every now and then he'd do something that could only be construed as possessive. He'd drape his arm around her, touch her neck, lean in closer than was proper and lay his eyes on her in a way that was undeniably sexual. He was good at this. There were moments when she thought every touch, every inviting look, was real.

"Your partner is really getting into his work," she said softly, casting a quick glance at Michael. The kid was flirting with Lizzy, who was spending her break at the corner table where Luther's partner sat. Lizzy was his excuse for coming in here every night, and the poor girl was eating it up.

"Mikey can be very dedicated," Luther said.

Cleo kept her eyes on the kid. "He's cute," she observed casually. "Looks kinda like Jon Bon Jovi—except that your partner obviously owns a comb."

Luther dropped his head and laid those dark eyes on her. "Cute?"

"Jealous, honey?" she teased, giving him a wide smile.

One eye narrowed. "Homicide detectives are not supposed to be *cute.*"

She leaned just a tad closer. "What are they supposed to be?" she asked.

"Dedicated. Tough. Determined."

He was all those, and more. "Sounds like the qualities one looks for in a hound dog, Malone."

"I am also learning that a homicide detective needs an infinite amount of patience."

"Am I testing you?"

Something deep in his eyes reacted to that question. "Most definitely."

Out of the corner of her eye, Cleo saw the door swing open. Thea strode in, composed, annoyed, nose in the air. Literally and figuratively. She made her way for Cleo, weaving past tables carefully so she didn't touch anything. The woman had been born with a bug up her butt.

"Visitation was tonight," Thea said as she passed the last of the tables and approached Cleo. "I expected to see you there."

Cleo shook her head. Visitation was for family. Friends. "I'll be at the funeral tomorrow."

Thea sighed, in a way so much like that of their mother. Could one inherit a *sigh?*

"At least Palmer and I were there to represent the family."

"Thank you." She glanced toward the door. "Where is Palmer?"

"Yeah," Luther said. "Where *is* Palmer?"

He was putting up a marvelous front of being territorial. Palmer was probably sitting in the car, terrified to face Luther again. For that, she could thank him.

"Palmer didn't feel well, so he went back to the hotel. I just wanted to come by and make sure—" her expression softened, just a little "—that you're all right."

Cleo laid a hand on her sister's arm. She and Thea were as different as night and day, and no one got on her nerves the way Thea did. But no matter what happened, she knew her sister would be there for her, if she needed help. And if Thea ever admitted that she might need help, Cleo would be the first one to her side. "Thanks. I'm fine."

Eric was already giving her the eye from stage. He hated to be late getting started, and he didn't like Luther. Poor Eric. She'd told him so many times that she was not interested in dating, and here she was hanging all over Luther. She considered telling him it was all for show, but in truth she hoped maybe her "relationship" with Luther would give Eric a push toward a more suitable woman.

"Stick around," Cleo said, smiling at Thea. "My set starts in a few minutes."

Thea shook her head, then moved down the bar just a little bit to order a drink from Edgar. A Vodka Collins. "I'll just drink this and then head to the hotel. I'm quite tired."

Cleo glanced at her sister, then at Eric, and then down the bar to Edgar. So many people who loved her, each in his or her own way. People who would protect her. She grabbed Luther's wrist and pulled him a couple of feet toward the end of the bar, where she could be sure no one would overhear. She'd put this off for too long.

She lifted her head, aiming her lips for his ear, and he dutifully leaned down.

"I have something to tell you," she whispered, gripping his wrist too tightly.

When she hesitated, he urged her on. "Go on. Can't be that bad."

She swallowed. He had no idea. "The night Jack was

killed,'' she said in a breathy voice. ''I wasn't here with Edgar and Eric. Don't be mad,'' she added quickly. ''They were only trying to protect me. They meant well. I just…didn't want to lie to you anymore.''

His hand rested at the back of her head, holding her close. His mouth moved to her ear. ''Thank you for telling me,'' he said. ''But I've known all along.''

Luther hated funerals. Crying women made him feel helpless, and that was a feeling he did not like. Not at all. Randi, Jack's latest and last girlfriend, sobbed openly, occasionally wailing as she threw herself over the closed casket. There were a number of weepy women in the small crowd, and even Thea dabbed at her eyes occasionally with a lacy handkerchief.

Cleo didn't cry. She hadn't worn red and she didn't dance, but she was not pretending to mourn the man who had hurt her.

Luther admired her honesty.

She wasn't always honest, though. A couple of days ago, when she'd given him that sassy *''Can't dance and can't kiss,''* she'd been lying. He knew, not because he was an expert with women, but because he had seen the light in her eyes when he'd pulled away from that kiss. She hadn't looked so tough, for a moment. She hadn't looked at all invincible.

Besides, the kiss had blown him away. That could absolutely, positively not be one-sided.

And last night, she'd confessed that her alibi had been false. He'd known from that first night. When Edgar and Eric had given Cleo an alibi, the expression on her face had given them all away. No, she wasn't a very good liar.

He knew Cleo had not killed her ex, but the false alibi had bumped Eric and Edgar up on his suspect list. Had they lied to protect Cleo, as she thought, or to protect themselves? As soon as Luther had more information on the two, he was going to have a nice, long talk with them, one at a time. Until then, he'd let them get comfortable. When the time came, he didn't want them on their guard.

He'd followed Cleo home after her last set, Wednesday night and last night, too. He'd walked her to the door, as any decent suitor would. But he hadn't gone in and he hadn't kissed her again. Both of them had known it would be too dangerous.

Now, they stood at the back of the largest room in the funeral home, watching the crowd, waiting for something to happen.

"Randi with an *i* is going to faint before this is all over," Cleo said softly.

"Wanna bet?"

"Five bucks."

He placed an arm around her, a move that might appear to be consoling to anyone watching. "You're on. See anyone here who looks familiar?"

She glanced around the room. "A bunch of Jack's old girlfriends. A guy from Nashville he did business with on occasion. Oh," she said, lifting her hand to point furtively to a man who was making his way to the coffin with a confident swagger. "That's Corey Flinger. Jack cheated him out of more money than he did me. I'll bet another five dollars that he's here just to make sure Jack is really dead."

Luther made a mental note to check out the leather-jacketed Flinger. The man's thick dark hair was flawlessly styled and looked like it had been sprayed to death. His jeans were too tight and the toes of his black cowboy boots too pointy. "Is he a musician?"

"Yeah. Corey's kind of an unbalanced, low-rent Roy Orbison."

"Unbalanced?"

"Given to temper tantrums, on stage and off," she revealed.

Definitely a suspect, then, but why would he go to the trouble to point the finger at Cleo? Why the damn grapefruit? Corey surprised them all when he sat down next to a sobbing Randi and put his arm around her shaking shoulders.

When the time came for everyone to take their places, Luther and Cleo sat in the back row. She wanted to be inconspicuous, and he wanted to be able to see everyone else. To his surprise, Thea and Palmer scooted into the same aisle, and Thea sat beside her sister.

"You should have worn black," Thea whispered, checking out the stylish blue-green dress Cleo wore.

"I should have worn red," Cleo shot back. "And I would have, but I lost my best pair of red shoes."

"Behave," Thea said, before the service began.

The service was short, the minister who gave the sermon blessedly to the point. *Life is precious. We should not judge others.* Luther noted that there were no kind words about Jack's days on this earth. Maybe there weren't any to be said.

Near the end of the service, Randi stood up, cried out and fainted into Corey Flinger's arms. Immediately, Cleo's hand shot out, palm up.

"Pay up," she whispered.

"Later."

Cleo dropped her hand into her lap and left it there. Once, when she thought no one was looking, her pale, slender fingers closed into a tight fist, then gradually loosened. Her face was stony and told nothing of what was going on in her mind.

As soon as the service was over, Cleo jumped to her feet. "Let's get out of here."

Luther took her arm and led her out of the room where

people talked and lingered. Thea and Palmer were right behind them.

"Are you all right?" Thea asked, as they stepped from the funeral parlor into the parking lot, where a blast of cool air slapped them.

Cleo didn't slow down as she headed for his car. "I'm fine," she said, without looking back. "I mean, it was *Jack.*" Her voice only cracked a little.

"I knew you would be upset," Thea said, rushing past Luther to walk beside her sister. "That's why I came."

"You came because it was the right thing to do," Cleo said.

"I came because I love you."

Both women stopped behind Luther's car, turning to stand face-to-face. Cleo had to tilt her head back and look up. "Thank you," she said, reaching out for a sisterly hug.

Luther watched, confused, as Thea and Cleo embraced one another tightly.

"I can stay awhile longer," Thea offered as she rested her head on Cleo's shoulder. "If you need me, I will."

"I have to get back—" Palmer began.

"Shut up, Palmer," Thea said. He did.

"I'll be all right," Cleo said as she backed away and dropped her arms. "It's not like I loved him anymore."

But she had once, hadn't she? Somehow he had forgotten that, and had remembered only that Cleo's ex was a thorn in her side.

"Are you sure?" Thea asked.

Cleo nodded, they hugged again, and Thea headed for her own car, Palmer in tow.

Luther opened Cleo's door, saw her situated, and then walked around the car to the driver's side. He dropped into his seat and turned to look at her. "Okay, I'm confused."

"About what?"

Too many things to list, at the moment. Best to settle for

just the one confusion. "Thea. I thought you two hated each other."

"No," Cleo said, with a sad smile. "We're different as any two women could be, we get on one another's nerves like no one else can, and we don't agree on anything. But she is my sister. I love her."

"What about Palmer?"

"He's one of the many things we disagree about." She offered her palm. "Where's my five bucks?"

"Stop trying to change the subject."

"I thought we were here to find the man who killed Jack, not investigate my dysfunctional family."

She was right. "Did you see anyone who didn't belong?"

Cleo shook her head before turning to look away from him, as the other mourners left the funeral home. "I did hate Jack, you know."

"I know."

"But there at the end of the service, I suddenly remembered what he was like when I fell in love with him. I remembered how it feels to love someone so completely that they become your whole life." She turned her head slowly to look at him again. "The man I loved died a long time ago, but I just buried him today. Does that make sense?"

"Sure it does," he said, trying to understand.

"Have you ever loved anyone that way?"

He shook his head.

"Don't," she warned. "It steals a part of your soul."

Friday nights were always her busiest. Already the place was packed. Edgar usually brought in an extra waitress for the weekend, and both girls were busy now, hustling through the tightly packed tables, delivering drinks and sandwiches and making chitchat with the customers. Lizzy, with her long brown ponytail and bright smile, and Paula with her short blond bob and laugh that carried across the room.

Cleo scanned the faces in the crowd. Was one of them a murderer? Was one of them her secret admirer?

Michael had come in, a while back. He pretended not to know her, but had struck up yet another conversation with Lizzy. She hadn't been teasing when she'd told Luther his partner was cute. The kid had a pretty face and a great smile, and Lizzy was obviously a little bit taken. What would Lizzy do when she found out that Mikey was a cop on an assignment? That his flirting with her was part of the job?

Maybe she should warn the poor girl. Luther was trifling with her, the same way Russell trifled with Lizzy—but at least Cleo knew *why*.

Luther walked into the club, shaking off the cold as the door closed behind him, glancing around the room with eyes that didn't miss much. When his eyes landed on her, he smiled and started toward the bar with that long-legged, lazy walk of his. A few women turned to watch, but he didn't notice. The guy probably didn't even know he was a heartbreaker.

He didn't waste time with a traditional greeting, but raked his eyes over her quickly. "The red dress."

"The very same."

He stood close. "Are you okay? You could always take tonight off."

She shook her head, not bothering to try to explain that she needed to sing tonight more than ever. "I'm fine."

She backed away and caught Edgar's attention with a wave of her hand. He came quickly. "There's a package under the bar," she said, eyes on Luther.

Edgar came up with the neatly wrapped gold foil package. "This one?"

"That's it." She took the small, oblong package and offered it to Luther.

"What's this?" he said, without touching the box.

"It's a gift. Strictly for show," she added, with a smile.

He took the package as if it were a snake.

"It's not a bomb," she said. "Open it."

He did, taking his time, unwrapping the package methodically and then lifting the lid. "A tie," he said as he took her selection from the box. "A *red* one."

"If you're going to hang out with me, Malone, you're going to have to snaz up your wardrobe." She pointed at the blue-and-gray-striped tie he wore. "That's just awful."

He held the new tie in one hand and lifted the tail end of the one he wore. "I paid four dollars for this tie."

"I don't doubt it."

"It was on sale."

"This one," Cleo said, running her fingers over the new tie, "is silk."

"And it's *red.*"

"Do you have something against red?" She reached out and began to unknot the tie he wore, her fingers easily working the neat knot.

"Not when you wear it," he grumbled.

"Every man needs a power tie."

"I'm a cop, not a lawyer. I don't need a power tie."

She slipped the unknotted tie from around his neck, sliding it slowly from beneath his starched collar and then dropping it onto the bar. He didn't protest, when she took the new tie from him and draped it around his neck, then began to work it into place. Her fingers touched his neck, brushed against his shirt and the firm, warm skin beneath.

"I have a reputation to uphold, Malone," she teased. "I can't be seen with a man who wears four-dollar polyester ties."

"I have a seven-dollar tie at home."

"Humor me," she said as she straightened his collar around the new tie.

He stood stock-still, while she knotted the tie. Her fingers skimmed his chest, the back of her hand sensed the heat beneath that plain white shirt. And suddenly what she was doing seemed terribly intimate, and not at all for show. Her heart started to beat too fast. Her breath caught in her throat. As she finished with the new tie, she patted it softly.

"See there?" she said, doing her best to sound nonchalant. "That's much better."

The jukebox was playing. For most of the night someone had been punching in remakes of the old tunes, the stuff she sang these days. But the jukebox carried an eclectic selection, and while she stood there patting Luther's new tie, an old, slow, country song started playing.

"Dance," she said, taking Luther's hand and dragging him to the dance floor.

"I don't—" he protested.

"You can learn," she said, stopping at the corner of the dance floor. Two other couples danced, huddled together and oblivious to those around them.

She stared at his chest. "It's not difficult, Malone," she said. Her arms came up. So did his. "Dancing is like breathing. You feel it, deep inside. You don't think about each step, you don't count in time with the music. You just let the music seep inside you, and you move." The hand he enfolded over hers was warm and firm, a man's strong and tender hand. Her other hand rested on his shoulder, his arm snaked around her waist, and he pulled her close. Very, very close.

He took a deep breath and took the first step. A very small, cautious step. Cleo let her head fall against his shoulder, and she rested her cheek against the warm fabric of his dark blue suit. Her eyes drifted closed. She did as she had instructed him to do: she let the music wash over her. It washed away everything. Jack. Thea. The funeral.

After a few cautious steps, Luther relaxed. "This isn't so bad," he muttered.

Cleo smiled. "Told you so." She loved the way he smelled, the way his arms were firm and still tender. She loved the way his warmth wrapped around her. She didn't get this close, not anymore. She didn't let anyone hold her this way. But for a while, she wanted to pretend that it wasn't pretend.

"What are you doing Sunday?" Luther asked.

"The club is closed on Sunday. I usually sleep late, take Rambo to the park, and sometimes Syd and I will go out to eat."

"Would you do me a favor?" he asked carefully, sounding almost sheepish.

"If I can." He sighed, and she felt it. Oh yeah, she felt it.

"My ex-partner and his wife have invited me to Sunday dinner."

"Don't worry about me," she said, feeling a little disappointed. "You don't have to watch over me all the time."

"I was wondering if you'd go with me."

Cleo lifted her head and looked up at Luther. He stared down at her with those dark brown eyes that were sad and deep and sexy, all at the same time. "If you want me to."

"Grace is always trying to fix me up," he grumbled. "It's like a mission with her, to see me settled down. When Ray called this afternoon, I told him I'd be there, but that I'd bring my own date, thank you very much."

"A date," she repeated.

"If anyone's watching closely, it'll look strange if I desert you over the weekend and meet someone else at Ray's for Sunday dinner."

They always had to keep in mind how things might *look.* She had almost forgotten that.

"Besides," he added with a smile, "if Grace thinks I have managed to snag my own woman, maybe she'll lay off for a while."

Cleo laid her head against Luther's chest, so he wouldn't see her face. Why *didn't* he have his own woman? Luther Malone probably had a long string of females, never letting anyone get too close, never caring enough to make a commitment.

"Still willing?" he asked.

She should refuse. Why should she spend Sunday, her only day off, pretending to be in a relationship with Luther so his friends would get off his back? All she had to do was tell him she'd rather have peanut butter sandwiches with Syd and Rambo than sit down to a meal with him and his friends and continue to pretend…

"Sure," she whispered.

The music came to an end, and they stopped. Cleo lifted her head, Luther looked down.

"Maybe I could learn how to dance, after all," he said.

"You're off to a good start."

He stared at her mouth, his eyes darkened, and he didn't let go. When he moved his mouth toward hers, she knew she should back away before it was too late. But she didn't move.

Again, he kissed her. Soft, sweet, his mouth lingered over hers. The music, a faster tune, replaced the slow country song, and still Luther kissed her. And she kissed him back. How could she not?

His hand climbed to tangle in the fall of hair at her back. Her hand clenched the fabric of his jacket sleeve. She felt this kiss the way she felt the music. Down deep. It was as basic and primal and necessary as breathing.

His lips parted, and he very subtly slipped his tongue

between her lips. Testing. Arousing. *Can't dance and can't kiss.* Had she really said that to him?

Finally he broke the kiss, drawing slowly away, leaving his hand enmeshed in her curls. She didn't release her hold on his jacket. Not yet. Her knees were too weak to let go.

"Guess I need a little work on that, too," Luther said as he draped his arm around her and led her back to the bar.

Eric stood at the end of the bar, a scowl on his pretty face as he glared at Luther. Edgar just shook his head in what looked like fatherly dismay.

Luther chose a table at the back of the room, even though he was tempted to drag a chair up to the stage. He could watch the crowd well enough from the back, and that was why he was here. Right?

Cleo sat on stage, all great legs and womanly curves and tempting black curls. He could still feel her mouth on his; he could still feel the way she moved against him. Dancing was undeniably sexual, and it was only natural that he had found himself turned on. But hell, the last thing he needed was to fantasize about Cleo Tanner any more than he already did.

Still, Cleo was a woman made for fantasies, he mused as he fingered his red tie.

No matter how large the crowd in her place, she mesmerized them all. The room was quiet as she sang, all eyes turned to her. After a while he quit studying the crowd and allowed himself to watch her, too. Yeah, she was definitely a fantasy woman.

She finished one bluesy number, and smiled as the crowd applauded. Her smile died when a drunk who sat on the opposite side of the room from Luther shouted out, "Jeremiah was a bullfrog!"

A few of the patrons at tables near the man tried to shush him.

"I'm tired of hearing that old crap. That's my granny's kind of music. I want to hear something snappy!"

Cleo, apparently unperturbed, looked down at the heckler and lifted her eyebrows. "First of all, 'Jeremiah was a Bullfrog' is not the title of any song."

"Is, too," the drunk argued, and then he began to sing. Off-key.

"If you're going to request a song," Cleo continued, "you could at least go to the trouble to find out what the title is."

Edgar moved quietly around the room, heading for the heckler.

"You know," the drunk said, enjoying all the attention that had been shifted to him. "You're not even very good. I came in here looking for a few snappy tunes to make me feel better, and you've depressed the hell out of me! If you don't know 'Jeremiah was a Bullfrog,' how about something fun like…like I wanna party all night and party every day. Something like that. I like that one."

Cleo smiled down at the man. "You know, I don't come to your place of business and tell you how to do your job."

The drunk scoffed.

Cleo stared at the man with wide, innocent eyes. "I don't stand over you and say, 'The fries are done! The fries are done!'"

The crowd laughed, and the drunk stood up in disgust, pointing a wavering finger at the stage. "You're a lousy singer. I shoulda gone somewhere else to get cheered up." Instead of heading for the door, the drunk walked to the stage.

He didn't get there. Edgar grabbed one arm and Luther grabbed the other. When the drunk protested, Luther pulled back his jacket and showed the man his badge and gun. The sight very quickly took the fight out of him.

"Let's go, buddy," Edgar said gruffly.

''I didn't mean it,'' the drunk said pitifully. ''I just wanted to hear 'Jeremiah was a Bullfrog.'''

The three of them busted through the club doors and onto the sidewalk.

''I'm going home,'' the drunk said, trying to reach for his pocket with the hand Edgar had immobilized. He didn't seem to understand why he couldn't reach his keys.

Luther pulled a twenty from his pocket and handed it to Edgar. ''Put him in a cab and take his keys. He can reclaim them tomorrow, at Precinct B.''

''I'm perfectly fine,'' the drunk said, trying very hard not to sound intoxicated and failing miserably.

''What's your name?'' Luther asked.

''Bob Smith,'' the drunk said, with a wobble.

The door behind them opened, and Russell stepped out, his favorite cocktail waitress in tow. ''Everything okay out here?'' he asked, reaching for a cigarette in his breast pocket.

''Everything's fine.'' Luther nodded once. Russell, who didn't smoke, lit up a cigarette for him and for his new friend, Lizzy. They stepped a few feet down the sidewalk and talked in subdued voices.

Luther returned his attention to the drunk. ''Okay, Mr. Smith, let's see some ID.''

''All right,'' he snapped. ''My name is Willie Lee Webb. I didn't do anything wrong. You can't arrest me for not liking the songs that woman sang.''

Luther tightened his grip and lowered his voice. ''I can arrest you on any number of charges, if I have a mind to. You want a list of charges, or do you want to go home like a good boy, before I change my mind and haul your ass in?''

''I'm going home,'' he said grudgingly.

Luther left the surly drunk in Edgar's capable hands. A

cab was parked down the street, and at Edgar's signal it pulled down to the front of the club.

Luther stepped back into the warm club, his eyes quickly landing on the woman on stage. She sang as if she didn't have a care in the world, as if she hadn't sparred with a heckler who'd insulted her and interrupted her show.

Usually Cleo kept her eyes above the crowd, but as he stepped to his table, her gaze found him. It lingered there, a moment longer than was proper, and then she tore it away.

Chapter 7

Tonight Luther followed her in. She wasn't sure that was a good idea, but giving him the boot at the door didn't seem like such a good idea, either.

"Does that happen often?" he asked as he closed the door behind him and bent to dutifully scratch Rambo's head.

She immediately thought of the dance, the kiss. *Never.* "What are you talking about?" She kicked off her shoes.

"The heckler."

She shook her head and walked toward the kitchen in her stocking feet. "No. Every now and then someone will wander in looking for a different kind of music or a different kind of atmosphere. Usually they just leave quietly. Every now and then..." She shrugged and took a glass from the cabinet.

Luther stood in the kitchen doorway, leaning against the frame and watching her closely. Too closely.

"You handled him well."

"Guys like that don't bother me."

"What does?"

She watched the suddenly fascinating swirl of juice in her glass. *You, Malone. You bother me.* "Nothing," she said, sounding like she meant it. "But the worst is when someone in the crowd recognizes me and asks me to sing 'Come Morning.'"

"Why is that so bad?"

"Come on, Malone, you heard it," she snapped. "It's a stupid, heart-on-my-sleeve love song."

"I liked it," he said, with a shrug.

"Well, I don't sing it anymore." It reminded her of who she'd been and how she'd been hurt. Besides, there was no such thing as a love as powerful as the one she'd written about. Made her feel like such a sap…. "Do you want some juice?"

Luther shook his head.

"I guess you have to be going." *Please.*

Again, he shook his head. "I don't know if anyone is watching or not. I haven't seen any sign of surveillance, but I can't be sure. It would be best if I…stayed a little while."

"Have a reputation to live up to, is that it?"

He smiled, not too widely. "Something like that."

Suddenly thirsty, she finished her juice quickly. "Well, make yourself at home. I'm going to change into something comfortable."

His eyebrows shot up, but she ignored him.

As she changed clothes, she told herself again that this was all for show. Malone didn't really like her. No matter how he looked at her or danced or kissed, he didn't want her. She was a job. A means to an end.

When she walked into the living room, warm and comfy in her flannel pants, and baggy T-shirt and thick socks, Luther grinned at her from the couch. "This is not what happens in the movies when a woman disappears into the bedroom to make herself more comfortable.''

''Sorry to disappoint you, Malone, but this is not a movie.''

''Too bad.''

And if it were a movie, it would be rated PG. She was almost sorry. Her entire life was PG, and until Malone had walked through her door she'd liked it that way.

She didn't take her favorite chair, but sat on the floor, legs crossed, and called Rambo to her. The traitorous dog cast a longing glance at Luther before padding over to join Cleo.

Cleo raked her fingers through Rambo's fur. ''What you said at lunch the other day, about your mother and father. Was that true?''

The easy expression on Luther's face died. ''If we're going to talk about my childhood, I'm going to need something stronger than orange juice to drink.''

''Sorry,'' she said, with a crooked grin. ''I didn't mean to pry, I was just...curious.''

He hesitated for a moment, and then answered. ''Yeah, it was true.''

''What happened to your father?''

''It depends on what story I choose to believe.''

She raised her eyebrows in a silent question.

''My mother was never married,'' he said. ''When I got old enough to ask about my father, I got a different story every time. They were childhood sweethearts. He went off to Vietnam before he knew she was pregnant, and never came home.'' His own eyebrows lifted. ''He was Elvis.''

''Elvis?''

''Yep. She actually told me once, when an old Elvis song came on the radio, that Elvis got her pregnant.''

Cleo shook her head. ''Didn't she ever give you any other name?''

"Sure," he said, trying to sound as if he didn't care. 'She said I was named for him, so for a long time I thought is name was Luther, too. But one night she mentioned im, and she called him Trent."

Cleo relaxed, leaning her back against the chair, and ooked up at Luther. "You never tried to find him."

He shook his head. "Why should I?"

"What's the father's name on your birth certificate?"

He held up both hands, palms outward, patience rapidly isappearing. "What difference does it make?"

"Sorry," she said, turning her eyes down to a relaxed Rambo.

She went back to petting Rambo, wishing Luther would eave. Praying he wouldn't. Not yet.

"Unknown," he said quietly, when he finally spoke gain. "When I asked her about that, she said she was fraid my father's family would try to get custody, if they new about me. She said they weren't bad people, they vere just grieving over the loss of their only child and apable of doing anything."

"And yet she named you after him?"

"And moved away from the small town in Georgia vhere she grew up, when I was not yet a year old."

Cleo tried to piece it all together. "Anything else?"

"I don't think about it anymore," he said sharply. "It's ncient history."

"You should think about it now," she said. "What ou've told me could all be true. Luther and Trent could oth be right. She might've called him Trent sometimes, he way I call you Malone and you call your partner Russell. They might've been childhood sweethearts, and he night've gone off to war—"

"And Elvis?"

Cleo was not dissuaded. "Maybe they were listening to

one of his songs when they made love. I don't know but—"

"It doesn't matter," he said.

Somehow, she thought it *was* important. He was a detective. He could have investigated his own past at any time. Why didn't he?

Time to change the subject. "Why do you carry such a small gun?"

He lifted his jacket by the lapel and glanced at the snub-nosed revolver in his shoulder holster. "Size doesn't matter," he said wryly. "It's what you can do with what you have that counts."

"You are so bad," she said, with a smile.

"Hey," he said innocently, "I'm a great shot."

"Have you ever actually shot anybody?"

He shook his head. "No."

"Ever been shot?"

Again, he shook his head.

"Good," she said absently.

While Cleo stroked Rambo's back, the dog lifted her head and looked up at Luther, her eyes pleading. And then she gave a short, low bark.

"What does she want?" he asked suspiciously.

"I think she likes the way you scratch behind her ears."

Luther dutifully left the couch and sat on the floor, on the other side of a lazy Rambo. He began to scratch. "Spoiled dog," he muttered.

"I'm gone so much," Cleo said. "When I'm home I like to give her lots of attention." She stroked Rambo's back and Luther scratched behind the dog's ears. After a moment, Rambo growled in sheer delight.

Surely Luther had been here long enough to satisfy anyone who was watching. She doubted anyone was watching anyway. Whoever had killed Jack was probably long gone. It wasn't a secret admirer who was obsessed with her, 'as just someone trying to pin the murder on her so no ne would look in their direction. Someone like Randi with n *i.*

Without warning, Rambo rose up and lumbered content- dly into the kitchen.

"She must be thirsty," Cleo said.

Luther just nodded.

Cleo looked at the man who sat on the floor before her. he couldn't stand this much longer. "You've been here ong enough, right?"

"Probably," Luther agreed.

"You might as well—"

He reached out, cupped her neck in one hand and drew er toward him slowly. He gave her plenty of time to move way, plenty of time to tell a joke to spoil the mood or turn er head or order him to stop. She did nothing. She allowed im to draw her mouth to his, and she not only allowed im to kiss her, she parted her lips and closed her eyes in heer delight, as she wrapped her arms around his waist.

It was amazing, what the simple touch of the right man's ps could do to a woman. She felt like melting butter. Her nees went weak, her entire body reacted to the kiss. She ngled, from the top of her head to her curled-up toes.

She held on tightly and let herself be swept away. If she llowed herself to consider love, if she wanted a man in er life—

It was Rambo, trying to wedge herself between them, at interrupted the kiss. Luther pulled back slowly, looking s dazed as Cleo felt.

"What was that for?" she whispered. "No one's here to e."

"Since I'm such a lousy kisser, I figured I could use the ractice."

"Practice," she breathed.

"I have to go." Luther rose slowly.

Have to. Not want to, not need to. *Have* to. "Okay." She didn't get up.

"I'll drive you to the club tomorrow afternoon," he sai as he backed away. "I'll pick you up about three."

"Okay," she agreed, feeling oddly complacent.

He walked slowly toward the door, and Cleo watche her hands in Rambo's fur, as Luther slowly took his leav turning to study her more often than was necessary.

When he reached the turn in the foyer that would tak him out of sight, she jumped up to follow, rationalizing th she needed to make sure he'd remember to lock the fro door. Like he'd forget. She caught up with him quickl before he laid his hand on the knob.

"Luther," she said, as he opened the door.

"What?" He glanced over his shoulder, his eyes me hers, and in that instant Cleo's heart jumped into her throa

She smiled. "The tie looks good."

When you had a case like this one, you didn't take Sa urday off. Sunday, either, if you had a lead. In the Jac Tempest case, they had plenty of leads. The problem wa none of them actually went anywhere.

Luther banged on Randi Rayner's door. Since it was nin o'clock on a Saturday morning, and Luther was wound s tightly he felt like he was about to explode, he put ever thing he had into the pounding of his fist.

Finally, a tinny voice yelled, "Just a minute!" followe by a *very* unladylike obscenity.

Mikey grinned. "Why are we here again?" he aske casually.

"Because Jack Tempest was a snake, I'm ninety-nin percent sure he was cheating on Randi, and Miss Rayne doesn't seem like the kind of girl who takes that sort thing lying down." And she hated Cleo. That much wa clear in every conversation he'd had with her, in every heated glance.

Finally the door opened, just a crack. Randi, fresh from her bed, was raccoon-eyed. Her blond hair stood straight up. The Bride of Frankenstein had nothing on her.

"Good morning," Luther said, smiling. "If you have a few minutes, I have a couple of questions for you."

"Now?" she whined. "Can't you come back later?"

"Sorry," he said. "I have a full day planned."

She sighed and looked over her shoulder...and in that instant Luther knew she was not alone.

"Just a minute," she said, closing the door in their faces.

Luther turned to Russell and nodded, whispering, "Wait here."

He slipped around to the back of the apartment building, stepping around a rusted tricycle and over a discarded basketball that had gone flat. There were no windows on this side of the building, but surely at the back... He rounded the corner just in time to see a cowboy boot at the end of a blue-jeaned leg stick out of one of those windows.

Corey Flinger, slipping out the window, didn't look much better than Randi had. His shirt was unbuttoned, the dark hair that had been so well sculpted yesterday at the funeral stuck out at odd angles, and he needed a shave. Luther let him get halfway out the window before rounding the corner.

"Mr. Flinger," he said. "Just the man I wanted to talk to."

Flinger glanced back at Luther, lost his balance and fell out the window.

"Damn," the man mumbled, as Luther stood over him and glared down.

Luther offered Flinger a hand and pulled him to his feet. "You look like you could use a cup of coffee."

Once Flinger was on his feet, he looked like he wanted to run. Too late for that. "I guess."

"I know just the place."

Luther leaned against the bar at the club and sucked on a peppermint. He didn't really want it. What he really wanted to suck on was Cleo.

He was more and more attracted to her with every passing minute. Bad idea. She had crawled under his skin, in a way no other woman ever had, and he thought about her often. Hell, he thought about her all the time. For the first time in years, he wanted a woman so much, he ached with it. All he needed was a few days in bed with Cleo; which in spite of everything seemed like a very *good* idea.

This morning's interrogation of Corey Flinger and Randi with an *i* had gotten him nowhere. Flinger was easily intimidated, not too bright, and guilty of nothing more than sleeping with Randi. His alibi for the night of the murder was solid, smashing Luther's theory that Randi had suckered the poor guy into doing the dirty work for her.

He'd spent the afternoon here, mulling over how he should proceed. Cleo had been going over the books. For a while he'd sat in the office with her, but the tension had gotten to be too much. She kept looking up, and he found himself staring at her so hard it hurt. And remembering the way she kissed. If Rambo hadn't interrupted last night, he would've ended up making his move right there on the floor.

He had no right. This was business, an assignment. And making a move on Cleo could cost him his job.

So he'd eventually left Cleo to her books and spent the rest of the afternoon talking to Edgar. Picking Edgar's brain about the man who had sent Cleo notes and flowers. According to Edgar, this was not Cleo's first secret admirer. And wouldn't be her last.

Edgar seemed inordinately protective of Cleo. Protective enough to kill for her? Eric adored her, openly and with a youthful passion. Did he love her enough to kill for her? Luther wanted to believe that someone not related to Cleo had killed Jack...but he didn't. He just couldn't put his finger on the reason *why.* The killer had murdered a man known for hurting Cleo, but then he had pointed the finger at her with that grapefruit. That made whatever relationship the killer had with her complicated. A love-hate relationship she knew nothing about.

Cleo changed in her office, slipping out of her cream-colored pants and sweater and into a black, clingy dress that showed off all her curves. When she walked into the main room of the club, he was sure his heart would stop beating.

Women didn't affect him this way. Not ever. They came and went. They served a purpose, and when things got too close he severed the connection. Already he was closer to Cleo than he'd been to any other woman.

A broken heart had driven his mother crazy, hadn't it? Why else had she told all those stories about his father? Why else had she devoted her life to her only child, to the exclusion of everything else...until it killed her. Thirty-year-old women didn't have heart attacks for no reason.

Ray had been miserable for years, all because of a broken heart. Things with Grace were fine now, but for a while it had been rough. And look at Cleo. Jack's betrayal had made her build a shield around her heart. That smart mouth, the sassy smile—he knew they weren't the real Cleo, because he'd kissed the real Cleo last night.

The real Cleo wore flannel and cotton and looked as gorgeous in those baggy clothes as she did in clinging satin. She adored her dog and cared about people and kissed with all her heart and soul. The real Cleo needed someone to love her more than anyone he'd ever met.

"Hi," she said, walking slowly toward him. "Sorry I took so long. I hate numbers."

"Hire a CPA."

She shook her head, sending long black curls dancing. "I don't trust anyone else with my money."

Thanks to Jack, she didn't add.

There was already a small crowd gathered in the club. Eric tinkered with the piano. A few couples had ordered sandwiches and beers and talked, while Eric played softly. Edgar got the bar ready for another busy night.

"I have something for you." Luther didn't bother Edgar, but circled the bar to collect the box he'd left there.

Cleo's eyes widened as he returned with the large, gaily wrapped box in his hands. "Another gift? Let me guess. Diamonds?" she teased.

Luther hefted the large box once before placing it on the counter, shaking his head. "On a cop's salary?"

He had tried to do a better job of wrapping this time, and still Cleo picked at the messy spot on the side.

"I misjudged when I cut the paper," he explained. "So I just cut another square to cover it up."

"I never would have known," she said.

"Just open it, smart-ass."

She did, ripping at the paper, and laughing when she saw the writing on the side of the box.

"A coffeepot."

"Yep."

"For someone who doesn't drink coffee."

He leaned close. "If I'm going to spend time at your house, you *will* have a coffeepot. Coffee's in the car."

"You think of everything." She rounded the bar herself, walked slowly to the other end, and reached around Edgar to grab something on a low shelf. She placed the box on the bar and slid it toward him. It scooted down the bar, and he caught it.

"Too big for a tie," he said.

Cleo walked slowly toward him, her amber eyes smiling, her walk…painful to watch. And he couldn't tear his eyes away.

"Open it," she said as she reached him, standing on the other side of the bar and leaning on it.

He did as she commanded, wondering what on earth she might have bought him this time. Couldn't be any more ridiculous than the bright red tie.

He was wrong. "It's purple," he said, slowly lifting the shirt from the box.

She grinned. "You must have something in your closet besides white, starched shirts."

"White matches everything."

"Purple is more fun."

"I have no desire to dress like a grape."

"It'll look great on you." She reached into the box and grabbed what he'd missed, a tie just a shade darker than the shirt. "You can wear this with your black suit."

"When did you buy these?"

"I went shopping this morning."

"We might've run into one another."

She picked at the price tag on the coffeemaker. "Unlikely. I didn't buy your new clothes at Wal-Mart, Malone."

He leaned over the counter toward her. "But it's purple."

"You can't take it back," she said softly. "I burned the receipt and cut off all the tags."

"You *burned* the receipt?"

She smiled and nodded, and he couldn't help himself. He kissed her. He was too far away to hold her, too far away to do anything more than give her a light, friendly kiss. It wasn't enough.

"Thank you for the coffeepot," she whispered, when h
took his mouth from hers.

"Thank you for the purple shirt and tie."

"Will you wear it?"

"Probably not."

"For me?"

He sighed in surrender. Of course he would wear it fo
her. "Yes, I'll dress like a plum, just for you."

He would do just about anything to make her smile th
way she was smiling now, and the realization scared th
bejesus out of him.

It was an oddly warm night for February, and the
walked toward her door slowly. Luther carried the coffee
maker box, and she carried the coffee.

Before they reached the door, she stopped and looke
up. In summertime, the leaves on the trees in her yar
shielded the sky from view, but winter had bared th
branches. The sky above her was black and dotted wit
brilliant stars.

Luther stopped with her. "What's wrong?"

"Nothing," she said, her gaze remaining fixed on th
sky.

He tilted his head back. "What are you looking at?"

"Nothing," she said again. "Doesn't it make you fe
small?"

"What?"

"The sky. It's so vast, so…beautiful. Whenever I thin
my problems are going to overwhelm me, I look at the sky
In a universe so vast, Jack was nothing. A heckler? N
more than a speck of dust." *My own heartache? Insigni-
icant.*

When she took her eyes from the sky, she saw that Lu
ther no longer stared above. He stared at her. Too har

like he saw too much. She broke the shared glance and headed for the door.

He carried the coffeemaker to the kitchen and placed it on the counter. "I'll hook this up tomorrow. We're supposed to be at Ray's by noon, so I'll come by about eleven-thirty. That'll give me time to set up the coffeemaker before we go."

"Fine."

He started for the door, ready to leave in spite of the reputation he needed to protect, but Rambo got tangled up in his feet.

"I don't think she wants you to go," Cleo said from the doorway.

Luther lifted his head and stared at her. "What about you?"

Cleo shook her head, scared he'd leave her here all alone. Scared he'd stay. She was so tired of being scared.

Rambo padded off to the living room, leaving Cleo and Luther alone again. Luther closed the distance between them quickly, wrapped his arms around her and kissed her. Hard, deep, without the restraint he had called upon to this point. Her body fit snugly against his, tight and warm along the entire length, as he devoured her with his mouth.

"This is a bad idea," he said, in a brief moment when his mouth was not covering hers.

"I know," she murmured.

Luther pressed her back against the doorjamb and trailed his mouth down her chin, down her throat, down to the valley between her breasts. His mouth was warm and soft, the way he kissed her so hungry it took her breath away. His hands studied her shape, barely touching her breasts, skimming down her side, coming to rest on her hips. Her body throbbed. Her knees went weak.

She snaked her hand beneath his jacket, tried to absorb his heat and his passion. It was like looking at the stars.

Nothing else mattered at the moment. This was the only thing that was real. The way they touched, the way Luther made her feel.

Her fingers rocked against his back, pulled him closer, gently studied the muscles beneath his shirt in time with her heartbeat.

His hand slowly traveled lower, caught the hem of her skirt and raised it until his hand rested over her stocking-encased thigh. His fingers lingered there, and then he stopped and muttered a few choice words.

"Do you have a—"

"No," she said huskily. "Do you?"

"No, dammit. Are you on—"

"No."

He stepped back and ran his hands through his hair. Neither one of them was prepared for this. He had no condom in his wallet, she had nothing stashed under the bathroom sink.

"We can't..." she began softly.

"No, we can't." Luther took her face in his hands and stared down at her. "I have to ask to be taken off this case."

"No," she said quickly. "I..." How much could she tell him? Deep inside, she knew it wasn't smart to give too much of herself to any man. But deep inside, she was also very tired of being alone. "I don't trust anyone else but you."

He closed his eyes. "Don't trust me, Cleo."

"I can't help it." She didn't want him walking away because he wasn't comfortable with what was happening between them, and she wouldn't make it easy for him. "What are you going to do if you quit? Assign Mikey to play my lover?"

"No." His fingers brushed her cheeks. "I don't want to pretend anymore. Surely you know that. But I can't con tinue to investigate Jack's murder and...and stay with you at the same time."

"I understand," she said, going cold. It would be easier for him just to walk away.

"So I'll hand the case to Russell and take a vacation. I'm due."

Her heart hardened. "That makes perfect sense." He was going to run from this. Because he liked her too much. Because he didn't like her enough.

"And as soon as I'm officially off the case, I'll be back. *Prepared* this time, Cleo, so if you have any doubts about this..."

Relief rushed through her. "I don't." She leaned into him, and he stepped toward her so his body rested tightly against hers again, so snugly she could feel his arousal. "Did you trade in your peashooter for a bigger gun?" she teased.

"Very funny," he muttered.

Knowing he wanted her made her want him all the more. "Are you sure you don't have just *one*..."

"There's an all-night drugstore on Whitesburg." Luther sighed against her neck. "I'll withdraw from the case Monday morning, bright and early."

"What are you waiting for—"

A knock interrupted them. They parted slowly, and Luther headed for the door.

"It's probably Syd," Cleo said. "Sometimes she stops by when she hears me come home."

"Ask who it is," Luther demanded, as they reached the door.

Cleo obeyed, and Syd's cheerful voice called out a late-night greeting.

A slightly disheveled Luther opened the door, and Syd smiled when she laid eyes on him. She did not look at all surprised to see him here.

"This was delivered for you this afternoon," Syd said, offering a long white florist's box. "I found them sitting on the porch when I got home."

Luther cursed and took the box from Syd, and the redhead's smile faded. "I'm guessing this means they aren't from you?"

Cleo said she'd see Syd in the morning, and Luther closed the door.

More red roses, she imagined. Luther set the box down on the foyer floor, and very carefully lifted the lid, trying not to add any more fingerprints.

When Cleo saw what was inside, she shuddered, just a little. Not red roses this time, but white. A dozen, like always. The plain card rested on top, and Luther read it aloud without touching the evidence.

"'How could you do this to me?'"

"Do what?" Cleo asked softly.

"I think he's talking about me."

Cleo dropped down to look more closely at the perfect blooms. "Red roses mean love," she said.

Luther nodded as he reached for his cell phone to make a call.

"White means death."

Luther's eyes snapped up to meet hers above the box of flowers. "You don't know that."

She nodded quickly. "Mother's Day, if your mother is alive you wear red, if she's dead you wear white."

"That doesn't mean—"

"People send white roses to funerals, Luther."

"People send all kinds of flowers to funerals," he said sensibly.

"If it doesn't mean anything, why change to white after all this time?"

He ended the cell phone call before he got an answer, moved the box of white roses aside without touching a flat surface on the box, and took her hand in his. Gripping her shaking hand firmly, he helped her to her feet.

"I'm not going anywhere," Luther assured her, as if he knew instinctively that that was her greatest fear.

Cleo rested her face against his chest and took a deep breath. "Good."

His hands settled in her hair, soft and easy. "You need twenty-four-hour protection."

She nodded silently.

"I'm it," he said. "There's no way I can step down now and hand this case over to someone else."

Something deep inside her slackened, as if a painful knot had come loose. She knew better than to trust anyone. She knew better than to put her faith in a man. But she was putting her faith in Luther, and it felt right. She wrapped her arms around him and held on tight.

Chapter 8

Luther had been tempted to cancel lunch with Ray and Grace, but by mid-morning it had been clear that he and Cleo both needed to get out of her house. The walls were closing in. The tension between them wasn't easing, it was gradually ratcheting up to a new level.

At least they had coffee, which was a good thing—since he hadn't been able to sleep more than two hours on Cleo's couch last night.

He'd turned the flower box over to the crime scene techs, but he was pretty sure nothing would come of it. Just as nothing had come of their dusting of her office. Cleo had been right when she'd said there would be numerous prints there. Everyone who worked there or ever had worked there had left their mark. It was easy to distinguish the newer prints, of course, but the only prints on the drawer from which the notes had been stolen were Cleo's.

On the way to Ray's, they'd stopped by his apartment so he could change and collect some clothes and toiletries, enough for a few days. This detail wasn't official, and if anyone found out he was moving in…

Since it was his day off, in a way, he dressed in jeans and a black T-shirt, and clipped his gun and badge to his belt. Cleo had looked him over and then commented that she'd have to do a little more shopping for casual clothes. He could only imagine.

She had dressed more casually herself today. He was accustomed to seeing her dressed for the stage, or for relaxing at home. Her emerald-green pants and matching blouse were classy and surely expensive, and showed off her figure in a more subtle way than the dresses she wore to perform in. A gold clip held her wild black curls back on one side, her makeup was more understated than usual. The look suited her.

Grace and Ray opened the door together, both of them obviously curious about the woman Luther had been able to procure on his own. Grace was particularly curious, grinning widely and raking her eyes from Cleo's head to her toes. Ray seemed more amused than anything else.

"You look like you're about to pop," Luther said, as they stepped into the house.

"Luther!" Cleo said, admonishing him.

"Well, she does. When are you due?"

"Any day," Ray said with a wide grin. "She's already started dilating, and if her water breaks…"

"Whoa," Luther said, holding up a hand to silence his ex-partner. "More than I need to know. Just tell me when the kid is here, and if it's a boy or a girl. I don't need specifics on how it *gets* here."

"Dinner will be another twenty minutes or so," Grace said, waddling away and leading them into the living room. "It's a casserole, which is about all I can manage these days. Mix everything up, put it in the oven and wait."

"We shouldn't be here," Cleo said kindly. "You should be resting, not cooking for company."

Grace—who was, Luther had to admit, radiant these days—glanced over her shoulder and smiled. "It's no trouble. Besides, dessert was easy. Krispy Kremes."

Cleo laughed lightly, already at ease with Grace. He could easily see them being friends, as different as they were. They each had a warmth about them, something intangible and soft…and dangerous.

"We can sit and talk until the casserole is ready." Grace very carefully lowered herself into a fat chair near the window. Since it sat a little bit higher than the couch and the only other chair in the room, he imagined it was her favorite place to sit these days. She settled in with a sigh.

Ray took the other chair, leaving the couch for Luther and Cleo. Luther stared at Grace's stomach as he sat beside Cleo. "Are you sure you're not having twins or triplets or something? You're *huge*."

Cleo laughed, but she slapped him on the arm and said, "Luther!" again, in that familiar, chastising tone.

"That's okay," Grace said, smiling. "He's right. And he's a good enough friend to tell me the truth."

"Which is why he's here," Ray added, in a cautious tone that set Luther's nerves on edge.

They wanted something. Something big. "What does that mean?"

Grace and Ray exchanged a look, one of those meaningful glances that made it seem they were reading each other's minds.

"You ask," Grace finally said.

Ray didn't hesitate. "Luther, we want you to be godfather to the baby."

"That's so sweet," Cleo exclaimed.

"Sweet," Luther grumbled, knowing that he was being

put on the spot. How could he say no? "Doesn't that mean that if anything happens to you two..."

"Yes," Grace said. "We can't agree on anyone else. We don't trust anyone else with our child."

Trust, again. How did he do this to himself? "Can I think it over?" Maybe if he thought long enough, he'd be able to come up with an acceptable way to refuse.

"Sure you can," Grace said, her happiness only slightly dimmed by his obvious reluctance.

Ray changed the subject. "Where did you two meet?"

"Cleo's club," Luther said. "She's a singer."

Ray lifted his eyebrows slightly. "A singer? Really. Ever sing any Lyle Lovett songs?"

"Not usually," she said. "But if you two ever drop by the club, I'll see what I can do."

"I can't possibly go anywhere until after the baby is born," Grace said. "I can't even go to the grocery store anymore without my ankles swelling."

"We can go hear Cleo after the baby is born," Ray said.

"We'll need a baby-sitter," Grace said skeptically.

Ray grinned. "Luther can baby-sit."

Enough was enough. "Luther cannot baby-sit," Luther said testily. "Luther doesn't change diapers, coo or wipe up spit."

Grace and Ray both laughed, but Cleo maintained her composure. "You do coo," she said meaningfully. "On occasion."

He looked at her, saw the laughter in her golden eyes. "I do not."

"You coo at Rambo."

"I do *not.*"

"Who's Rambo?" Grace asked.

Cleo looked at the impossibly large pregnant woman and answered, "My dog. She loves Malone because he scratches behind her ears. And coos."

Luther leaned closer to Cleo. "I do not coo," he whispered.

"Sorry, tough guy," she answered. "You've been found out."

Cleo rolled up her sleeves and rinsed dirty dishes, while Grace sat behind her, perched on a kitchen chair.

"You shouldn't be doing that," the pregnant woman protested. "Ray can load the dishwasher later."

"I don't mind," Cleo said. "Besides, I think Ray and Luther wanted to talk alone."

"Guy stuff," Grace agreed.

Luther and Ray were in the living room talking about the case. Her case. They kept their voices low, and Luther paced a lot. When she'd gone in there to collect a couple of dirty glasses, she'd seen him stalk to the window and run his fingers through his hair in apparent exasperation. They hadn't said a word until she left the room. Oddly enough, she didn't mind. She understood the distinction: the smudged line between what was happening between her and Luther, and what was going on with the case.

Cleo ran water over a dirty plate and placed it in the dishwasher. How could Luther be so jaded, when he had friends like Ray and Grace? They loved one another so much that it was clear to see; they had a nice home, a baby on the way...everything every woman dreamed of.

Everyone but her, Cleo thought, the knowledge stealing a bit of the warmth from her heart. She simply wasn't cut out for domestic bliss. She had a few good friends and her nightclub, and she didn't need anything else. She could sing and run her place until she was old and gray, without ever again suffering from a broken heart.

All of a sudden she pictured herself, white-haired and wrinkled, sitting on stage and singing "My Funny Valentine." Alone still, heart unbroken but also unmended.

"Luther is a good guy," Grace said quietly, as if she were afraid the men in the next room might hear.

"I know."

"But he's also very tenderhearted," she continued. "You wouldn't know it to look at him, but he's one of those men who would go to the ends of the earth for a friend."

Cleo loaded the last of the dishes, closed the dishwasher and turned to face Grace as she wiped her hands on a yellow-and-white checked dish towel. "I know that, too."

The expression on Grace's face was wary. "I don't mean to pry, but Luther's never brought a woman to our house before. I've tried to fix him up a hundred times, but his relationships with women never last long. And I've never seen him..." She stalled midsentence and blushed.

"Never seen him what?" Cleo prodded.

"I've never seen him *look* at another woman the way he looks at you."

She didn't want to know that. It was easier to believe that she was one of a thousand women, that she and Luther could have their time together and then part without anyone getting hurt.

"I really shouldn't say that," Grace said quickly. "It's none of my business. But..."

"You don't want Luther to get hurt," Cleo finished for her. "And you know darn well I'm not the right kind of woman to—"

"No," Grace said sharply. "Well, yes to the part about him not getting hurt. But I like you. I think you could be good for him."

Cleo knew she wasn't good for anyone, least of all someone like Luther. "We're just friends," she said.

Just friends. Last night, if Syd hadn't shown up with those flowers, they would be lovers by now. She'd wanted it, he'd wanted it. But it wasn't right. The energy that danced between them was sexual, but it had nothing to do with love. It was sensuous, not lasting. But, oh, if she fell for Luther any harder than she already had, it was going to kill her when he left.

Luther muttered a curse as he lined up the drill. He wasn't a handyman. He had never actually used this drill.

The door next to Cleo's opened, and a red head peeked out. "What are you doing?"

"Putting in a security viewer," he said brusquely.

"A what?"

"A peephole," he amended.

"Oh," Syd said as she stepped onto their shared porch. "That's nice." She smiled as if she knew an amusing secret. "Getting serious, huh?"

"What?"

"Whenever a man shows up with tools, things have to be getting serious, right?"

The word *serious* in conjunction with any woman made the hair on the back of his neck stand up. "I'm just installing a peephole, so Cleo can see who's at the door before she opens it."

"That's very sweet," Syd said, not moving on or knocking on Cleo's door, but taking up residence on the porch.

"No, it's not," he said. "It's very practical. Every woman should have a peephole in her door. This is just an extension of my duties as a police officer."

"Great!" she said cheerily. "I don't have one, either."

He glanced at her closed door. "So I see." Again, he lined up the drill.

"What are you doing?" Syd asked.

Luther took a deep, calming breath. "I'm installing a—"

"No, I mean, why there?"

"Eye level," he said.

"That's your eye level, Detective Malone. If you put the

peephole there, you're going to have to get Cleo a step stool to keep by the door.''

She was right. It was a detail he would not have normally overlooked, but Cleo had his insides twisted in knots, his mind in a muddle. He wanted her, and he couldn't have her. Well, he *shouldn't* have her.

He repositioned the drill at a level that would suit Cleo. ''Thank you,'' he said grudgingly.

''You're welcome.'' The moment of silence that followed her response was too short. ''On a femininity scale of one to ten, with that girl on *Saturday Night Live* that you can't tell if she's a man or a woman being one, and Shania Twain in leopard skin being ten, where would you put Cleo?''

With a disgusted sigh, Luther dropped the hand holding the drill and turned to face Syd. ''What?''

''On a femininity scale of one to ten, with—''

''I heard you,'' he said. ''I just can't believe I heard you correctly.''

''She's my friend,'' Syd said, her smile fading. ''I just don't want to see her hurt by someone who doesn't properly appreciate her.''

''It's not like that. This is just business.''

She scrunched up her nose. ''That might be true, but I don't exactly buy it. See, I know Cleo better than anyone. She's tough, right? She's sassy and confident and can handle anything. But the truth of the matter is, Detective, she's not so tough, and she *can't* handle everything that comes along by herself the way she insists she can.''

''I know that.''

''Good,'' she said, pleased with his response. ''Now, on a scale of one to ten, with—''

''Fifteen,'' he said as he turned around and repositioned the drill, making sure the viewer would be at Cleo's eye level.

For some reason, Syd laughed.

* * *

She should not be sexy in baggy flannel pants and an even baggier T-shirt. She should not be irresistible with her hair piled on her head and her face scrubbed clean of makeup. She should be ordinary.

Cleo was definitely not ordinary.

He had been fascinated by the woman he'd met at the club, the sexier-than-any-woman-had-a-right-to-be, smart-mouthed vixen who captured hearts with a wicked glance and her siren's song. But this woman…this woman was extraordinary.

There was a light in her eyes, a softness to her mouth, a seduction in the very way she breathed. Man, he had it bad. All night, he'd looked at her and fantasized about what it would be like when they finally went to bed together. He tried not to, but he couldn't help himself. Cleo had crawled beneath his skin and he couldn't shake her. Hell, he didn't want to shake her.

She sat on the floor with Rambo's head in her lap, pretending to watch a show on television while she stroked the dog's fur. Neither of them had said a word for over an hour. The television played softly—an old movie she'd chosen—and the clock on the end table ticked softly. *Tick. Tick. Tick.* Occasionally Rambo, who was mad at Luther because he had ignored the request to join them on the floor as he had a few days ago, occasionally made a contented noise.

There was only one way to handle this. He'd withdraw from this case in the morning, take his damn vacation and spend it right here. He'd throw caution to the wind and tell Cleo that she was an extraordinary woman who had turned him inside out.

Handing her case over to someone else wouldn't be easy, but he would be here through it all. If she would let him.

Someone had to watch over her, and no one else seemed to be taking the white roses as a threat. Not even Russell. No one else in the department could take proper care of her. No one else in the world.

"When this is over," he said softly, "I might take a vacation."

Cleo looked up at him, her eyes wide and golden and tempting.

"Florida," he said. "Two weeks on the beach, doing nothing but sleeping and eating shrimp and... Maybe if I go, you'd like to go with me."

She smiled, but there was no humor in the twist of her lips. "Need female company for that last, unmentioned activity you plan to execute on the beach?"

"No," he said quickly. "Well, yes, but that didn't come out quite right."

Some of the light in her eyes dimmed, making her look calculating. Uncertain. "When this is over, Malone, you'll find some other woman in distress to take care of. That's what you do, right?"

"Not usually."

Cleo could very easily cut him down with a biting comment or a laughing refusal, but she didn't. She continued to stroke Rambo's fur while she stared up at Luther, her heart in her eyes.

"I like you," she said.

"I like you, too."

"Last night we almost..."

"Yes, we almost."

She shook her head gently. "I don't want to be a notch in anyone's belt, Malone. I don't sleep around, I don't get this confused about the way I feel. I certainly don't go to Florida with men I've known less than a week."

"By the time this is over, you will have known me at least...two weeks."

"Don't make light of this," she said sternly. "I don't want to be...convenient."

"I want you," he said. "There's nothing casual or *convenient* about it, you're not a damn notch in anyone's belt, and if you think you're confused you should take a trip through my head. Sleeping with you could cost me my badge."

"I don't want that," she said quickly.

"Neither do I, but right now it seems like an acceptable risk."

"It's not." Cleo jumped to her feet, turned her back on him and headed for the bedroom. "I would never do that to you. I'm going to bed."

Luther left the couch and followed her. "We're not finished."

"Yes, we are."

He thought about grabbing her before she reached the bedroom door, but he didn't. She had every right to walk away, if that's what she wanted. He just didn't believe that ending this here and now was what Cleo wanted. Or needed.

She turned before she reached the bedroom door, looked up at him with wide, amber eyes. "Believe it or not, I don't take risks. Not for myself, and certainly not where your career is concerned."

"Neither do I. Which is why tomorrow morning I'm taking myself off your case."

She went pale.

"I'm not leaving, Cleo," he assured her. "I just won't be on the case in an official capacity." He reached out and stroked her pale cheek. She was so soft and warm, so giving beneath his rough fingers. "I've already gotten too close."

She nodded. "I know what you mean."

He lowered his head and kissed her. The way they came together, so easy and right and natural, had scared him at first. But, oh, this was not something to be afraid of. Cleo kissed with everything she had, and he lost himself in her. Her lips parted, and he tasted her with the tip of his tongue. She held her breath, canted toward him and laid her hand at his waist.

Once he touched her, there was nothing in the world but his need for her and her unrestrained response. The need to feel her beneath and around him was overwhelming, undeniable. His body ached, his heart clenched. Something he had never experienced before, a certainty that this was right and real, consumed him as his desire for Cleo consumed him.

He was not a man easily consumed, but he surrendered easily. Gratefully.

The SWAT team couldn't drag them apart, not now. He was flying toward the inevitable, that joining of bodies that had been teasing and taunting him from the beginning. Had he known on some primal level, when he watched her walk away from her club that first night, that they would end up here? Maybe.

He cupped her breast, warm and full, and brushed his thumb over a nipple that peaked in response. A half moan, caught low in her throat, almost sent him over the edge. Cleo wanted him. She was flying, too. Never taking his mouth from hers, he took a single step toward the bedroom, guiding her gently.

"Luther," she whispered, barely raising her mouth from his to speak. "Do you have a...?"

"Yes, I do."

She sighed in relief and grabbed on to his belt buckle. "Good."

Chapter 9

Rambo was not happy to be on the other side of the door Luther kicked shut, but she didn't make much of a fuss. She barked once, then lumbered off to the kitchen and her food bowl.

Kissing and touching, Luther and Cleo danced across the rose-colored carpet to the edge of her bed. If she thought too much about what she was doing, she'd call an end to this, she knew it, so Cleo didn't allow herself to think. She felt. She reached out and touched. She got lost in physical sensation in a way she never had before.

Without taking his eyes from her, Luther removed his revolver and placed it on the bedside table.

He slipped both hands beneath her T-shirt and dragged his hands slowly upward, bringing the shirt with him. Cool air touched her skin.

"Let me turn off the light," she said, reaching for the low-watt bedside lamp that cast a soft light through the bedroom.

"No," he whispered, gently grabbing her wrist to stop her. "I want to see you."

Cleo swallowed hard. She wasn't model thin, she wasn't even what one might call slender. She didn't need a lifetime of motherly admonitions to know that. Her body had fleshy curves. With the right clothes, she could make the look work for her. But completely bare?

"What if you don't like what you see?"

"That's not even a possibility," he said, continuing to drag the shirt up, then pulling it over her head. The cool night air caressed her skin, and Luther smiled as he reached out to touch her bare breasts. "You're beautiful," he whispered. "The most beautiful woman I've ever seen."

She was afraid to think he might be telling the truth. "Malone, you are so full of—"

He kissed her to shut her up, and she didn't mind. He kissed so well, so thoroughly. While he moved his hungry mouth over hers, he reached up and blindly removed the scrunchy from her hair. The curls came tumbling down.

"Remember when I said you couldn't kiss?" she muttered against his mouth.

He hmmmed an affirmative answer.

"I was lying."

"I know." He threaded his fingers through her hair, kissed her deep and pulled her close. When he let his hands go slack, his palms skimmed slowly down her back and his fingers slipped beneath the elastic waistband of her flannel pants.

Cleo shuddered, deeply and completely. From the top of her head to her toes, she quivered.

Luther's fingers pressed against her backside, as they kissed. Moving gradually, he slid the flannel pants over her hips and down, his hands skimming her flesh as he completed the chore.

"Absolutely, positively, the most beautiful woman I have ever seen," he muttered.

He laid her on the bed, moving slowly, cradling her in his arms as he positioned her on the center of the soft mattress. She lay there, completely bare and as vulnerable as a woman could possibly be, while he sucked gently against her neck, her shoulder, and finally took a nipple into his mouth and drew it deep.

Shivers of sheer delight winked through her body, a promise of what was to come, a hint of the pleasure they would share. Her body throbbed.

"You are going to take your clothes off, aren't you?" she said, pulling on his black T-shirt as he took his mouth from her breasts. She worked the soft cotton up, while Luther nibbled at her throat and threaded his fingers through her hair.

She had always suspected he would be magnificent beneath his starched shirts and conservative suits, and the sight of his chest as she tossed the T-shirt to the floor confirmed those suspicions. Muscled and trim, strong and dusted with dark hair, he had a perfect male body.

"Beautiful yourself," she whispered.

He smiled briefly before covering her mouth with his once again. It was a possessive, demanding kiss. It was not the kiss of a friend, or of someone who might find her convenient. Her heart and soul were in that kiss, and so were his.

She reached for his belt buckle and began to work it blindly, and still he kissed her. The buckle came undone, and he slipped his tongue into her mouth. She lowered the zipper and laid her palm over the hard length beneath his briefs, and he moaned into her mouth.

She took her time, easing his jeans and briefs down, touching as she pleased, losing herself in the heat and desire they generated. Luther reached behind his back once, quickly, and snagged a single condom from his back pocket, catching it between his fingers and slipping it beneath her pillow.

"You didn't have that last night," she whispered.

"No. I grabbed it, and a few others, while we were at my apartment this morning."

"A few?"

"Enough, I think," he said as he lowered his mouth to her breasts again.

She continued to work at his jeans until he was as bare as she, and they lay entwined in the middle of her big bed. They didn't rush toward the joining they both wanted, but took their time touching, tracing curves and tasting, learning one another's most sensitive places.

Cleo held her breath, as Luther grasped her hips in both hands and sucked on her neck. Her body throbbed, she wanted him inside her so badly. And as the sensations grabbed her and started to spin out of control, she was tempted to tell him that she hadn't been with a man in years, not since Jack. She wanted to tell him that she hadn't chosen him lightly. That she had never thought to feel this way again.

But she remained silent, reaching down to touch him intimately, and forgetting everything when he laid his hand on her in the same way.

Finally, he retrieved the condom he'd stashed beneath the pillow. He opened the foil package quickly covered himself, and spread her thighs with gentle fingers. He hovered above her, all man, passion and wonderful heat, and put his mouth over hers as he guided himself to her.

He entered her slowly, and her body gradually opened to take him inside. She wrapped her legs around Luther, snaked her arms around his neck and rocked against him. He satisfied one hunger, with his long, slow plunge, and aroused another: a hunger for the thrill of completion, for a pleasure so intense and perfect it would change their world.

He stroked her slowly, deeply, and the new pleasure began to grow. She sparked inside. She forgot everything and listened only to the demand of her body and her heart.

She threw her head back, and Luther laid his mouth against her bared neck. And still he stroked, slow and steady, deep and complete. She held his head in her hands, cradling him against her, rocking her hips in time to his. The light of the bedside lamp he had insisted on leaving on cast a soft glow across their joined bodies. Hers soft and yielding, his hard and powerful. Cleo was glad he had left the light on. The sight moved her, filled her with wonder.

When Luther began to move faster, he lifted his head and looked down at her, his eyes so deep and dark they pierced her. She laid her palms against his arms, skimmed them up to grasp his shoulders, and closed her eyes as completion hit her with a force so powerful she could not breathe, could not scream. She felt Luther come with her, his body shuddering, his invasion deep.

When she could breathe again, she opened her eyes and saw Luther staring down at her. Still again. She reached up and threaded her fingers through his dark hair, guided him down so that his head rested on her shoulder.

What could she say? It seemed that she should say something. *Thank you.* He wouldn't understand. *I love you.* Even if that were true, and she wasn't sure that what she felt was love, she wasn't looking to scare him off. Not just yet.

"Can't dance, can't kiss...I'm happy to know you're good at something," she said in a lightly teasing voice.

Luther lifted his head and glared down at her. Even in the soft light, he looked unrelentingly hard. It was the harsh lines of his face, she reasoned, the glint in his dark eyes.

"Don't make light of this," he whispered hoarsely.

"I'm not." She reached up to trace his jaw with her fingers. It was a fine jaw, she mused.

"We should have waited until I officially took myself off this case, but…dammit, Cleo—" he sounded more than a little confused "—I've never lost control before."

"Never?"

"Never."

She draped her arms around his neck. "Then, I guess it's about time."

He didn't sleep with women, not literally. He never spent the night, he didn't stick around for breakfast. But it was going on four in the morning, and he woke in Cleo's bed, her warm, naked body curled against his.

He told himself that since he had planned to spend the night on her couch again, anyway, it just made sense to sleep in a soft bed that was wider, softer and made for sleeping.

But it wasn't the bed that kept him here, it was her. He didn't want to let her go, he didn't want to move a foot away from her, not if he could help it.

The room was dark, the only light coming through the window—soft moonlight—and from the faint glow of the bedside clock. It was just enough to allow him to see her outline, to see the mass of dark curls spread across a white pillow.

His fingers itched to touch her, but he didn't. She slept soundly, in spite of everything that had happened this week. Rambo slept just as soundly on her bed in the corner of the room.

Luther couldn't sleep. What if she was right, and the white roses were a subtle threat? No one else saw it that way. One detective had even suggested that because Valentine's Day was coming up, the price of red roses had gone out of sight. The moron suspected they had a cost conscious secret admirer on their hands.

The roses had not come from the usual florist. Luthe had checked on that first thing. The week before Valen tine's Day, every discount store, grocery store and floris shop was lousy with roses. They'd probably never trac down that particular purchase.

Cleo had looked at those flowers and thought of death Was the man who had sent her white roses someone clos enough to her to know how she'd react? And was her ad mirer the man who had killed Jack? Luther still couldn' be sure.

In a few hours it would be someone else's problem. H couldn't be involved with Cleo and remain on the case And he couldn't not be involved with Cleo.

"You should be sleeping," she whispered, movin slightly against him. Her skin brushing against his, so sof and warm, aroused him all over again.

"I didn't mean to wake you."

"You didn't." She sighed and draped her arm aroun his waist.

"You should go back to sleep." He put his arm aroun her, and she curled up against him, closer than before. H liked it. He liked it too much.

"Maybe," she murmured. "I was thinking," she added "I think you should say yes."

"Yes to what?"

"To being godfather to Ray and Grace's baby."

Oh no, not that. One more decision he wasn't ready t face. "I don't know. It's a huge responsibility."

"They love you, and I think it would be a great weigh off their minds if you agreed to raise their child, if anythin ever happened to them. Odds are, nothing will ever hap pen..."

"You don't know the Madigans," he muttered. "Anything is possible."

Cleo raised herself slowly and laid her hand on his face. She was a shadow surrounded by black curls, a soft glimmer of pale skin in the night. "What are you afraid of?"

She didn't miss much, did she. "What I see every day makes a man wary of…of taking on anything as important as a child. There are so many disasters, there's so much sorrow. Have you ever seen a mother bury her own child? Or a father watch as his son goes to prison for the rest of his life? I didn't know that kind of pain existed. I'm just not anxious to put myself in a position where—"

"Malone," she said sweetly, laying her head on his chest. "That is so much crap."

"Excuse me?"

"I know you see the worst of people, the saddest moments in some people's lives, but I also know that you're smart enough to realize that what you see in your job is a small slice of life." Her fingers absently caressed his side. "There's a flip side," she said. "Watching a child learn to walk and talk, birthday parties and graduations, soccer games and going to the circus."

"Yeah, but…"

"What are you really afraid of?"

He turned Cleo onto her back and held himself above her. In the dim light, he saw her gentle smile. "I'm afraid of nosy, bossy, mean women."

"Mean?" Her hand skimmed down his side.

"A gorgeous, mean woman can drive a man crazy, you know."

"Gorgeous, mean, nosy *and* bossy. Sounds like a handful."

"You better believe it." He laid his mouth on the side of her neck and tasted, flicking his tongue over her warm flesh.

"I never thought of myself as mean," she murmured. She touched him and found him ready. Her fingers lingered. "But I *can* be bossy."

"Do tell," he muttered as he lifted his head to brush his lips over hers.

"Make love to me," she said.

"Yes, ma'am."

An insistent pounding on the front door woke him and Cleo. She sat up with a start, brought the comforter to her chest and jerked her head around to look at the clock. It wasn't even six-thirty yet.

"Something must be wrong," she said, jumping from the bed and grabbing her clothes from the floor. She threw on the flannel pants and T-shirt as she made her way out of the bedroom.

"I'll answer the door," Luther said, trying to dress as he followed her. He didn't like what that pounding implied any more than Cleo did.

She was peeking through the new peephole in her door, when he caught up with her. "It's your partner."

"Mikey?" He reached past her and unlocked the door, swinging it open.

Detective Russell was not happy. He stood there in his neat suit and expensive shirt and tie, and glared.

Caught. "What do you want?"

Russell didn't wait to be invited in. He brushed past Luther, glanced at a disheveled Cleo and groaned.

"This isn't what it looks like," Luther said.

"You're not sleeping together?"

"Okay, it is what it looks like, but I'm going in this morning to take myself off the case."

Russell shook his head. "No, you're not."

"I have to."

"Remember Willie Lee Webb?"

Luther nodded, and Cleo moved to his side. "Who's he?"

"He was your heckler Friday night," Russell answered.

"Did he file a complaint when he picked up his car keys?" Luther asked, running his fingers through his hair to tame it.

"Not that I know of." Mikey headed away from the door; Luther and Cleo followed. "Willie Lee Webb was found murdered this morning."

"What?"

"At just after five this morning, his body was found draped around a plastic clown at a fast-food drive-through. Someone had stuffed what appears to be several large orders of French fries down his throat." He turned to watch Luther and Cleo enter the living room behind him.

Cleo gasped and automatically leaned into Luther. He placed his arm around her.

Russell continued. "Someone choked him with French fries. What do you want to bet he was drugged with the same stuff Tempest was, so the deed could be accomplished?"

"Luther," Cleo whispered, "oh my God, this is all my fault."

"No," he said, pulling her close. "It's not."

The kid shook his head and groaned again. "You guys can't do this, not now. I covered your ass this morning when you didn't turn up at home where you were supposed to be."

"Thank you, Mikey."

"If you want to thank me," the kid said sharply, "stop calling me Mikey. And don't expect me to continue to cover for you."

Luther glared at the oddly indignant Russell. "Why didn't you just call here? Or page me?"

"Wanted to see for myself if I was right when I guesse where you were."

"Great detective work," Luther said sharply. He had t remind himself that Russell hadn't done anything wrong "Like it or not, I have to take myself off the case."

Russell shook his head. "You can't. We're shorthande I haven't been in homicide long enough to handle a cas like this one on my own, and the captain is not going t let his senior detective off what has the potential to be serial killer case."

"Bohannon in burglary..."

"...is a good cop who has no experience in homicide Come on, Luther, you know you can't step down now."

Like it or not, Russell was right. Someone had kille twice, and both bizarre murders had come right out o Cleo's act. He couldn't fool himself into thinking tha maybe Tempest's murder was committed by someone un related to Cleo, someone who chose her as a convenien patsy. The damn grapefruit hadn't been a red herring, afte all.

And his list of suspects had just gotten smaller.

He looked down at a terrified Cleo. "I'm going to get twenty-four-hour detail on you. I won't leave until it's done deal and the uniformed officers are here."

Russell piped up again. "The captain will never author ize—"

Luther sent the kid a silencing glance. "For twenty-fou hours, he will. By tomorrow morning, I'll have someon else on bodyguard duty." He wished Grace wasn't due t deliver any day. Ray would be perfect for this.

"Bodyguard?" Cleo said softly.

Luther turned to her and placed his hands on her face "'Round the clock, until this guy is caught."

Russell passed them. "I'll call a unit in from the ca and then I'll wait. Try not to be too long, Malone."

The door closed behind Russell, and when he was gone, Cleo reached up and placed her hand on Luther's face. "You need a shower and a shave. Better hurry."

"I'm not leaving until a patrol car gets here."

She let herself fall against him, gently and easily. "Now I'm scared," she confessed.

"Me, too."

"It's my fault," she said. "Jack, that drunk heckler who just wanted to hear some old song..."

"It's not your fault."

She lifted her head and stared up at him with frightened golden eyes. "Will you be with me tonight?"

"I shouldn't."

"I know."

He brushed a curling strand away from her face. Who was he kidding? Staying away from her would be the hardest thing he'd ever done. "I'll be at the club this afternoon, as soon as I can. If nothing else, we have to keep putting on a show for your secret admirer." He let his fingers tangle in her hair.

"And when the show is over?" she pressed.

He didn't like this, he didn't want this, but what choice did he have? "We're going to have to put what's happening with us on hold until the investigation is over."

She obviously didn't like the idea any more than he did, but she nodded gently and sighed in acceptance.

"Hurry up and find this guy, will you, Malone?" she said, not nearly as brusquely as she obviously intended.

"Count on it."

Chapter 10

Crime scene tape and well-positioned patrol cars wit flashing lights kept the public away from the area. Goo thing they'd gotten to the victim before the television sta tions and newspaper arrived. This was not a picture anyon wanted on the front page or the noon news.

Luther stood back and studied what was left of Willi Lee Webb, while crime scene photographs were made Webb had been draped around the plastic clown and tie in place with sturdy rope. His legs and arms were in un natural positions, so he'd most likely been unconscious o already dead when he'd been placed here. A few frie peeked out from Webb's mouth, just a hint of the bizar murder method.

Most murders were cut and dried. Robbery, crime of pas sion, execution. This…was different. He thought he'd see everything, but this gave him a serious case of the creep

Russell stepped up beside him. "Sorry I lost my co earlier," the kid said, calmer than he'd been when he' come to Cleo's door.

"You had good reason," Luther said, his eyes never leaving Webb.

"I was just surprised, that's all," Russell explained. "I always thought of you as a strictly by-the-book cop."

"I am," Luther muttered. "Usually." He reached into his pocket and pulled out a peppermint, played with it a moment and then dropped it back into the pocket. "It's not what you think."

Russell sighed. And Luther turned his head to look at his young, optimistic, gung-ho partner. Yeah, Mikey was just a kid.

"It's never happened before," Luther said. "I don't make a habit of getting involved with women who are a part of a murder investigation." It was the cardinal rule, the one he had never thought he'd even be tempted to break. What was happening with Cleo was not casual or careless. It was so much more than that.

The kid scoffed. "You're gonna marry her?" he said sarcastically.

Luther returned his attention to the body. The crime scene techs were almost finished. Married? He hadn't thought that far ahead. He hadn't been able to think past the fact that Cleo was somehow different. That she'd crept beneath his skin and would be there always. It wasn't like him to be so sentimental, to think about a woman when he had work to do. Webb had a family. Co-workers. Neighbors. Even though Luther knew this murder was related to Cleo, somehow he had to cover all the bases.

"That's what I figured," Russell said, taking Luther's silence as a negative response. "You know, she's a nice lady. You shouldn't take advantage of her like—"

Luther snapped his head around. Russell stood there, indignant and righteous and stiff-spined. "Is that what this is about? You're worried about Cleo. You think I'm taking advantage of her."

"Aren't you?"

"No."

"You expect me to believe this thing with Cleo is serious?"

Photographs done, evidence collected, the techs began to untie the latest murder victim. "Ask me again after we catch this guy."

Luther stood back and watched as Webb was bagged and tagged, and Russell knew him well enough to keep his mouth shut while the wheels turned. Webb's death changed the focus of the investigation. There was no longer any reason to look at Randi Rayner, Tempest's business associates, or musicians he had cheated out of their rights the way he'd cheated Cleo.

Someone was killing the men who hurt her. Jack, with his constant harassment, and Webb with his unkind words. And the method...the method of murder said *I'm doing this for you.* Sooner or later the killer would expect Cleo to thank him for his work. That realization scared the crap out of Luther.

Both murders had been on a Sunday night. The murderer had been in the club on Friday. He'd witnessed Webb heckling Cleo.

"Compare their phone records," he ordered. Tempest had gotten several calls on Sunday afternoon. One had been from a pay phone not far from the building he'd been thrown from. All the other calls had been traced to business associates and personal friends. "See if Webb got a call from a pay phone last night."

Russell nodded, taking mental notes.

"I don't want the coroner dragging his feet on this one," Luther said. "I'm not going to wait days for the results this time. This case gets priority. If I have to stand over him—"

"Got it," Russell said.

"I want to talk to Eric and Edgar this afternoon. Not at

the club. I want them downtown where I can make them sweat.''

''Do you really think—''

''I think we can't rule them out.'' Even though Cleo had told him the truth about the alibi her friends had provided for her, and for themselves, they were sticking to their story. When Jack had been killed, Edgar was cleaning the bar and Eric was practicing on Cleo's piano. Luther didn't believe either one of them.

The only other possibility was that the killer was a stranger. Someone who sat in her club and fabricated a relationship with Cleo that did not exist. Luther didn't care for that possibility: if that was the case and the secret admirer simply disappeared, they might never catch him.

Cleo jumped when the door opened, as she had jumped all evening every time a customer entered the club. Monday nights weren't the busiest, but she usually had a decent crowd in here six nights a week. Lately, she'd been looking at all her regular male customers and wondering...is it him?

Watching Luther walk into the club, so at home here and so undeniably beautiful, eased her heart and made her smile for the first time today. He headed first for the cop that was seated in the corner. A word or two from Luther, and her guardian for the day was dismissed.

When Luther turned and came toward her, their eyes met and her heart melted. She hadn't realized how much she missed him until now. How did a man become so important so fast?

''How are you?'' he asked as he reached her.

''Better, now.''

Luther placed his hands on her face and kissed her, once quickly, and then more deeply. The touch of his mouth on hers was a relief, and more. She needed it. Craved it. How had she made it through the day without this touch?

''Just for show,'' he said unconvincingly as he took his mouth from hers. ''People are watching.''

''How was your day?''

His eyes darkened. ''I got nothing from Webb's family and acquaintances, but then I didn't expect to. We know who did this.''

She shivered, and he answered by placing his large hands on her upper arms and stroking gently, warming and soothing her. ''I understand you spoke with Eric and Edgar this afternoon?''

''Yeah,'' he said.

They had told her all about it, indignant that their alibi was being questioned, incensed that Luther thought either of them would dare to frighten her. They'd both confessed that they had no alibi for last night. Both had been home alone. But they had been here when Jack had been murdered. They'd both told her so, and she believed them.

''Why would you suspect my friends? They would never—''

''I can't talk about this,'' Luther said gruffly. ''Don't ask me questions I can't answer.''

She laid her head against his chest. ''All right,'' she said gently, accepting his limitations easily as her cheek settled against the crisp whiteness of his shirt. Maybe it was good for the show for her to reach for Luther this way, but that's not why she listed into him and held on. She needed this. Needing Luther, needing any man, frightened her. She'd guarded her heart for so long. Why did she capitulate now?

''I have something for you,'' he said, reaching into his pocket and pulling out a small velvet box.

Cleo backed up slightly and laid her fingers on the soft case. ''This box is much smaller than the one the coffeemaker came in.''

''Yes, it is.'' The velvety box remained on his palm, offered and waiting. ''I was going to give it to you on

Valentine's Day, but..." He hesitated, and even in the dim light she could swear he blushed. "I couldn't wait."

She opened the box, expecting anything, and still her heart jumped when she saw the pendant inside. A gold treble clef studded with diamonds hung from a delicate chain.

"They had lots of hearts," Luther said, his voice too low for anyone listening to hear. "But I saw this and it reminded me of you."

"It's beautiful. And perfect." She would not cry, not over something like this! She fought back the tears. "Put it on." She spun around and lifted her hair, taking the time to gather her wits about her while her back was to Luther. She only sniffled once, and very softly, as he fastened the chain around her neck.

When she turned back around, calm and dry-eyed, he reached out and picked up the diamond-studded treble clef that hung on her chest, the backs of his fingers brushing familiarly against her.

"Thank you," she whispered. "I love it. And I have something for you."

Luther's smile faded. "Uh-oh."

Cleo grinned and signaled Edgar with a wave of her hand. The bartender knew what she wanted, reached beneath the bar for the purple-foil wrapped box and place it on the counter. Instead of carrying it to them, he gave it a shove toward them. Cleo stopped the sliding package with her hand.

"Don't you trust me?" she teased.

"Let's see," Luther muttered. "Cherry-red tie, purple shirt... No, I'm terrified of what might be in that box."

But he unwrapped it, anyway, and lifted the lid cautiously. He peeked inside, then replaced the lid quickly.

"Aren't you going to study your gift more carefully?"

"No."

"Come on, Malone. It'll be great for the show."

He sighed and flipped the lid off. Using only two fingers, he lifted the silk boxers. "The hearts match my new tie."

"I know," she said with a grin. "There's another pair in there."

"I'm afraid to look," he said, glancing into the box. "Hmm. I didn't know they even made cowboy underwear for grown men."

"See?" Cleo said, lifting out the second pair of boxers. "Little sheriff's stars, and six-shooters, and horses..."

"Put that back," he ordered gently. "People are watching."

Cleo dutifully laid the silk cowboy boxers in the box, and Luther dropped the gray silk boxers with the red hearts on top, replacing the lid as quickly as possible.

"I wish you were going to stay with me tonight," she whispered, fiddling with the pendant Luther had given her.

"So do I." He reached out to run his fingers through her hair, barely touching a long curling strand. "But until this is over..."

"I understand." She leaned in so close, her nose was almost on his shoulder. She felt the heat radiating off his body, and closed her eyes as she breathed deep and he filled her. His scent was arousing, and she remembered, too well, what it was like to have him close. Closer than this. Closer than anyone had been in a very long time.

"But I want you to know something," she whispered. Her heart climbed into her throat, but this was important. He needed to know, and she needed to confess. It had been so long since she'd trusted anyone with the truth: letting it go was more difficult than she'd imagined. "I haven't been with anyone since the divorce. Not until last night."

Luther said nothing, but his hand settled more firmly in her hair.

"For a long time, I didn't trust any man enough to let

him that close. If you're just..." Her heart clenched. She couldn't bear it if he didn't feel the same way she did, if she was nothing more than a quick, convenient lay. But she had to know. "If this is just..."

"It's not *just* anything," he whispered hoarsely. "I don't like waiting, but dammit Cleo, I want to do this right."

She smiled and rested against his shoulder, her cheek against his conservative dark jacket, her hands settling on his waist. "Right is good." She hadn't had anything right in her life in so long, would she recognize it? Appreciate it properly? Yeah, as long as Luther was a part of that right, she would love it. She would love him.

She hadn't thought she'd ever love anyone again, and what she felt now scared her. But she also knew, without reservation, that it was worth the risk. She would risk her heart, her life, her soul, for the rightness Luther promised.

"Will you stay with me tonight?" she asked.

He shook his head. "I can't. I'll take you home, but I can't stay."

She sighed.

"I've hired someone to keep an eye on the house overnight. You'll be safe."

"I'm not worried about being safe, Luther."

She was much more worried about being alone again. A few days ago, living single and unfettered had been her way of life, but right now she already dreaded crawling into her bed tonight without Luther. He belonged there. She needed him.

Edgar interrupted their private moment, grumpy as he placed a cup of black coffee on the bar. "Something to eat, Detective?" he snapped.

"A sandwich," Luther said as he faced the bar, one possessive arm around Cleo.

Edgar didn't much care for the appearance of Detective Malone in their lives, and neither did Eric, she knew. This afternoon's interrogations had done nothing to change that. They would come around, when the real killer was caught and they realized that Luther cared for her. When they knew, as she did, that for once in her life everything was going to work out *right,* they'd be happy for her.

Russell flirted with Lizzy, but not with as much enthusiasm as usual, Luther noted. The kid was beginning to take this case too much to heart, and the worry showed on his young face.

As she sang, Cleo unconsciously fiddled with the pendant Luther had given her. She liked it. Since he had never done Valentine's Day before, he was relieved. Every time she caressed that gold clef, he felt as if she was touching him. Thinking about him. Wishing they were somewhere else, alone and with none of this god-awful mess between them.

Cleo didn't constantly stare above the crowd, as she usually did. Often, she looked at him. Sometimes she even smiled.

She hadn't been with anyone else since Jack. Knowing that Cleo had put aside her hurt and mistrust for *him* added an unpleasant weight of responsibility to his gut. What if it didn't work? What if, like everyone else, they screwed this up? Everything seemed perfect, at the moment, at least as far as the two of them were concerned—but he knew damn well "perfect" didn't last.

At the same time, knowing she had waited for him made her all the more his. He wanted her harder, deeper, in a place he hadn't known existed.

Out of the corner of his eye, he saw the longhaired thug walk in. With tight jeans, leather jacket, black boots, and that long dark hair, he looked not at all like Cleo's regular clientele. The guy belonged in a biker bar.

He took a table in the corner, ordered a beer from Lizzy

and turned his eyes to the stage. And grinned. Luther did not like that wicked grin.

A few minutes later, the beer quickly disposed of, the man's eyes met Luther's. He nodded once and stood, tossing a bill onto the table and bursting through the front door and into the cold night. Luther followed.

"Not a bad gig," the man mumbled as the door closed behind Luther. "She's a looker."

Luther turned to watch, as the man lit a cigarette and leaned casually against the brick wall that fronted Cleo's.

"This is a hands-off job, Sinclair," Luther said.

Boone Sinclair smiled and blew out a long puff of smoke. "Too bad."

Of all the people he could have called, why this man? There were other private investigators available, some of them specializing in bodyguard assignments. Truth was, he had called Boone Sinclair because he trusted him, and because the man was as tough as they come. He wanted the best man possible to be watching Cleo when he couldn't be there himself. But the way Boone smiled was enough to give Luther second thoughts.

"I can call in someone else..."

Sinclair lifted a hand to silence him. "No. I owe you. That's why I'm here, Malone. You know this isn't the kind of job I usually take. And if you say hands off—" he spread his hands wide "—then you got it."

"How's your sister, Shea?" Luther asked, anxious to change the subject.

Sinclair sneered. "Married. Pregnant. Working for CNN."

"That all sounds good."

Boone shot him a disbelieving glance. "*Pregnant,*" he said again.

"That seems to be going around."

The Birmingham PI snorted. Now he was the one who

wanted to change the subject. ''You didn't tell me much about the case over the phone. Fill me in.''

Cleo stood with her back to her front door, Luther blocking the cold wind. He'd insisted on driving her home, and had also insisted that he could not stay. He wouldn't even come inside, not tonight, but he wasn't any more ready to let her go than she was to allow him to walk away.

His arms bracketed her head, his hands pressed against the door behind her. ''You have my phone numbers, and the pager number, and you have 9-1-1 on speed dial.''

''Yes,'' she said, leaning close to him to cut the night's chill. If she thought it was fair, she'd try to convince him to come inside and stay the night. But she didn't. He wanted to do this properly. Maybe that meant what they had was as important to him as it was to her. She certainly wanted to believe that was true.

''Sinclair is watching—''

Luther nodded to the van that was parked down the street. With its dark tinted windows, it looked deserted. She knew it was not.

''He'll be here all night and he'll make regular rounds of the property. He'll watch you until I can make it to the club, then he'll catch a little sleep while I stay with you.''

''Is all this really necessary?''

''Yes.''

''I hate for him to stay out in the cold all night.''

''He's used to it.'' Luther lowered his head slowly, obviously intending to kiss her.

''You know what I think?'' she asked, as his lips barely brushed hers.

''What?''

''I think you have a new oral fixation.''

He brushed his mouth against hers. ''Oh, you do?''

''I haven't seen you reach for the candy all night.''

He made a noncommittal sound. "Hmmm."

She nibbled lightly at his lower lip. "Do you crave this?" she whispered.

"You know I do."

She wrapped her arms around his waist. "I have a feeling I'm much better for you than peppermint and jelly beans."

"Me, too."

The kiss turned deep, and there was no more talking. No more teasing. Luther caught her up against his body and held her there, tight and secure. She grabbed on to his jacket and kissed him back with everything she had. She didn't want to stop; she didn't want to let him go, not ever.

But eventually they fell apart, before they arrived at that point where there would be no stopping, before they passed the point where she opened the door and he followed her inside.

She was so close to that point. "Maybe you should come inside and take a look around, before you go home. Just in case." She didn't really think anyone had broken into her home. In spite of the white roses, there had been no real threat to her life. Only to those who hurt her.

"Sinclair already took care of that."

"I didn't give him a key, and there's no spare hidden under my mailbox anymore."

"Sinclair doesn't need a key."

Having met the man, she wasn't surprised. He looked more like a criminal than the ex-cop Luther said he was. "Did he find anything alarming?"

"Yeah. A dog who tried to love him to death."

"Some guard dog Rambo is. She doesn't live up to her name at all, does she."

Luther kissed her again, his mouth coming to hers as if he couldn't help himself. A quick kiss, a nibble, a too-brief connection to stir the heat within them both, and then he backed away just slightly. "You better go inside before I change my mind."

She fished her key out of her purse and turned around to slip it into the lock. Luther took the opportunity to nose her hair aside and kiss her neck.

The sensation of his mouth on her neck almost pushed her over the edge. She wanted him to come inside with her, fall into the bed and love her all night. He wanted that, too. She could feel it.

"Why do you have to be such a good guy, Malone?" she asked huskily. "Why did I have to fall for a guy who always plays by the rules?"

He reached around and cupped her breast with one easy hand. "I swear, Cleo, I never had such a hard time playing by the rules before. If there was anyone else to hand this case over to, if there was any other way…if I could forget the rules just this once—"

"Don't apologize for being a good guy," she said softly. "It's so much a part of who you are." She leaned her head back against his shoulder. This was easier when she didn't have to look him in the eye. If anyone asked her if she was brave, she wouldn't hesitate to say yes. But she didn't feel brave at the moment. She was terrified. "It's a very big part of the man I'm falling in love with." With that she unlocked the door, turned to kiss Luther quickly on the mouth, and then stepped inside and closed the door before he could respond. Yeah, she was really turning into a coward.

Would he run from her now that she'd actually said the *L* word? Had she scared him off with her honesty? She peeked warily through the peephole, and smiled when she saw that Luther was still there on her porch, leaning against the door and looking as if she'd knocked the wind out of him.

Then he laid the palm of his hand against the door, a silent goodbye, and glanced back quickly, his face clear just long enough for her to see that he was smiling, too.

Chapter 11

Cleo awakened from a deep sleep to the sound of someone knocking lightly but frantically on her door. She recognized the knock, as she stumbled toward the door, but looked through the peephole, anyway. A familiar head of red hair filled her line of vision.

She opened the door, and Syd hurried inside. Her friend closed the door behind her and locked it quickly before turning around, then leaned against it taking a deep breath.

"What's wrong?" Cleo asked sharply, coming instantly awake.

"Someone's watching you," Syd whispered.

Cleo's heart jumped into her throat. "Watching me?"

"I saw him a few minutes ago, skulking around the house. He got in a van down the street, but he didn't leave. He's still there." Syd took a wicked-looking kitchen knife from the inside pocket of her denim jacket and wielded it clumsily. "Isn't Luther here?"

"No."

"Well, call him, or call the police. Call somebody!" Syd said breathlessly. "This guy that was walking around the house, he's pretty scary looking. Long hair, leather jacket, and one time when I peeked out of my bathroom window while he was around back, I saw that he had a gun stuck in his pants."

Cleo breathed a sigh of relief. "That's Boone Sinclair. Luther hired him to keep an eye on the place when he can't be here."

"Why can't he be here?" Syd asked, letting her hand and the kitchen knife fall.

Cleo shook her head and turned around to walk slowly toward the kitchen. Syd followed. "He's investigating the case, I'm the ex-wife of the first victim—it's just not—"

"*First* victim?"

Cleo nodded. "Did you hear about the body that was found at that fast-food restaurant on Whitesburg?"

"Yeah."

"My heckler. Luther thinks the same man who killed Jack killed the heckler." She shook her head. "He has to concentrate on the case, not on us. There can't be any *us* as long as he's on this case." She hated it, she hated it so much, but what was she supposed to do?

"You're not still a suspect, are you?" Syd asked.

"No." At least, she didn't think so. Luther never would have gotten this close if he'd thought for a moment that she was involved. "But still…I suppose it might look bad." *Might* look bad? Who was she kidding?

She offered Syd chocolate chip pancakes, and they ate a big breakfast before Syd had to run to open her shop by ten. Cleo showered, then dressed in a casual, dark purple outfit that hung loosely and comfortably on her body.

When she heard footsteps outside her window and peeked out the front window to see Sinclair rounding the corner, she opened the front door and called him in.

The big man, all dark hair and denim and leather, stopped on the front porch. He didn't look like he'd been up all night, except for the fact that he was in bad need of a shave. "Is something wrong?"

"No. Are you hungry?"

He shook his head. "I'm fine. I'll grab something this afternoon, once you're settled in at the club."

"Chocolate chip pancakes," she said.

"Okay," he said, giving in quickly and stepping inside, as she moved back to make way. "Nice place," he said, looking around as if seeing it for the first time.

Cleo headed for the kitchen. "Don't play dumb with me, Sinclair. Luther told me you checked the place out yesterday."

Sinclair grunted.

Rambo, who had been sleeping in the kitchen, bounded forward to greet Sinclair as if he were a long-lost friend.

"You need a new lock on the back door," the PI said, as Rambo licked his hand voraciously. "The one you've got was too damn easy to work past."

"Thank you," she said as she began to gather the ingredients. "I'll take care of having it replaced."

"I told Malone. He'll probably set you up with a new one by this afternoon."

Her next gift, she imagined. A gaily wrapped dead bolt.

Sinclair ate the pancakes with relish, but didn't care for her coffee and didn't mind telling her that it tasted like dishwater. Oh, if she was going to start cooking for a man, she needed to know how to make decent coffee! And other things, too. *She* didn't mind eating peanut butter and jelly sandwiches for dinner or grabbing a sandwich at the club. But she'd have to learn to feed Luther. More than that, she *wanted* to feed him. She'd never given a fig about feeding anyone before, not even Jack.

"This is kind of a boring job, I imagine," she said, as

Sinclair dumped out a pot of weak brew. He was going to show her how to make good coffee. He laid out the necessary ingredients—a filter, coffee grounds and a spoon—and she watched carefully as he measured, using twice as many grounds as she had.

"Most stakeouts are."

"I don't imagine anything exciting will happen. No one's really threatened me, except for..." She was no longer sure those white roses were a threat. Not everyone looked at white roses and thought of death. That might've been a coincidence. "Luther's being overprotective."

"Except for what?" Sinclair asked as he started the fresh pot.

"I've been getting red roses from a secret admirer for months, and Luther thinks he might be, you know..." She hated to say it out loud. *The man who's been killing people on my behalf.* "Last week, I had a delivery of white roses, and I thought..." She shrugged off her concern. "It's probably just me."

Sinclair leaned against the counter while the coffeemaker gurgled. "Malone took the threat seriously enough to call me in."

"He's just being cautious."

"Better safe than sorry." Sinclair gave her a lady-killer grin. "I don't blame him for being careful where you're concerned. If I was the kind of man who enjoyed a fight, I'd give Malone a run for his money. Okay—" he shrugged "—I do love a fight. But I like Malone, so I'll behave. Sweetheart, you have a voice that would knock any man flat on his ass. Not my kind of music, you understand, but still...dynamite."

"Thank you, I think."

"Besides, Malone's got that look in his eye. You don't mess with a man's woman when he gets that look."

"What kind of look?"

"That dangerous, *permanent* kind of look."

She couldn't help it; she blushed.

Sinclair waggled his eyebrows. "You kinda got that look yourself. God help you both."

Boone waited around until Luther arrived at the club, and then he split. Luther knew he wouldn't be able to keep the PI on the case for more than a few days. Not only was this not Sinclair's usual missing or runaway child case, but stakeouts got boring, fast. Sinclair wasn't a man who would stand for such a tedious assignment for very long.

Luther had thought about Cleo all day. While he'd been interviewing Webb's co-workers, going over the details the crime techs had come up with, bugging the coroner for an autopsy report and jumping down Mikey's throat, he'd been thinking about Cleo. No matter how he tried, he couldn't set her aside, he couldn't...dismiss her.

"Hi," he said, dropping her heavy gift on the bar. "How's everything?"

"Fine. Nice and quiet." She picked up the package and shook it gently. "This is heavy," she said, placing an ear to the sloppily wrapped box. "And quiet. I'm guessing..." She placed her playful gaze on him, and he was caught by her amber eyes. "A new lock for my back door."

"You've been talking to Boone."

She nodded gently. "I was going to pick up something new for you, but Boone didn't want to go to the mall. Do you have a yellow tie?"

"Yellow? I'll have to thank Sinclair when I see him tonight." He hadn't kissed her yet. There weren't that many people about, since it wasn't late enough for a crowd to have gathered. Cleo wasn't even dressed for her show, but the purple outfit she wore looked fine to him. He really should wait...yet somehow he reached out and kissed her gently, quickly. To anyone watching, and there were a few people about, it might appear to be a friendly, intimate kiss between two people who were becoming comfortable with one another.

She draped her arms around his neck. ‘‘Okay, how about orange?’’

‘‘Yellow would be better.’’

She rested her forehead against his and closed her eyes. ‘‘I missed you today,’’ she whispered.

‘‘Me, too.’’

Eric bounded off the stage and joined them, his eyes flashing angrily. ‘‘Sorry to interrupt,’’ he said curtly, obviously not at all sorry.

‘‘It's okay,’’ Cleo said, wrapping her arm around Luther's waist as she faced her piano player. ‘‘What's up?’’

‘‘Can I talk to you privately?’’ the kid asked, nodding toward the office.

‘‘Sure…’’ Cleo began, trying to disengage her arm.

‘‘No,’’ Luther muttered, grabbing her and gently drawing her back. He didn't like the kid. More than that, he didn't like the way the kid looked at Cleo, all moony eyes and broken hearts. The kid was fairly high on his list of suspects, but all Luther had in the way of proof was an apparent schoolboy crush. Eric didn't look at all like a cold-blooded killer. But there was one thing Luther had learned in the past several years: looks could be deceiving.

Cleo turned to him, smiled and came up on her toes to kiss him briefly. ‘‘I missed you, I thought about you all day, I could spend all night right here. But this is business. I'll be right back. Edgar,’’ she called in a louder voice, ‘‘fix Luther a cup of coffee and a sandwich.’’

Eric led the way to her office, and Cleo followed the kid. God, he loved to watch her walk away….

When the two of them were in the office, Luther walked quietly down the hallway and stopped outside the almost-closed door. Eric mentioned a song he'd like to play, one night soon, and Cleo agreed. They talked about the set for Valentine's Day, and then Eric lowered his voice. Luther strained to hear, wondering if he should interrupt, but then Cleo spoke, a smile in her voice.

"That's great," she said.

Luther made his way back to the bar. Like Cleo had said, strictly business.

Edgar placed the coffee and sandwich before him in a matter of minutes. Instead of moving away, as he usually did, however, the bartender took up residence on the other side of the bar, a scowl on his face and one eye almost shut, he squinted so hard.

"What are your intentions toward Cleo?" the older man finally asked, practically spitting out the words.

Luther finished what was in his mouth and took a long swallow of coffee. "Are you asking me if those intentions are honorable?"

"Yep."

"What are you, her father?"

Edgar's nostrils flared. "She doesn't need some cop coming around, acting like he has the right to take what he wants with no concern for her feelings. She has feelings, you know."

"I know." He almost felt guilty for suspecting Eric and Edgar. They cared about Cleo and made no bones about it. It would be easier, for her, if the killer was a stranger. Someone she could easily and gratefully dismiss from her life, once the guy was behind bars. If it did turn out to be someone she considered a friend…

"She deserves better than to be manhandled by the likes of you."

"I don't…" Luther began. His beeper went off, and he grabbed at it impatiently. *Ray.* He snagged his cell phone from an inside jacket pocket and dialed the number.

Ray answered his own cell phone. "We're going to the

hospital!'' he shouted over the sound of traffic in the background.

Luther's heart almost stopped. Not again. ''What's wrong?''

''Nothing's wrong. Grace is in labor.''

Luther breathed a sigh of relief. Of course. ''Great. Call me when it gets here.''

''This is a baby, Luther, not an *it.* And I will not call you when he or she arrives. We want you to be there.''

His sandwich did a little dance in his stomach. ''I don't have to actually be *there.* Do I?''

Ray laughed. ''No, we'll let you pace in the waiting room, you coward. But we do want you there. Bring Cleo, if you want.''

''Okay.''

''Luther,'' Ray said more solemnly. ''You still haven't given us an answer.''

''I know.''

''We're counting on you, man.''

Luther shook his head. He didn't want anyone counting on him, not personally. Give him a crime to solve, a bad guy to crack, a job to do. That he could handle. But this...first Cleo and now the Madigan baby. It was almost more than he could stand.

''I'll be there.'' He hit the end button and headed for Cleo's office. Without knocking, he pushed open her door. Eric sat on one side of the desk, Cleo sat on the other. They both jumped when the door flew open.

''Grace is having her baby,'' he said. ''Come with me.''

''Sure.'' Cleo rose gracefully. ''Eric, you can perform solo tonight. Try out that song you wrote. I'll look over the lyrics later, and we'll use it next week, for sure.'' She looked at Luther again. ''Do we need to go now?''

He nodded. ''Yeah. I need to make a stop or two on the way.''

* * *

Luther wouldn't tell her what was in the huge bag he carried. In fact, he had been oddly silent since they'd gotten to the hospital. He paced as if he was about to become a father himself.

She almost wondered why he had asked her to come along, but every now and then he looked at her and she could tell that her presence calmed him, somehow. So she was happy to sit and smile and read outdated magazines until the middle of the night.

Finally, a grinning Ray came into the waiting room. "It's a girl," he said.

"Of course it is," Luther said, giving a relieved smile.

"Come on back." Ray led them down a hallway and into a room where Grace sat up in bed with a tiny pink-wrapped bundle in her arms. She looked exhausted but happy. Beaming, in fact.

"Is everything all right?" Luther asked, placing his large bag on the floor.

"Everything went great," Ray said. "Grace was wonderful, and I got to cut the cord."

Luther grimaced. "Isn't that what you paid the doctor for?"

"Come and look at her," Ray said, grinning widely. "Angel Madigan."

"Angel," Luther said as he bent cautiously over the bed to get a look at the baby's face.

Ray was not satisfied. He carefully lifted the baby from Grace's arms and handed her to Luther, before he could move away or protest. After a moment of sheer terror, Luther relaxed and even smiled.

"Lucky for you," Luther teased, "she looks like her mother." He turned around and walked toward Cleo.

She felt like an intruder here, among people who had

been friends for so long. "I should wait outside," she said softly.

"Don't you want to see it?" Luther asked.

"Her," Ray and Grace said at the same time.

"Sorry. Don't you want to see her?"

"Sure." He held the baby close, and Cleo was fascinated by dark blue eyes, a little bow of a mouth and full cheeks. Even more, she was fascinated by the way Luther held the baby. His arms were so big, with that tiny baby snuggled in them. But he was sure and steady as a rock. "She's gorgeous."

Luther lowered his voice. "She's red and her head is shaped like a melon."

"I heard that," Ray said, apparently taking no offense.

"Quit eavesdropping and open your present," Luther said, nodding toward the bag he'd left by the door.

Ray collected the bag and placed it on the single chair in the room. He reached inside and pulled out something large and black and bulky.

"A bulletproof vest," he said, sounding confused.

"I'll get you another one next week," Luther said, his eyes on the baby. "You each need your own."

Ray set the vest aside and dug down in the bag. "And vitamins."

"His and hers," Luther mumbled. "Take them. Every day."

Grace smiled. "Does this mean your answer is yes?"

"Do you have air bags in both vehicles?"

"Yes," Grace said, almost laughing.

"Then, the answer is yes." He handed the baby to Cleo, his movements deliberate and cautious. "You want to hold her?"

"I shouldn't," Cleo said, as he deposited the baby in her arms. Oh, but it felt right. Red faced and melon headed and all, Angel Madigan was a beautiful baby. Little Angel opened her eyes, cast a glance up and settled comfortably in Cleo's arms.

So completely trusting, Cleo thought with wonder. Had she ever trusted anyone so much? She had spent the past few years waiting to be dropped, she knew that much. And she had never even considered the possibility that she might one day have a child of her own. But now she was thinking…maybe. One day.

"Uh-oh," Ray said, moving forward. "Cleo's getting that maternal look. I'd better rescue her while I can." He gently took the baby, kissed Angel on the forehead and settled into the chair beside Grace's bed. "They're contagious, you know," he teased. "You see one of these babies and before you know it you're having your own."

Cleo shook her head gently. "I think I'll just visit yours."

"Anytime."

Grace looked exhausted, with good reason. "We should go," Luther said, taking Cleo's arm. "I'll come by tomorrow."

"Great," Ray said. "And Luther—" his happy smile disappeared "—thank you. You have no idea what this means to us."

Luther was obviously embarrassed. "Just…take the damn vitamins."

"You got it."

Chapter 12

Luther sent Boone home and knocked soundly on Cleo's door. He hadn't slept much last night, and he was feeling crankier than usual. He wasn't supposed to dream about the way Cleo looked holding a baby; he wasn't supposed to wake up in the night reaching for her.

She opened the door with a smile on her face, so he assumed she'd used her peephole to see who had come knocking. Her black curls were a mess, and she wore those flannel pants and a baggy T-shirt. She wasn't just out of bed, but she hadn't been up long. She had that warm, rumpled look about her, a trace of dreams left in her eyes. And God, she was beautiful.

One long look at him, and her smile slowly died. "What's wrong?" she asked softly. Rambo joined her, tail wagging, tongue lolling.

"Nothing. I'm here to take you to lunch." He realized, as the words left his mouth, that he hadn't asked her, he'd ordered. Like a drill sergeant. "You haven't already eaten, have you?"

She backed up and made way for him to enter. ''No. Lunch sounds great.'' He hesitated. It would be best if he waited here on the porch while she got ready. Best and much, much safer.

He followed her inside, glancing around warily as he closed the door behind him and reached down to pat Rambo's head. ''We need to talk.''

''Sure,'' she said. ''Let me make you a pot of coffee. You can have a cup or two while I dress.''

She'd made coffee for him once before, and it had been pretty bad. He had no idea how to tactfully tell a woman she had done something wrong. Seemed safer to just drink the damn coffee and keep his opinion to himself. ''Great,'' he muttered from the kitchen doorway.

Smiling, she began to gather together what she needed. Rambo carried her favorite ball to Luther and dropped it at his feet. Luther knew what was expected; he kicked the ball into the living room, and Rambo gave chase.

''Or...I can make coffee while you get ready,'' he offered.

''No, I need the practice,'' she said as she measured out the grounds. ''Boone showed me what I was doing wrong.''

''Oh, he did?'' Suddenly Luther wished he'd hired some little old man to watch over Cleo. Sure, he trusted Boone with his life and Cleo's—but could you trust any Sinclair with your woman? Probably not.

But his unease didn't last long. Even if he didn't trust Boone, he did trust Cleo. The realization struck him like a hammer between the eyes. He had never trusted a woman before. Never. They were flaky like his mother, telling one tale this minute and another tale the next. They were deceitful, like the women he came across in his line of work. They ran when the going got rough, the way Grace had once run from Ray.

But he didn't believe Cleo would do any of those things.

In fact, he knew she wouldn't. She was honest, sometimes painfully so. She was solid, in a way the other women he'd known were not. And she freely confessed that she was falling in love with him, a fact that scared and encouraged him at the same time.

She got the coffee started and turned to him with that come-hither smile that grabbed his heart…and other regions, too. Yeah, he definitely should've waited on the porch.

"Where are we going?" she asked as she walked slowly toward him. "I need to know what to wear."

"Tim's Cajun Kitchen," he said. "If that suits you. I have a craving for gumbo."

"If you're having cravings, you've been spending way too much time with Grace."

"We can go somewhere else, if you'd like," he said, as she met him in the doorway. He really should step back and let her pass, but he wasn't ready to do that, not just yet.

"Are you kidding? I'd walk over broken glass to get to Tim's bread pudding." She smiled as she said this, then cocked her head and set her eyes on his mouth.

The time for him to step aside had come and gone, and still he stood here, blocking Cleo's exit, staring down at her and doing his best to look his fill. He couldn't get enough of her; he didn't want to move. Ever. Behind her, the fresh coffee gurgled and filled the room with its fragrant aroma.

One kiss, he decided as he reached out and brushed a long strand of curling hair away from Cleo's face. One kiss wouldn't be so bad. Besides, he needed that one kiss. He absolutely, positively had to have it.

She took the final step that brought her to him. Close enough for touching, close enough to feel her heat. Her body barely skimmed his, her hand snaked beneath his jacket and reached around to caress his back through the thin fabric of his shirt. His arms encircled her possessively, and when he lowered his head to kiss her, just once, she came up on her toes to meet him halfway.

Their lips touched and he lost it. He forgot everything else but this. How could a kiss be comforting and arousing at the same time? Cleo's was. How could a woman kiss decadently and innocently at the same time? Cleo did. Her eyes remained trustingly closed, her hands and mouth were as greedy as his. He felt the shudder that snaked through her body, the tremble of her hands at his back.

He spun her around as they kissed and pressed her back against the doorjamb. He tasted her, deep and then with the tip of his tongue against her lower lip. His hands dipped to rest on her hips, to hold her against him while he plundered her mouth.

He couldn't break away, didn't want to. The kiss fed something inside him, something more than sexual. He hadn't known he could feel this way, hungry and on the edge of control. Wanting to fall over that edge, willing to risk anything to have this woman beneath and around him.

It was the catch low in her throat that almost sent him reeling. He could so easily say to hell with the rules, pick her up and carry her to bed where they'd stay all day and all night. He had never in his life wanted anything as much as he wanted to do just that.

He took his mouth from Cleo's, and she dropped her head to his shoulder, finding the side of his neck with soft, caressing lips. ''This isn't fair,'' she whispered.

''No, it's not.''

''I've waited for you for so long...''

And he had waited for her, hadn't he? He tangled his hands in her hair. ''When this is over, you're going to close the club for a couple of weeks, or else put someone else in charge.''

"I am?"

"Yes, you are. We're going to Florida on vacation, and I hope we can get a room with a view, because if we don't we might never see the ocean."

She sighed, long and sweet, and he took that to mean that she liked the idea. Her head fell back, and she looked up at him with dreamy eyes, those well-kissed lips as tempting as anything he'd ever seen.

Rambo pawed insistently at Luther's leg, and when he looked down, the dog dropped the ball at his feet.

"Your timing is terrible, mutt," Luther murmured as he kicked the ball into the living room once again.

Cleo dropped her arms and slipped past him. "I'll get dressed. The coffee's almost ready."

Coffee would not cure what he had a hankering for now—but what choice did he have?

They were obscenely stuffed with Cajun food and Tim's fabulous bread pudding. Cleo had a suspicion the slow walk they were taking around the park would do nothing to burn those calories. At the moment, she didn't care. Lunch had been great, and walking with Luther beside her was wonderful. The weather was almost springlike. A sweater over her cream-colored pants and blouse was plenty to keep her warm, and the sun shone on her face, promising warmer days to come. She couldn't remember the last time she'd been this happy. Not giddy-happy, but deep-down content.

"How much longer?" she asked softly, as they rounded a bend in the path and came upon a gathering of ducks at the edge of the pond. "Do you have any idea who killed Jack and the heckler?"

Luther didn't answer right away, so Cleo jumped in quickly. "I guess you can't tell me. That's okay. I'm just a little impatient." She shot him a smile. "I haven't been to Florida in ages."

He draped an arm around her shoulder and pulled her close. "We don't have nearly as much as I'd like. We're discreetly checking out as many of your regulars as we can. Mikey's been taking pictures on the sly. I've got someone checking into Palmer, though I really think he's a long shot. I've done a little digging into Randi's past, as well as Corey Flinger's. He has an alibi for the night Jack was killed. It's not great. If I keep digging I might be able to shake it loose. But I can't see why they'd bother with Webb, unless it was strictly to send us in the wrong direction."

"I'm sorry things aren't going well."

He stroked her arm, warming her. "I wish you had an alibi," he said.

"Being in bed with the homicide detective in charge makes for a pretty good one, I imagine," she teased.

"Don't remind me," he muttered. "But I was talking about Jack, not Webb. You have more motive than anyone. I know you didn't do it. I know you couldn't. And like you said, your alibi where Webb is concerned is airtight."

She tried to smile, but it wasn't easy. Until this crime was solved, they couldn't possibly move forward. For the first time in ages, she wanted to move forward. She wanted to know what came next, what the future held.

"You don't want to hear it, I know," he said. "But we have to consider the possibility that Edgar or Eric, or maybe even both—"

"No," Cleo said. "They wouldn't." She held on to Luther more tightly as they stopped by the pond and gazed out over the water. She wanted the murderer to be a stranger. Someone who could be taken from her life without leaving a hole.

"I think we're going to have to smoke him out," Luther said almost casually.

"How?"

He looked down at her, tried to smile but didn't do a

very good job of it. "So far, both victims have been men who hurt you. You made jokes on stage about them, and a couple of days later they're dead."

She took a deep breath. "If I had known..."

"I'm not blaming you, just laying out a plan." He pulled her closer, held her tighter. "You and I are going to break up, and on Friday night—"

"No," she said, her heart leaping into her throat.

"There may be no other way. We haven't found a single usable print, the commercial furniture polish that was used to render the victims unconscious is commonly used, and with every hour that passes the killer is closer to getting away with two murders."

"But—"

"I thought you wanted to go to Florida."

"I do," she whispered. "But I don't want to make you a target, Luther. I...I can't. I can't stand up there and pretend that you've hurt me and purposely put you in danger."

He brushed a finger under her chin. "I can take care of myself."

"I don't doubt that."

"And when this guy is caught, we can put this behind us and go to Florida."

There was so much promise in that phrase. *Go to Florida.* It meant starting over. Together. It meant a new, fresh start. It meant love. She had thought she'd never know love again, and now here it was, staring her in the face and offering things she'd given up on. Love, family, waking to find a man she adored in her bed.

"All right," she said finally. "If there's no other way."

"Friday," he said, with a nod of his head. "Whoever he is, he always seems to be there on Friday."

Boone was back on the job by that afternoon, and Luther reluctantly left Cleo in the PI's hands. Luther was more and more certain that she was not personally in danger, but he wasn't going to take chances. Not with Cleo's life. The man who had killed her ex-husband and the heckler was obsessed with her. Obsession could quickly turn to hate, he knew that too well.

He had interviewed Randi, and the cowboy singer who had been hanging around her place since Jack's funeral, several times. He could see why Cleo was suspicious of the woman, but he didn't see Randi with an *i* as a killer.

But when Randi came into his office on Wednesday afternoon, she definitely had murder in her eyes. "Now are you going to arrest her?" Randi snapped as she tossed a manila folder onto his desk.

"Arrest who?" he asked calmly, indicating that Randi should take the seat on the opposite side of his desk. Corey Flinger stood supportively behind her.

"Cleo, that's who." Randi tapped a finger against the folder. "If hating Jack's guts wasn't motive enough, this is. I want her arrested!"

Luther remained calm, while the two people on the opposite side of the desk quickly worked themselves into a tizzy.

"Yeah!" Flinger said, crossing his arms over his chest and puffing out.

"What's in the folder?" Luther asked.

"Jack's will. He changed it six months ago, and the bastard didn't tell me. He left his ex-wife the publishing rights to 'Come Morning,' and all those other songs she wrote for her stupid album."

Seemed only fair to Luther, since Cleo had written the songs. Maybe Tempest had hidden a small shred of decency somewhere deep inside. "Well, I can't see how there'd be enough money in those songs that are—what, almost eight years old?—to constitute a motive."

Randi shook her head in a show of greatly tried patience.

"You have no idea how the music industry works. It just so happens that 'Come Morning' was recently chosen to be the main theme for a Hollywood movie. A big one, with major stars and major financing. The song will be in the movie itself, in the soundtrack, and the country-and-western star who's recording it for the movie is also going to feature it on her next CD." She slid the folder across his desk. "We're talking major money here, Detective Malone."

Randi with an *i* didn't sound much like a bimbo at the moment. She seemed to know exactly what she was talking about.

"That's interesting."

"Interesting? Detective, this is a hell of a lot more than interesting. It's a damn good motive."

"Yeah," Flinger said again. His limited vocabulary was really starting to get on Luther's nerves.

Luther opened the folder, noted the lawyer's name at the top of the first page, and leafed through the simple will. Sure enough, there was Cleo's name.

"I'm sure Ms. Tanner has no idea that her ex-husband changed his will—"

"I think she did know," Randi said curtly. "I think Jack told her that she'd get back the rights to her songs when he was dead, and the temptation was more than she could stand."

Luther wasn't going to sit here and tell Randi and her moronic cowboy friend how he knew Cleo wasn't guilty. "Thank you," he said calmly. "I'll look into it."

Randi snatched her folder off the desk and rose swiftly. "You'd better."

"Yeah!" Flinger muttered.

Cleo rested her cheek against Luther's shoulder, and they danced to the sad music droning from the jukebox. Maybe they couldn't be together until this was over, but she was beginning to love pretending for those who watched. It was all she had, for now.

He hadn't said much tonight. He'd come in, relieved Boone and asked her to dance.

"Are you by chance wearing one of the gifts I gave you?" she asked softly.

"Obviously not," he said absently. "I just can't bring myself to wear a bright red tie or a purple shirt to work."

"I meant one of the *other* gifts."

"Oh," he said. "No. What if I got shot, and they rushed me to the hospital and cut off my suit and found cowboys or hearts. I'd bleed to death, while the doctors laughed over my—"

"Don't say that," Cleo said, lifting her head to glance up. "Don't even joke about it."

He had been teasing her, she knew, but he looked serious tonight. The lines on his face were more pronounced, his eyes were dark. "Sorry. Cleo, we need to talk."

"Talk away."

"Not here." He glanced around the sparsely populated room.

She was tempted to give him his Valentine tonight. Oh, she couldn't wait to see his face! But, no. She wanted to do this right, and that meant she would wait until Valentine's Day, when they were alone.

"My office." She took his hand, and they left the dance floor in mid-song. His hand wrapped around hers, and he didn't let go. To anyone watching, it might look as if they were headed to the back for a little hanky-panky. She wished that were true.

Luther closed the door behind him, and Cleo made her way across the small room. She turned to face Luther and leaned against the desk.

"Randi with an *i* came to see me today." He didn't keep

his distance, as he knew he should, but came directly to her and brushed aside a curl that touched her cheek.

"I'm sorry," she said, just a little caustically.

"She thinks you killed Jack, or that you at the very least had something to do with his death." He backed up, perhaps realizing it was dangerous to stand too close, and dug around in his pocket to come up with a strawberry candy. Instead of unwrapping the candy and putting it in his mouth, he played with it as he talked. "Those publishing rights for 'Come Morning'? Tempest left them to you in his will."

"It's an old song," she said dismissively. "Hardly worth killing anyone over."

"Randi mentioned a movie," Luther continued. "A soundtrack, some country star's new album."

Cleo felt the blood drain from her face. "Oh, dear."

"Is that worth a lot of money? I have someone checking on the specifics, but—"

"It should be enough to keep me in peanut butter and dog food for a *very* long time," Cleo said.

Luther nodded. "We have to find this guy, and fast. If I didn't know better, I'd be looking at you real hard, Cleo. I know you didn't kill your ex or Webb, but if I remained distanced in this case, like I should, I'd have to suspect that you might be somehow involved."

She shivered, and Luther saw her response. "We'll get him," he assured her in a low, deep voice that wrapped around her and did, amazingly, make her feel better. Warmer. Not alone, after so many years of being alone.

"I know."

He came to her because he knew she needed it, she supposed. His hand drifted back up to brush her hair, her cheek, to trace her lips. "Don't be scared."

"I'm not," she said.

"You are," he said gruffly.

She shook her head. "I'm worried, that's all. You want me to make you a target. How am I supposed to do that and make it look real? How can I pretend to hate you?"

He moved near, so near that she closed her eyes and savored the almost touch, the way his aura skimmed hers. She didn't usually have such fanciful thoughts, but right now…yes, something definitely merged. His heat and hers. The energy that danced around them.

She reached out blindly and found him, her searching fingers touching his chest, her palm resting there. His fingers trailed down her throat, the gentlest caress she had ever experienced.

Her own hand skimmed up to touch his neck. She needed to touch him, even if it was just in this way. She needed to feel his heartbeat and his warmth. Her eyes drifted open. She wanted to see his face, to see her pale fingers against his tanned neck, to watch the way his dark eyes went almost black.

His fingers dipped gently beneath the collar of her little black dress, brushing the swell of her breasts as he leaned his head down to kiss her neck. Her body throbbed in time with that kiss.

Something horrid happened to her, then. Oh, she really was falling in love with Luther! She couldn't imagine a life without him in it. He touched her and she had hope for the future. She hadn't dared to hope in so long. Physically, she wanted him here and now. On the desk, on the floor, against the wall…she didn't care. She craved him.

In a deeper place she had ignored for too long, she wanted more. She wanted to know that Luther would be there forever. She wanted to awake and find him in her bed every morning. Babies. Girls like little Angel Madigan and boys who would have their father's dark eyes. She wanted that, too. She wanted Luther to love her the way she loved him: so deeply it hurt.

For the first time in years, she wanted everything. And she had the faith to believe that what she wanted could one day be hers.

Luther lifted her off her feet and placed her so she sat on the edge of the desk. He stood between her thighs, and her legs wrapped around his as he took her mouth deep, with a craving she tasted and savored. His fingers speared through her hair, and he held her there while he plundered her mouth.

She cradled Luther's head, holding him to her. Her legs tightened around him, drawing him close. His fingers dipped lower into the bodice of her dress, finding and barely teasing a nipple that hardened at his touch.

Cleo's body throbbed and moistened, and she felt Luther's insistent erection pressing against her. Her clothes and his kept them apart, but those annoying bits of fabric could so easily be disposed of…

Someone knocked on the office door casually and quickly before throwing it open.

"Lizzy wants next Friday—" Edgar began.

Luther jumped back, and Cleo slid off the desk, landing on her feet. Luther did offer a steadying arm, one she gratefully took.

Edgar stood in the open doorway, an expression of disgust on his face. "We can talk about it later. I just wanted the name and phone number of that girl who filled in last time."

"I'll take care of it," Cleo said, trying to sound calm and cool, and falling far short.

Edgar snorted and left, leaving the door wide open.

Luther glanced down at her, passion still burning in his eyes. "You make me crazy," he said.

It wasn't a declaration of love, but it wasn't bad, either. "*You* didn't lock the door."

He looked as if he was considering kicking the door shut

and taking up where they'd left off, which would be fine with her.

"Cleo," Eric's bright voice called as he slipped into the room. "What do you think? Can we..." He cast a suspicious eye at Luther and curled his lip. "I guess we should talk about this later."

"No, go ahead," Cleo said, just a tad more in control.

"Just wondering if we can give my song a run-through tomorrow night."

"Absolutely," she said. "It's fabulous."

He pointed toward the main room. "And one of the regulars, that old guy Charlie? He's asking about you. Might be nice if you went out and said hello."

"I'll do that. Just let me fix my makeup first."

"Yeah," he said as he turned and stalked out of the room.

Luther leaned close. "Florida is sounding better and better."

Chapter 13

Luther arrived at work in a very bad mood. He hadn't slept more than three hours, and the last of those three hours had made him late. Russell sat at his desk, well-dressed, bright-eyed, and looking like he'd had a good eight hours' sleep. God, that kid really knew how to get on his nerves.

An array of pictures that had been taken in Cleo's club lay across the kid's desk. All they needed was one previous arrest for harassment, a history of violent behavior. Something to point them at the right guy.

"Find anything?" Luther asked as he headed for the coffeepot.

"Not yet," Russell said cheerfully. "But I think we might be on the right track."

Last night he had come damn close to losing control with Cleo. Again. A few more minutes and he would have been screwing her on the desk. Every one of his reservations forgotten. All his caution thrown out the window.

If not for Edgar and Eric interrupting, one after the other...Cleo didn't want to believe her friends were suspects, but Luther definitely did. Eric was obviously smitten with Cleo, but did he have a harmless crush or was he obsessed? Edgar seemed to be the stern, fatherly type. Did he love Cleo enough to kill for her? Did his fatherly protection go that far?

Something would happen tomorrow night. He and Cleo would stage the big breakup, she'd say something caustic to her adoring crowd, and then they'd wait. If their killer held true to form, on Sunday night they'd know who he or she was.

He didn't like it, but something niggled at him. In the beginning, Cleo had let Eric and Edgar give her an alibi. She had come clean after just a few days, and hearing her admit that she had not been with them hadn't been a surprise. He'd seen the truth on her face, that first night.

Had she known that? No, he didn't believe so.

As a cop, he lived with deception every day of his life. He definitely didn't need it from the woman he...the woman he—what? Wanted? Dreamed about? Loved? He shook off the fantasy. Cleo had a great body, a gorgeous face, a come-hither smile and a voice that could seduce an angel. And Luther Malone was no angel. Had she been working at wrapping him around her little finger from the moment she'd first laid eyes on him and realized what trouble she was in? He didn't want to believe it might be true, but everything he knew of women told him that he shouldn't trust her.

And yet, he did. Against all reason, he did believe her. He trusted her. He wanted to draw her up against him and protect her from all this. His brain was screaming for caution, but his heart...for the first time in his life his heart was putting up an argument.

* * *

The club wasn't opened yet, but they were all here. Edgar, setting up the bar for the night, Eric tinkering with the piano, Lizzy wiping down tables and taking down chairs, and Boone sitting in the corner half asleep. She didn't expect the PI would be here much longer. Bodyguarding duty obviously bored him, and this afternoon he'd been getting a lot of calls on his cell phone. She had a feeling he'd be called away soon, for a more exciting, more interesting assignment.

Cleo found herself humming ''Come Morning'' as she stood at the bar and went over the order for more glasses and mugs, double-checking Edgar's figures. She hated the song, right? It was sappy and sweet and opened up her heart.

But it was hers again, or soon would be, and at the moment it didn't seem too sappy at all. Instead it seemed uplifting, a celebration of offering her entire life to the person she loved with all her heart. Right now the song didn't make her feel vulnerable and foolish the way it usually did. It made her feel whole.

If she and Luther could get through this and still be together, then they could get through anything.

''Cleo!'' Eric called from the stage.

She turned and leaned back against the bar. Eric continued to play, effortlessly, without flaw. He was really much too good to stay here much longer. Replacing him, when the time came, would be tough, but she wanted the best for him. He'd been here more than a year, but he was too talented to be stuck in her tiny club.

''Same set as last Valentine's Day for tomorrow night?''

''Sure,'' she agreed, still remembering last year's selections. She'd sing happy love songs only, and would open and close with ''My Funny Valentine.'' She'd wear her red dress, and there would be heart-shaped Mylar balloons floating above the stage. An idea made her smile, and she almost unconsciously reached up and caressed the pendant she wore, the one Luther had given her. "I have some sheet music for you to look at."

"Something new?"

Cleo nodded. Tomorrow night, for the first time in years, she'd sing "Come Morning." And it wouldn't hurt.

She rounded the bar to give Edgar the approved glassware order. He was perfectly capable of managing all the ordering on his own, but he always insisted that she look everything over and give it her personal thumbs-up. She usually barely glanced at the numbers.

"Looks good," she said, tossing the paperwork onto the bar. He stood in front of the small refrigerator that was set beneath the bar on his end. "Would you pour me a glass of juice?"

He nodded and bent down to open the fridge.

"A small glass," she said, leaning forward. As she looked down the length of the bar, a flash of shiny red caught her eye. Something had been hidden behind a row of flavored syrups. She bent and peeked over the bottles, and smiled when she saw the telltale sloppy wrapping of a small box. Luther's Valentine present to her, a surprise in addition to the necklace, hidden until tomorrow night? The wrapped package was the size of a shirt box, so maybe he was giving her lingerie. Something sexy with hearts on it. Something to match his silk boxers.

She carefully maneuvered the box out and placed it on the counter. She couldn't help but smile as she ran her fingers along the thick, misshapen seam on one end. If she opened it and had a look, Luther would never know. Curiosity was eating at her, and her fingers literally *itched.*

She slipped a fingernail beneath the tape on the end and lifted it gently, being careful not to tear the paper. In the corner of the room, Boone ended a phone conversation and stood slowly.

"Cleo?" he said suspiciously. "What is that?"

She waved off his concern. "It's from Luther."

He nodded once and retook his seat, but his eyes stayed on her as she carefully unwrapped.

"Don't tell," she added as she carefully unfolded the red foil paper. "I'm not supposed to be snooping, but I'm sure you understand."

Boone frowned. Lizzy smiled and Edgar shook his head. Eric kept playing.

Cleo set the paper aside so she could rewrap the package without Luther ever knowing. She placed both hands on the lid, and carefully lifted it.

The box was empty but for one square sheet of paper with a single word written on it.

Boom.

Rambo sensed Cleo's agitation. The golden mutt had been restless since they'd arrived home a few minutes ago, Cleo and Luther both shaken and off center.

Luther tried to offer her some comfort, he did his best to get her to calm down, but he was so angry he did a poor job of it.

"They're going over the building top to bottom," he said. "Just to be safe."

Cleo nodded. Her face was so pale, and she shook as she sat on the end of the couch and curled up, drawing into herself. "I could've killed everyone," she said. "Edgar and Eric and Boone and Lizzy. If there really had been a bomb in that box—"

"But there wasn't," he said. "That bastard is just trying to scare you." Boone had checked her house carefully, looking for signs of an intruder. He'd found everything in order.

The white roses had been subtle, but no one could deny that this was a threat. Boone and Russell were both posted on the street, and a patrol car was parked on the street behind, where they had a clear view of the duplex's backyard.

And Luther was here for the duration. He didn't care if it cost him his job, he didn't care about anything anymore, except keeping an eye on Cleo until this SOB was caught.

"I was so sure the package was from you," she whispered, settling back and closing her eyes. "You use that kind of paper, and it was so sloppy at the ends."

"You were snooping," he said gently.

She sniffled. "Yes."

The fact that the package had been under the bar, and that it had been wrapped so much like his own gifts to Cleo, confirmed his suspicions that whoever was doing this had been watching closely.

He sat beside Cleo and wrapped his arm around her. She didn't hesitate to melt against him and sigh deeply.

"My heart stopped when I saw that note," she said.

Mine, too. Instead of confessing anything so telling, he cursed.

Cleo rested her head on his shoulder, and Rambo rested her chin on his knee. All three of them calmed down together, one heartbeat at a time.

He had never known anything like this before, and it threw him more than a little. Cleo needed him; not to catch the bad guys, not to solve the crime, but to hold her like this, to assure her that everything was going to work out fine.

"I'm so scared," she said.

"You know I won't let anything happen to you."

She snuggled against him more securely, and he caught the beginnings of a smile that didn't last.

"I know. Believe it or not, it's not the killer that has me scared."

He threaded his fingers through her hair and held on loosely. "Then, what?"

"I'm more than a little afraid of you, Malone."

"Me?"

She lifted her head and looked him in the eye. "Yeah, you. I learned a long time ago to stand on my own two feet. I learned the hard way, and for years I managed just fine without...without *this*."

He knew what *this* was, and it scared him, too.

"I don't lean on other people," she whispered. "I most especially do not lean on any man. I don't get giddy about silly little presents, or crave a kiss at the oddest times, or think about a certain person all the time. I don't run to anyone when there's trouble. I take care of myself, always." She laid a hand on his cheek. "And now here I am, running to you, craving a kiss, thinking about you all the time. I love it," she added. "I love the way being with you makes me feel."

"Why does that scare you?"

Her lovely smile dimmed. "I'm afraid it's going to go away."

He drew her close, cupped her head and pulled it to his shoulder. Like it or not, he knew how she felt. "It's not going away."

"But what if..."

He tilted her head back and stared into her eyes. Amber eyes, so full of life and energy and love that they seemed to shimmer. He kissed her, laid his mouth over hers and closed his eyes while he gave in to the craving he'd had since rushing to the club to find her on the sidewalk outside. She was with the others who had been ejected by the squad searching the building for a real bomb. Shaking with fear as much as with the February cold. Waiting for him and so absolutely and clearly relieved when he arrived.

"Staying out of your bed this week has been the hardest

thing I've ever done,'' he admitted, taking his mouth from hers briefly, returning for another quick kiss.

She nodded, murmured an agreement, and laid her hand on his thigh as she nibbled on his lower lip.

''I knew that first night,'' he said, drawing her body across and over his, ''that you were mine. Don't ask me how I knew. I just did.''

She draped her arms around his neck. ''You annoyed the crap out of me that night,'' she said, giving a small smile. ''You blew into my life and crept under my skin and took up residence, and I knew there would be no shaking you free.''

''If you had any tender feelings for me when we met, you hid them well.''

''I did, didn't I.''

''I could have sworn you hated my guts.''

''I did,'' she said. ''I hated you because you slipped around my guard. I can handle wacko secret admirers, annoying ex-husbands, and hecklers much better than I can handle…getting involved again.''

''Falling in love,'' he corrected. ''You said it once. Why shy away now?''

''Because the harder I fall, the more it'll hurt when this ends.''

''Who says it has to end?''

He didn't look for permanence with women; he didn't speak from the heart and make promises that might not work out, no matter how much he wanted them to. But he couldn't imagine ever letting Cleo go. He couldn't imagine not coming home to her at the end of the day.

''Everything ends,'' she whispered.

He laid Cleo down on the couch and hovered above her. The skirt of her slinky royal-blue dress was too tight, she was wearing those damn pantyhose, and it seemed that everything was getting in their way. Including the nose of an overly friendly dog.

"Not everything." He kissed her. Once, twice. Again. They were wedged onto the couch. Cleo could barely move, thanks to the snug fit of her dress, and he wasn't in much better shape. And all he could think about was being inside her, claiming her as his own as was right and proper. To hell with the rules, to hell with caution. Nothing was as important as this.

He pressed his body to hers, his erection against her mound, his hand on her hip urging her to him. Layers of clothing, his and hers, impeded them, but he couldn't stop. He raked his length against her, and she answered with a low moan.

Another sound intruded, a whimper and a soft growl as Rambo tried to join in.

"Can't we put the dog outside?"

"I don't have a fenced yard," Cleo said breathlessly.

Luther turned his head and stared into big, brown eyes. "Go away."

Rambo cocked her head and continued to stare at him, so innocently.

The doorbell rang.

Luther cursed as he leapt from the couch. "I hope this isn't a sign," he said as he headed for the front door.

Cleo stood slowly, her laugh as husky and inviting as her voice when she sang and swept a roomful of people away. "I'm going to change into something comfortable," she said, heading for her bedroom. "If that's Syd at the door, tell her I'll see her in the morning. And then lay out some doggie treats in the kitchen for Rambo."

She closed the bedroom door, as he looked through the peephole and saw Russell standing on the front porch.

"What do you want?" Luther asked as he opened the door.

"You're not staying here all night," the kid said with a sanctimonious air.

"I am."

Russell shook his head. "This is such a bad idea. Can I at least come in for a minute?"

Luther stepped back and let his partner enter.

"The club is clean," Russell said as he looked around. "No real explosives of any kind, no sign that anything's been tampered with. So tomorrow is a go."

"Great."

"Looks like we might have one usable partial print off the package that's not Cleo's. It's on the underside of a piece of tape, which will be sufficiently incriminating if we can come up with a match."

Luther nodded. He wanted this case solved *now.* The sooner the better.

Russell laid accusing eyes on Luther. "The captain is going to hit the roof when he finds out about this."

"I don't care."

Russell sighed. "I understand, I really do. She's a beautiful woman, sexy as they come. I can see why any man might—"

"When this is all over, we're going to go away together," Luther interrupted.

Russell's eyes went wide. "What?" He shook his head. "I hope you know what you're doing, Malone. You're too good at what you do to make this kind of mistake."

"It's not a mistake."

"Okay." Russell headed for the door. "I hope you're right about this."

"Don't worry about me, kid."

When Russell was gone and the door was locked behind him, Luther headed for the kitchen to lay out a few treats for Rambo. Something to keep the mutt occupied for a while, hopefully. Cleo was going to walk out of that bedroom in her flannels and her T-shirt, and with any luck they'd pick up right where they left off.

If she hadn't changed her mind. If she hadn't come to her senses back there, while he'd been foolishly confessing to Mikey that he had something more substantial than a one-night stand on his mind.

"Luther?" she called softly from the kitchen doorway.

He laid out the last of the treats by Rambo's food bowl and turned around—

And almost dropped the bag of fake bacon in his hand. "Good God," he muttered.

No flannels tonight. Cleo had brushed out her hair, discarded the blue dress, and donned a long, silky, lavender nightgown that was cut to her navel and hugged every delicious curve.

"Do you like it?" she asked almost shyly.

"Of course I like it." He looked her up and down, noting the pebbled nipples, the way her breasts rose and fell, the dip of her waist and the swell of her hips. "What's not to like?"

She smiled. "I found it when I bought your silk boxers, and...I couldn't resist."

He closed the distance between them, as Rambo bounded into the kitchen and discovered her treats.

His fingers brushed lightly over the seductive nightgown, tracing the hard nipples, cupping the fullness of her breasts. "I think the mutt will be occupied for a few minutes."

"Good." Cleo came up on her toes and kissed him, sweetly seductive. "Luther," she whispered, closing her eyes and taking a deep breath. "What are you doing to me? I never thought I'd feel this way. Never."

He wrapped his arms around Cleo, lifted her easily and walked into the bedroom, closing the door behind them with an easy kick. They kissed along the way, quick easy pecks broken by the occasional deep kiss that grabbed his heart and twisted.

He gently placed Cleo on her feet beside the bed. A soft bedside lamp burned low, lighting her swollen lips and eyes hungry for him. He cupped her chin in his hand. ''How did I live without you, so many years?''

She smiled. ''The same way I did, maybe.'' She grabbed onto his belt. ''Half alive. Never quite whole. Hungry for something and never knowing exactly what.''

''Still scared?'' he asked.

Her smile didn't fade. ''Not so much, at the moment.''

Chapter 14

Luther slipped one finger beneath the strap of her nightgown and shifted it off her shoulder, the backs of his fingers raking across her skin. He released the strap and it fell, the silk caressing her skin as it tumbled downward to reveal one breast.

There was no rush in the way he touched her. They had all night. They had forever. She had never thought to have forever with anyone.

Impatiently, he shrugged out of his jacket and removed his shoulder holster, tossing them both over a chair.

He gently lowered her to the bed, his arms around her, his mouth skimming down her throat, down to the valley between her breasts, and then to the exposed breast to take the nipple into his mouth. She threaded her fingers through his hair, holding him to her, simply holding on. She didn't ever want to let him go.

Her hands left his hair and slipped over his shoulders. While he sucked her nipple deep into his mouth, she caressed the muscles in his arms, absorbed his heat, marveled at his strength.

He lifted his head, laid his hooded eyes on her face and dropped his mouth to hers.

The insistent throb of her body was rhythmic, musical, and she felt so wondrously light, as if she and Luther might, still kissing and touching, float up off the bed and hover there. This was magic, and real life—rules and danger and fear—had to make way for magic. It was only right.

Moving subtly, she urged Luther over and onto his back. His arms remained around her as they rolled, his mouth continued to devour hers. When he lay beneath her, she lifted her mouth reluctantly from the long kiss and began to work the knot at his tie.

"Another four-dollar tie?" she asked.

"I'll have you know I paid almost eight dollars for this tie." His hands settled possessively on her hips, as he lay there and allowed her to tug at the tie. When it was unknotted, she drew it slowly from beneath his shirt collar and dropped it to the floor.

"From now on, I buy all your ties," she said as she began to unbutton his white shirt. The buttons slipped through her fingers easily, and as she worked her way down, those fingers brushed his chest. Such simple contact, and yet it made her heart pound even harder.

She spread the shirt open and laid her head against his chest, her lips teasing one flat nipple, the tips of her fingers caressing a hard chest dusted with dark hair, edging downward to rest over his belt buckle. She hesitated there a moment, and then her hand slipped lower to caress his erection, her fingers light over his trousers as she barely touched the hardened length beneath.

He wanted her; she wanted him. But there was more than wanting here. Tonight was important. She had never given herself so completely to any man. Her love for Luther was so deep it really did scare her, she hadn't been lying about that. That love changed her a little bit every day. Filled the empty places inside her, gave her such wondrous hope.

Cleo blindly unfastened Luther's belt buckle, while he reached out to caress her breasts, fondling tenderly, teasing the nipples with gentle fingers. She lowered the zipper slowly, then feathered her fingers inside the opening to caress the silk-covered evidence of his desire for her.

“Six-shooters or hearts?” she asked.

“Six-shooters,” he said huskily. “It's been a busy week, and I got a little behind on my laundry.”

She let her fingers explore the silk boxers she'd given him—one of their many gifts for show.

But this wasn't a game, not anymore. No one was watching. This moment was just for the two of them.

Luther rolled Cleo onto her back and hovered above her, long and lean and hard, dark in the half light, his heat wrapping around them both. He pushed her nightgown up, his hand caressing her thigh as he moved the silk out of his way.

When he stroked his fingers over her intimately, she closed her eyes and reveled in the sensations his touch brought to life. Burning need, unstoppable desire. And more than that, the undeniable knowledge that he was hers and she was his, that this was not only right, it was destined.

She reached down and slipped the silk boxers and loosened trousers over his hips, freeing him to enter her, raking her palm over his erection and then closing her fingers around him.

He kissed her, demanding, his tongue mimicking the act that was still to come. She held on tight, guided him to her and wrapped her legs around his.

He didn't plunge fast and deep, but entered her body slowly. She opened to accept him, adjusted to his size with every magnificent second that passed. He loved her that way. Languidly. Gently. If making love were a dance, then this was a long, slow, romantic waltz. The world stood still; there was only his body and hers and this magnificent, sacred dance.

The world had a rhythm. Her heartbeat and his, the way their bodies moved together, the thrum of their blood. It all worked together until there was nothing outside this room, nothing beyond this bed.

The dance gradually changed, grew wildly fevered. What had been romantic was now primal. What had been sweet was now a hunger that demanded to be satisfied. Luther drove deep, deeper than before, and Cleo shattered. She cried out, and clutched at his heated body as completion racked her and stole her breath.

Luther groaned, drove himself deep once more, and found completion with her. She felt him, deep inside, giving over to a pleasure like no other. His body tensed and shook, and when the moment passed he laid his head against her shoulder and kissed her neck, and moved inside her one more time.

"I really did intend to get all our clothes off first," he said, slipping his hand beneath her nightgown to caress her breast.

Cleo rested her hand against Luther's head, cradling him to her with a deep sense of possessiveness she hadn't known was possible. "Next time."

He lifted his head and stared down at her, his own hand traveling to her hair and brushing a long strand away from her face. "You're so beautiful, sometimes it hurts to look at you."

Cleo smiled. She hadn't felt beautiful for a very long time, but Luther, looking down at her this way, made her feel special. Beautiful and loved.

"I love you," she said.

He answered with a kiss.

* * *

He couldn't sleep, and it wasn't the threat to Cleo or the possible danger to himself, once the public breakup took place, that niggled at his brain and kept him from finding rest with the most beautiful woman in the world nestled in his arms.

Cleo slept like a baby, satisfied, content, feeling safe in this room.

She had told him that she loved him, and he didn't doubt that it was true. She found some kind of joy in that love, a release he didn't understand.

He didn't deny that he loved her, too, but…the words stuck in his throat. He didn't open himself up that way. He had already told her, in no uncertain terms, what she meant to him. He couldn't imagine going back to a life without her. She was a part of him, and always would be. She made him crazy. Wasn't that enough?

Love was tricky. He had seen love, when it went wrong, eat away at his mother. He had seen it almost destroy Ray, a man who was not easy to shake. At least a part of the problem was the words themselves. What did they mean? *I love you.* I want you. I need you. You are my obsession. The man who had been sending Cleo red roses for the past four months, the man who had threatened her subtly with white roses and not so subtly with the word *Boom,* written on a card, no doubt thought he loved her. That wasn't love, it was a sick delusion.

The truth of the matter was, telling Cleo he loved her would make him vulnerable. He'd feel like a sap, putting his heart on his sleeve that way, calling on words that had been overused since man first began trying to charm his way into the pants of starry-eyed woman, who would settle for nothing else.

He had never told a woman he loved her. Never. He

didn't lie, he didn't open up and spill his guts any more than he absolutely had to—and he left the charming bit to guys like Ray and Mikey.

He felt Cleo come awake long before she said a word or changed her breathing. She rocked one foot and traced her fingertips down his side. She was no longer completely relaxed; a mild tension worked its way through her body. He felt it.

Already he wanted her again. Could he ever get enough of her? Until he'd met Cleo, no woman had made him lose control. She smiled at him and he got a hard-on. She touched him and he forgot everything but the way they came together, the way she took him into her body and offered everything a woman could offer a man.

"Too much caffeine," she said.

"What?"

"You drink too much coffee. The caffeine is keeping you awake."

"It's not caffeine that's keeping me awake tonight."

"Then, what is it?"

Your life is on the line and so is mine. My life is changing so fast it makes my head spin. I don't know if I can love you enough. He couldn't tell her any of that, so he took her hand and gently guided it lower to touch his erection.

"Oh," she breathed, long and slow, as she stroked him with bold fingers. "We can take care of that."

This is what he got for taking Cleo into his apartment so he could shower, shave and put on clean clothes. A purple shirt, a purple tie and silk underwear with hearts on it. She had insisted…and damn if he could bring himself to deny her anything.

Tonight was the night. He didn't know if he could carry off the plan, after all. They were to have an argument in front of the usual Friday night crowd.

They sat at a table near the stage, talking in whispers, while Edgar set up the bar for the night. Eric wasn't here yet, and neither was Lizzy. Luther held Cleo's hand on top of the round table made just for two.

"Do we really have to do this?" Cleo asked. "I don't want him coming after you."

"It's the quickest way to end this."

She nodded. "I do want that." Her eyes met his, wide, amber eyes that could be cutting one minute and openly vulnerable the next. "Maybe you should hit me."

"I will not!"

"Well, it would be sure to send whoever's been avenging me into a tailspin. You wouldn't have to hit me hard, just—"

"No."

Cleo leaned over the table, bringing her face close to his Not close enough. "How am I supposed to pretend to hate you?" she whispered. "How am I supposed to look at you without everyone in the room knowing how I really feel?"

He reached across the table and cupped her cheek. Florida was sounding better and better. He was so tempted just to pack up, toss her over his shoulder and go. Someone else could solve the crime, and when it was all over…man, he had it bad if he was considering running away from this even temporarily.

The door swung open, and Boone came striding in. The PI glanced around the dimly lit bar, saw Luther, and jerked his head back indicating the front door. Then he turned and walked out, practically bursting into the mild afternoon air

"I think Boone wants me."

"He's not the only one," she teased.

"I'll be right back." He left her sitting at the table, hesitant to leave even for a few minutes.

Boone leaned against the red brick of the building, one leg cocked up so the sole of his boot rested against the wall. His head stayed down, eyes on the sidewalk. He got right to the point.

"When this is said and done, if you want to deck me, I'll understand."

Luther nodded. Boone was probably about to quit, and he wasn't surprised. This was tame duty for a Sinclair. "What's up?"

"Cleo and the piano player are up to something."

Luther shook his head. "No. I don't—"

Boone lifted his head and pinned dark, hooded eyes on Luther. "Let me finish, and then you can argue or ask questions or hit me, or do whatever else you need to do."

Luther's heart sank. He definitely didn't like the way this sounded.

"Last week, I saw Cleo hand the piano man a wad of cash." He raised his hand to stop Luther's argument. "It wasn't his pay for a week's work. She handles that by check, not by cash. I noticed that they kept…sneaking around. Sometimes they'd sneak back to her office, close the door and whisper for a few minutes, before Eric came back out again and they pretended nothing had happened."

Luther gritted his teeth.

"So I did some checking. I know you didn't ask me to check on Cleo or Eric, I was only supposed to be keeping an eye on her, but…something was up. I smelled it. I felt it." He took a deep breath and shook his head. Long dark hair danced around his hard face.

"What did you find?" Luther asked.

"Eric hired a private investigator to check into you. He was working on Cleo's behalf."

A cold wind whipped against Luther's face, chilling his blood. "Who did they hire?"

"Some guy out of a big firm in Atlanta."

If she needed a PI, why not go to Boone? Or Ray? And why in hell was she checking up on *him?* "What exactly was she looking for?'' Weaknesses and blackmail material no doubt.

''I don't know. The Atlanta PI refused to share specifics I can take a drive, find the guy and beat it out of him, i you want, but...''

''No.''

Boone shrugged and got quiet. Everything got quiet.

Luther took a deep breath of chilly air that burned hi lungs. He was an idiot. He had no right to continue on thi case, to continue as a homicide detective. Cleo had playe him like a worn deck of cards, and he'd fallen for ever line. Every lie.

Had she and Eric been working together on other proj ects, too? Like ridding the world of her ex-husband and a annoying heckler? Was he next? Why had he thought sh was different?

''Thanks,'' he said coolly, not letting on that inside h was falling apart.

''Don't thank me,'' Boone muttered. ''I didn't much lik what I found, and I sure as hell hated having to tell you.'

''Didn't have any choice,'' Luther said.

''Nope.''

Luther turned around and stormed back into Cleo's. Sh was still sitting at the table they'd shared, and when sh lifted her head to watch him walk toward her, she smiled If he didn't know better, he'd never believe she was any thing but the beautiful, loving woman he'd thought her t be.

He didn't see the deceit in her eyes, but it was there. I had to be. The gut he had always relied on for the trut had failed him this time. Cleo had found and taken contro of a whole other part of his anatomy.

He placed hands, palms down, on the table, leaned to ward Cleo and caught her eye. ''Game's over, sweetheart.'

Chapter 15

t took a moment for the anger in Luther's eyes to register. he anger was so cutting, Cleo felt it slice through her. Her mile faded quickly. "What's wrong?"

"What's wrong," he repeated. "Where do you want me start? I know, how about we start with you and Eric."

"There is no me and—"

"Don't lie."

She had never seen his face turn so hard. His eyes were ark, unreadable. His lips uninviting. "Luther…"

"If you wanted to hire a private investigator, why not ay?" he continued. "Why not Boone? Unless, of course, ou didn't want me to know you had someone checking e out. I'm such an idiot," he growled. "I practically egged you to lead me around by the pecker." He leaned little closer and lowered his voice. "What else did you nd Eric do together? How clever of you to arrange to be leeping with me when the kid did away with Webb."

Something inside her snapped. He could get angry, and

of course he didn't yet understand...but he had no right t
attack her this way. "You've found me out," she said.

A muscle in his jaw twitched, a sure sign he was abo
to lose it. "You and Eric were in this together all alon
weren't you."

"Yeah. We were in cahoots," she said sharply. "Isn
that how you'd put it? We conspired together. We plotte
and planned and sneaked around behind your back."

He shook his head, as Cleo leapt to her feet. "I can
believe I didn't see it."

"Neither can I." She headed for the bar, but Luth
stopped her with a steely hand on her wrist. She glance
over her shoulder to give him an icy glare, never letting c
that he'd cut her so deeply. She hadn't known the proce
of a breaking heart could take so damn long. She fell apa
bit by painful bit. She'd never let him see that pain.

"Afraid I'm going to run? Not in these shoes." Sh
tugged, trying to release herself, and still Luther didn't l
go. She couldn't stand for him to touch her, not this wa
He didn't loosen his grip. She tugged more frantically.

"Hey!" Edgar rounded the bar, tossing his towel behin
him and stalking forward. "Let her go."

"Stay out of this, old man," Luther seethed.

"Who you calling old man, you—"

"Stop it!" Cleo cried, silencing them both. "Edgar, tak
a break. I need to talk to Luther alone."

Edgar didn't like the idea, but he headed for the bac
room and a short break, promising to return in a matter
minutes. When he was gone, Cleo stared down at her han

"If you want your confession," she said, "let me go.
have what you're looking for behind the bar."

He finally released her, snapping his hand up as if touch
ing her had burned him.

Cleo held her head high as she walked to the bar an
rounded it, snatching her purse from underneath. She lai

the leather purse on the bar and opened it, never once letting on that her heart was pounding so hard she expected it to come through her chest. Never letting on that it was breaking into a million pieces. It *hurt.* She had never thought anyone could hurt her this way.

"You're right, of course," she said, almost calmly. "I went to Eric and asked for his help."

Luther stood by the table, half a room away, stony and unforgiving.

"He's a good friend," she added softly. "And he did as I asked without questioning my motives."

Malone grit his teeth, his jaw going tight.

Cleo reached into her purse and pulled out the fat envelope. "I suppose I could have given this to you earlier, but I wanted the timing to be right, and I didn't want anyone else to be around, since...I couldn't be sure how you'd feel about this."

"How do you expect me to feel?"

She ignored him and waved the thick envelope above the bar. "Your father's name was Trent Luther. Everything your mother told you was true, in one way or another. There's a picture in here of your parents at the senior prom, another of your father in uniform. They're not very good pictures, just faxed copies, but the originals are on their way."

Her club had never been so quiet. Nothing moved, neither of them breathed. Luther's stony face softened, just a little, and he closed his eyes in a long, pained blink.

Finally, he mumbled a foul word and took a single step forward. "I really am an idiot."

"Just stay over there," Cleo ordered.

He did as she asked, coming to a dead halt there where they'd danced, and laughed, and where she had begun to fall in love.

"You have a grandmother living," she continued crisply.

"Your father's mother. She lives in a small town in Georgia, and she doesn't know you exist. I told the PI to keep it quiet, since I didn't know what you'd want to do."

"Cleo..." He tried another step forward.

"Stop! You think you can give me that look and take everything back? No, it doesn't work that way." She leaned on the bar and wagged the envelope in his direction. "Do you know why you never found any of this on your own? You didn't even look, because you expect the worst of everyone. And if you had looked, you wouldn't have gotten far. You think so damn logically. There's no room in that linear brain of yours for fanciful notions of any kind. God, when you were a kid did you ever color outside the lines? Did you ever have an imaginary friend or dance without music, or..." She shook her head. "It never occurred to you that everything your mother said about your father might be true, in some way. Or that his name might be Trent Luther and not Luther Trent. Or that when I went behind your back it might be for some reason other than betrayal."

"I'm sorry."

"No," she snapped. "Don't apologize. It's best to find out now that you don't care for me enough to see the truth. You're always going to assume the worst, and I can't live that way." She tossed the envelope at him. It spun like a Frisbee and hit him square in the chest. He caught it as it ricocheted off his purple tie. "Happy Valentine's Day, Malone. Do what you want with the information the PI gathered, but do me a favor and trash the card. It's just a load of sentimental crap."

She was on the verge of tears. Tears! She didn't cry, she didn't plead...but she had been so sure that what she and Luther had was real and strong. A breeze of her own making had blown away what she had thought to be lasting

Luther's own distrust of everything and everyone around him was stronger than her notions of forever.

Hell, there was no such thing as forever. Why had she forgotten that?

"I'm so sorry," Luther said again, coming toward the bar with long, cautious steps.

"Get out of my club," she said firmly.

He shook his head. "I can't leave you here alone."

"Boone's outside, Edgar's inside, and soon my coconspirator Eric will be here. I'll be fine."

"I don't like leaving you, and you know damn well I don't trust Eric or Edgar."

"Neither of them could ever hurt me the way you just did."

"Cleo—"

"I don't want you here. Get out."

Finally he backed toward the front door, envelope in hand, well-deserved guilt written on his face. "I'll be back tonight," he said firmly.

Of course he would. He had a job to do, and the damn job came before everything else. At least she wouldn't have to *pretend* that he had broken her heart.

Luther leaned against the brick wall of Cleo's and looked at the picture of his mother and father. He almost didn't recognize his mother, she looked so young and happy in the photo. And his father…there was no denying that this man was indeed his father. The resemblance was uncanny.

"It never occurred to me," Boone muttered, adding a foul word or two.

"Me neither," Luther said, his eyes remaining on the grainy copy of the old prom picture. "What's wrong with us, that we never even considered the possibility that Cleo's hiring a PI might be completely innocent?" More than innocent, she had gone out of her way to give him the most

precious, heartfelt gift he had ever received. And how ha
he thanked her? By accusing her of being involved in tw
murders.

"We're so completely screwed up," Boone said. "I sti
think it was perfectly logical to assume that Cleo hiring
PI had something to do with the murders. Let's face i
Malone, we see that kind of thing every day. It's just na
ural to assume—"

"That's crap," Luther said. He glanced up to meet
surprised Boone's eyes. "That's what Cleo told me, once.
They'd been in bed at the time, naked and warm and to
gether. "She said blaming my cynicism on the job was ju
an excuse to keep everyone else distant, that there's mo
honesty in the world than there is deception."

"I don't see it, how about you?"

"I didn't at the time. Now..." He shrugged. "Not th
it makes any difference. You should have seen the expre
sion on Cleo's face when she realized what I was thinkin
what I was accusing her of. She'll never forgive me."

"Sure she will," Boone said, a note of false encourag
ment in his voice.

Luther shook his head. "I blew it."

One woman, one chance for something special and las
ing—and he'd thrown it all away because he couldn't trus

Cleo sat on a stool and leaned against the bar, starin
into a half-empty glass of orange juice. "Love stinks," sh
said succinctly.

"I know, sweetheart," Edgar said as he wiped down on
of the glasses he had lined up against the mirror behind th
bar.

"I really loved him," she said. "How stupid is that?
should know better by now. Dammit, I knew he was troubl
the first time I laid eyes on him."

"Me, too," Edgar said. "Cop or no cop, if he comes in ere again, I'll toss his ass out on the street."

Cleo shook her head. "You can't do that. He's still in-estigating the murders."

How was she supposed to get up on stage and sing love ongs tonight? How was she supposed to sit in front of all hese people and smile and not fly apart? "Maybe I'll close he place," she said.

"What?"

"Sell it if I can, shut it down if I can't."

Edgar placed two beefy hands on the bar. "You can't o that."

"I'll go back to Montgomery and...and sell cars in one f Palmer's lots or take up interior decorating and join the unior League—all the things my mother always wanted ne to do."

"Don't even joke about that," Edgar said. "It would be crime for someone with a voice like yours to quit sing-ng."

"I'll sing in the shower," she said. "Singing in public ever got me anything but hurt, Edgar. First Jack and now uther. My mother would say that none of this would have appened if I hadn't insisted on making a 'spectacle' of nyself."

"Don't think that way," Edgar said. "If you stop sing-ng, then the bastards like Malone win. Don't let him run ou out of town and off the stage. You belong there. You ave a rare gift, and you make people's lives better just by etting up there and opening your heart."

"I don't have any heart left," she confessed.

"Sure you do." He laid a large hand over hers. "You're o sniveling, heart-on-her-sleeve, whining female, but that oesn't mean the bastards can't hurt you. You deserve bet-er than that jerk Malone. And one day the right man will ome along, you just wait and see."

"Thank you, I think," she said, sniffling just a little
"But I still say love stinks."

He sat in the back of the room, hiding in shadows, an
scoped out the crowd. Cleo was, Edgar said, in her office
and would not come out until it was time to begin. H
would intercept her on the way to the stage, they'd have
few heated words, and then she'd make her way to the stag
to seduce the crowd with her voice.

And what a crowd it was. Many of the regulars he rec
ognized, but there were new faces, too. Older couples ou
for Valentine's Day, awaiting a journey to music from
time's past, a journey Cleo would take them on. There wer
new younger couples in the crowd, too, celebrating with
drink and a dance and shared moony-eyed glances.

God, he had always hated Valentine's Day.

Randi and her new friend, Corey, sat at the back of th
room, just a few tables away. They seemed chummy bu
not necessarily romantic. He knew that Flinger had com
forted the poor girl after Jack's funeral, but was that al
they had? Why were they here, of all places? Randi didn'
like Cleo any more than Cleo liked Randi with an *i*.

The door behind him opened, and a lone man wearing
hat low on his head slipped in and claimed one of the fev
remaining tables. Like Luther, this man choose a table tha
was lost in shadows. Every nerve in Luther's body wen
on alert.

Something about the man was familiar. The way he hel
his head, the width of his shoulders and the way he sat. A
Luther watched, the man removed the hat from his head
Palmer.

Luther stood and walked past tables where loving cou
ples celebrated this most disgusting of all holidays, an
took the chair across from Palmer.

"What the hell are you doing here?" Luther demanded

Palmer was taken aback. "I have every right to be here."

"Just passing through?"

Palmer sighed. "I'm in town to speak to a man who's thinking about buying a fleet of cars. I thought while I was here I might as well come by and hear Cleo sing."

"Do you come to Huntsville on business often?"

"Occasionally."

How easy would it have been for Palmer to change his appearance just a little, the way he had with the hat, and slip in on a busy Friday night? Cleo said he was handsy. Did his interest in her go beyond that?

"I don't like the way you look at her."

"Come off it, Detective," Palmer said testily. "She's a great singer, she's my sister-in-law, and I have every right to stop by her club when I'm in town."

Luther leaned over the table and lowered his voice. He was more than suspicious. He was furious. "Look at her wrong, and I'll kick your ass. Touch her, and I'll kill you."

Palmer's eyes went wide. "I should report you to your superiors."

"Have at it," Luther said, rising to return to his own table. What he'd just done might not be smart, but if Palmer was the man who'd been knocking off Cleo's tormentors, a little push wouldn't hurt.

Sounded good, but that wasn't the reason. When this was over he might never see Cleo again. But if he could spare her another uncomfortable moment with her grabby brother-in-law, well, he had to do it, didn't he? She deserved better than that. She deserved better than a cop who saw deception everywhere he looked, too.

All eyes turned when Cleo entered the room. Dressed in red, her hair perfectly styled and hanging in midnight curls down her back, red spike heels clicking on the floor, she was a vision. Show time. Luther met her, cutting off her path to the stage. No one could hear what he said, but the

look on her face was enough to tell anyone that she wa
unhappy. Angry. Ah, if looks could kill.

"Listen to me," he said softly.

"Get out of my way, Malone."

"I don't know any other way to say I'm sorry."

She looked up, her amber eyes clear and bright. "I don' want an apology. I don't want you to grovel and beg an swear it'll never happen again. I just want you out of m way." She brushed past him, heading for the stage.

Without thinking, Luther reached out and grabbed he arm, stopping her in her tracks.

Cleo turned slowly and stared down at his hand on he arm. "Let me go."

He did, and she turned her back on him to continue t the stage. The self-absorbed lovebirds in the audience migh not have noticed what just happened, but anyone wh watched Cleo carefully certainly knew something was ver wrong.

She didn't sit tonight, but moved her stool aside to pac restlessly on the stage. Eric was waiting for her, and h went into an intro Luther immediately recognized: "Com Morning."

On hearing the notes, Cleo spun around and waved hand to cut him off. She whispered something insistent, an the kid shrugged and began again.

The number that took the place of the romantic song sh had written was not the kind of song people might expec to hear on Valentine's Day. "Forever Blue" wasn't onl newer than the numbers she usually sang, it was heartrend ing. She sang well, but almost absently. Lost in a world o her own making, torturing herself.

Luther made his way to his table at the back of the room Plenty of people glanced up as he passed, whispered whe they thought he was too far away to hear. Yeah, most o them had noticed something was up.

Cleo finished her song and was rewarded with a round f confused applause.

"Sorry, guys," she said with a half smile. "I guess that's ot what you came here to hear, not today." She walked cross the stage, looking at everyone. "Valentine's Day. eople either love or hate it, you know? It's a great day if ou have a sufficiently adoring significant other, a lousy ay if you don't.

"There have been one or two years when I loved Valntine's Day," she said. "Usually I'm one of those who ates it. I mean, who are we trying to kid? Hearts and lowers. Sappy cards. Heart-shaped meat loaf."

Someone laughed, but it was a kind of nervous laughter.

"Heart-shaped meat loaf. That's what I was going to nake for a late romantic dinner tonight, and trust me, for omeone who doesn't cook it was going to be a real sacifice. Fortunately for me, my latest significant other turned ut to be a jerk like every other man I've ever had the nisfortune to fall for. I think I'll settle for a peanut butter andwich when I get home."

The same idiot twittered, and his girlfriend gave him the lbow.

At Cleo's signal, Eric began again. Cleo closed her eyes nd began to sing "Chances Are," the kind of song one night expect on Valentine's Day. She didn't get far before ier voice cracked. In the stage lights, Luther saw a single ear run down her face.

She stopped, Eric's notes trailed away, and Cleo opened ier eyes. "I'm sorry," she said. "I just can't…"

The room was deathly silent, and one young girl sniffled s if her own heart was broken. "Eric will play for y'all or a while. Best piano player in Huntsville," she said, with crooked smile that did not go well with the tears in her yes. She started to leave the stage, but stopped before she eached the steps.

“I guess I should try to leave on a happy note,” sh said, as if it had just occurred to her. “What’s the differ ence between a dead snake in the road and a dead cop i the road?”

There was a moment of complete silence.

“There are skidmarks in front of the snake.”

Chapter 16

Cleo sat on the floor with Rambo's head in her lap. Stroking the warm fur did make her feel better. A bit. She had a gut-deep feeling that she would never be completely better again. How foolish, to give a man that kind of power!

"I'm thinking of moving back to Montgomery," she said, never taking her eyes from Rambo's fur. Out of the corner of her eye, she saw Syd sit up straight on the couch.

"What?"

"Things have never worked out here, not completely. The club does okay. It keeps me in peanut butter and dog food, and I make enough to pay my bills on time, but…that's about it. Once the money from 'Come Morning' starts rolling in…" She shrugged. "I just don't need the aggravation."

"Aggravation? Hello? Remember your mother, and Thea and that creep Palmer?"

Cleo lifted her head and smiled at Syd. "Palmer was there tonight. He came back to the office after the show, apparently to make sure I was okay before he headed to his hotel.''

''Did he get fresh?''

Cleo shook her head. ''No. He kept his distance.'' Thank God. The mood she'd been in tonight, she might have actually done murder if Palmer had been his usual, pawing self. Once Palmer had gone, she'd exited by way of the back door, leaving Luther and Boone and Michael sitting in the front room, while she slipped into the alley behind the club and made her way to a pay phone, where she called herself a cab. For all she knew, her three protectors were still sitting in the club, sipping a variety of nonalcoholic beverages and waiting for her to emerge. The thought actually brought a wry smile to her face.

''You wouldn't leave me here all alone would you?'' Syd whined. ''If you move back to Montgomery, who will I talk to late at night? Who will I have dinner with and commiserate about men with and... No one else will ever understand the Barney Fife-Bruce Willis scale of masculinity.''

Cleo snorted. ''Do you have a stupidity scale? How about an insensitive Neanderthal scale?''

''I'll work on it,'' Syd said. ''Are you really thinking about leaving?''

''Yeah.''

''Well, don't make any decisions now, when you're upset.''

''I am not upset,'' Cleo said firmly. ''I'm...'' *Confused. Heartbroken. Angry.*

She didn't have to finish her sentence. Someone—she had no doubt as to *who*—began to bang on her door so hard the house seemed to shake.

''Cleo!'' Luther shouted. ''Open this damn door.''

''Go away, Malone,'' she shouted back.

''I—will—not!'' He continued to pound on her door.

She rose with a groan and headed for the door, Rambo at her heels. She threw open the door and stared up at a very angry homicide detective.

"You didn't use the peephole," he seethed.

"How do you know?" she snapped.

He simply stared.

"I knew it was you," she explained. "How could I not, with that big mouth of yours shouting my name? You probably woke the entire neighborhood."

"Someone could have been standing behind me with a gun, making me call you to the door."

She snorted, and did not step aside to invite him in.

"You left," he said, stating the obvious.

"Bravo, Detective," she answered. "And you were clever enough to find me. Give yourself a gold star." She gave the door a shove, intending to close it in Luther's face, but he stopped it with a quick, strong hand.

"We need to talk."

"No we don't."

"I made a mistake."

"Yes, you did." She turned and walked away from him, so he wouldn't see the tears that stung her eyes.

Luther didn't go away, damn him. He followed her inside, soundly closing the door behind him. Rambo, the traitor, was happy to see her pal Luther. And when she presented her head, Luther dutifully scratched and said hello.

"I have to go," Syd said, rising quickly from the couch.

"No, you don't," Cleo said. "Malone's not staying. He was just on his way out."

"Not until I get some answers," he said.

Cleo spun on him, her tears dried. "I don't owe you any answers."

Syd, the coward, said good-night and all but ran to the front door. Cleo took a deep breath. She didn't want to face him; she didn't want to be alone with him, ever again.

"Fine," she said. "Ask your damn questions."

"Why did you slip out of the club without telling anyone?"

"I wanted to be alone."

"Dammit, Cleo, it's not safe for you to run around town on your own!"

"I haven't really been threatened, have I? You're the one who should be worried. I'd be very careful crossing the street, if I were you." Her voice was sufficiently cold, but inside...deep inside she shivered.

"Palmer went back to your office and spoke to you tonight." A muscle in his jaw twitched.

"He didn't try anything," she said. "He was a perfect gentleman."

"I know. Russell followed him and watched through the open door while y'all talked. He said Palmer never came near you."

"Then, what do you want to know?"

"What did he say?"

Cleo shrugged. "He just wanted to make sure that I was okay."

"Did you buy it?"

Strangely enough, she did. She answered with a nod.

"About this afternoon—" Luther began.

"I don't want to talk about this afternoon," she said sharply. "I should be glad I found out what you're like before this thing with us went any further."

"I lost it," he confessed. "Boone told me you'd hired a PI to check on me..."

"And you automatically assumed the worst," she finished. "What a horrible way to go through life," she said. "I thought I was cynical, but compared to you I'm a regular Pollyanna."

He took a step toward her, and she stepped back, maintaining the distance between them. "What do you want me to say? I said I'm sorry, I tried to take it back."

She laughed harshly. "You think you can take something like that *back?*"

He didn't try again to approach her, but stood there staring at her strangely. "So that's it?"

"That's it."

"You can't forgive me."

She shook her head. "You know, the terrible thing is, I think I could forgive you, in time. But I don't think I could ever forget. I think this afternoon would always be between us." She shook her head. "I need more from the man I share my bed with. I need trust, and friendship, and love. All that and more. I don't think you have it to give."

He didn't argue with her. How could he? He knew, better than she did, that he would never change. He would always expect the worst, he would always be suspicious and cynical, and if they stayed together she would forever wonder when the next blowup was coming.

"I never thanked you," he said softly.

"For what?"

"For the pictures and the names."

This was a safer subject, at least. "Are you going to go see your grandmother?"

"I don't know." He gave her a sad, crooked smile. "Maybe I should just let it be."

"That would be safest, I suppose."

Safest. Luther Malone was nothing if not cautious.

He turned away from her. "Don't run off again," he barked over his shoulder. "You almost gave Boone a heart attack."

When the door slammed she sank to her knees, put her arms around Rambo's neck and cried until she didn't have any tears left.

* * *

Luther fiddled with the candy in his hand, stared down at it, and then tossed it across the room. As an oral fixation, peppermint was a poor substitute for Cleo.

His apartment had never seemed so small. Ray had invited him over to see the baby, his goddaughter Angel, even though Grace and the baby had only been home for a couple of days. That fact was enough of an excuse for Luther to politely decline. But it wasn't the reason.

He wasn't ready to look them in the eye and tell them he'd blown it with Cleo. He'd blown it big-time.

Boone was keeping an eye on Cleo, and Russell was parked at the end of the street, keeping an eye on traffic that came and went into Luther's apartment complex. They'd wanted to put a couple of marked cars on him, an idea Luther had vetoed. If they surrounded him with cops, the killer would never make his move! No one was on alert just yet. The past two murders had taken place on Sunday night, late.

Regulations demanded backup, even though Luther was confident he could handle the killer himself. Still, if he had to have someone watching his back, Mikey would do. And like Cleo said, he'd have to be very careful crossing the street.

He tried to think of something else he might have said to her last night, something that would make everything right. Nothing seemed to work, not even in the recesses of his muddled, sleep-deprived brain. Cleo was right: she deserved better than what he had to give her.

His phone rang, and he glanced down at the caller ID, hoping, more than a little, that Cleo's number would come up. It didn't, but this might be almost as good. It was his florist calling.

''Malone.''

''This is Ginny, from the flower shop?'' she said breathlessly, her voice low. "You wanted to know when someone placed an order to be delivered to Cleo's?"

"Yeah." He stood up and grabbed his car keys and jacket, while she finished.

"He's here right now. Red roses, no card. Kimmi is trying to stall him, but I don't think she can keep him here much longer."

He ended the connection and ran to the door, bounded down the stairs two at a time and headed for his car. Russell would see him and follow, he knew. He tossed the red light onto his dash and took off, flying out of the parking lot. He was a good ten minutes from the mall. Could Kimmi stall the man long enough?

His heart pounded, and with adrenaline pumping he drove past cars that moved aside for him. This needed to be over, for Cleo's sake. He needed to catch this guy. *Now.* He glanced in his rearview mirror once, to make sure Russell was right behind him. He was.

He pulled up to the curb at the mall entrance closest to the flower shop, and left his car at a run. Russell was not far behind him. Two girls, one he recognized and one he did not, waited in the flower shop entrance.

"There he is!" the girl he remembered said, jumping up and down.

Luther followed the girl's pointing finger, just as a face he recognized as one of Cleo's regulars looked over a broad shoulder and panicked.

Luther took off running, and so did the man. Cleo's secret admirer knocked aside a woman who was too busy to be aware of what was happening around her, and Luther didn't stop. He skirted the fallen woman and kept on running. He glanced back once to see that Russell was checking to make sure the woman who'd been knocked down was all right.

The man who'd ordered the roses turned onto a narrow

corridor that led to a back entrance. He was a big man—more than strong enough to drag Tempest to the roof and toss him over—but he wasn't very fast. Luther caught him as he reached the glass-doored exit. He tackled the big man and they both fell. Hard.

"I didn't do nothin' wrong," the man on the floor said in a surprisingly whiny voice.

"Then, why did you run?" Luther asked breathlessly.

Before the man he had pinned to the floor could answer, Russell was there. Luther stood and dragged the man to his feet. *Henry,* he realized as he got a better look at the man's face. He'd heard Lizzy call this one by name.

"Why did you run, Henry?"

The big man blushed. "I want my lawyer."

"Fine."

He cuffed Henry and read him his rights. Henry had clammed up, but his chin quivered as if he were about to cry. Jeez.

And the man had asked for his lawyer already, so they couldn't do a damn thing.

"Let's go," Luther said, dragging Henry along with him as he headed down the corridor. He was almost to the car when his cell phone rang. He handed Henry over to Russell and snagged his phone from the inside pocket of his jacket.

He glanced at the number on the caller ID before answering. "What's up?" he asked without preamble.

"Something's going down," Boone said tersely. "A kid just delivered four dozen red roses to Cleo's door. And one white rose. He says a man paid him to deliver the flowers. Fifty bucks."

Luther glanced at Henry. "I'll be right there."

"Cleo doesn't want you here," Boone snapped, before Luther could hang up the phone. "Sorry man, she specifically said—"

"All right," Luther said. "I'll send Mikey—Russell," he amended. "I'll send Russell over there to check it out."

"That'll work," Boone said, calmer now. "You know, I think she might have been right about those white roses before. This one white rose in all the red ones, it creeps me out."

"I know what you mean," Luther said before ending the call. He gave Henry a shove. "You've been busy this morning, haven't you?"

"I don't know what you're talking about."

"Of course you don't," Luther said.

Deep inside, Cleo shook. Her bones quivered, her knees knocked. She made very sure no one would know it, to look at her. She made the rounds and said hello to all the regulars, ignoring Luther, who sat in the back of the room wearing his usual sour expression and a black suit with a white shirt and a cheap tie.

She herself had gone all out tonight. Her dress was white and snug and low-cut, her matching heels were high. The white rose in her hair, the single white rose that had been in the massive bouquet delivered to her home early this afternoon, was tucked behind her right ear. And tonight, unlike last night, she'd been able to get through her set. Luther Malone might be able to take a lot of things from her, but her voice was not one of them. She wouldn't allow it.

They had her secret admirer in custody, which was a relief. When Luther had told her, she'd thought, for a moment, that this was over. Her bodyguards, all of them, could take a hike. She'd never have to see them again.

But Luther, never satisfied, couldn't be sure that the man they had in custody was the killer. While he had suspected that her secret admirer might be the man who had killed

Jack and the heckler, he couldn't be sure. Apparently Henry had confessed to sending roses, but not to anything else.

But he was the one, she knew it. Soon this would be over. When tomorrow came and went and no attempt was made on Luther's life, they'd know for sure that Henry was their man.

Palmer was here again tonight and so was Corey—without Randi with an *i*. Luther, Boone, Michael—their familiar eyes seemed riveted on her. Cleo looked around the room and her head swam.

She wished Luther wasn't here. She could handle anything else, everyone else, but to look at him and pretend it didn't hurt was the hardest thing she'd ever done. So she did her best not to look at him at all.

"Hey, sweetheart," Corey called, smiling at her as if they were old friends and lifting his hand to wave her over to his table.

Her first instinct was to turn and walk away without acknowledging him at all, but like it or not everyone was a suspect, and the sooner this was over with, the sooner Luther Malone would be out of her life.

She made her way to Corey's table with a smile she didn't feel, and sat across the small round table from him. The light from the glass-encased candle in the middle of the table lit his almost-handsome face too well.

"You're alone tonight," she said. "What happened to Randi?"

He shrugged. "She didn't want to come." He gave her what might pass with other women as a charming grin. "But I love to hear you sing, even if it's this old stuff."

"Why, thank you," she muttered.

"I'll never understand why you quit writing and singing country for this. Where's your audience, Cleo? The way you look and the way you sing, you could be a star."

She'd never wanted that. Jack had. Everyone she'd met

in Nashville had shared the same dream. Not her. "I like what I do," she said.

Corey had something to say. He wasn't good with words, and he was apparently fighting with a few of them now. "I'm doing a new album," he finally said.

"Congratulations."

"I want it to do well. It really has to do well, or else I'll be shopping for a new label."

"That's the way it goes."

He leaned over the table, bringing his face close to the yellow light of the candle. "What I need is a showstopper. I had this really great idea. How about if you write us a song, a really sexy duet. You can sing it with me on the album, and we'll make a kick-ass video, and—"

"No thanks," she said, before he could say more. "I appreciate the offer, but I really can't."

Corey bit his lip and flexed his fingers. "But once 'Come Morning' is rereleased, you'll be a star again."

"I'm not recording it for the movie," she said. "They got a big name to do that."

"Yeah, but you can sing circles around her. When the song comes out and makes it big, radio stations will be playing your version, too. People will start talking about you again, wondering where you are, and it would be the perfect opportunity for you to break back into the business."

"But I don't want to break back into the business," she said testily, annoyed at the prospect that he might be right. She didn't want to hear herself on the radio as she drove to work, she didn't want customers to start requesting "Come Morning" every damn night. The occasional requests were tough enough.

She stood. "I have work to do in the office. Thanks for the offer, but—"

"Think about it," he said, glancing up at her with hopeful eyes. "It would really be great."

Cleo turned and walked away from the table without another word. She'd said no. Sooner or later that would sink through Corey's thick skull.

She headed for the office, wanting nothing more than to sit at her desk, lay her head down and breathe deeply. She hadn't been able to breathe deeply all day.

She had her hand on the door to the office, when she caught a glimpse of Luther entering the hallway. Her heart hitched.

"What did he want?" Luther asked as he came up behind her.

"He wants me to write a hit song and record it with him."

"Did you accept?"

"No," she said. She didn't turn around to look up into Luther's face. She couldn't. She didn't open the door, either, because if she did he would follow her inside and close it. She didn't think she could bear to be behind closed doors with Luther ever again.

Not because she didn't love him, but because she still did. No matter what. And that just wasn't right. She couldn't live this way, waiting for the next accusation, the next hurt.

"Are you okay?" he asked.

"Fine," she said shakily.

Luther placed a hand on her shoulder and gently forced her to turn around. She didn't fight him. To fight would reveal too much. So she slowly turned, and lifted her head to look at him.

Luther laid his hand on her cheek. "When this is over," he whispered huskily, "I'll be back."

"Don't bother," she said, trying to sound tough.

He shook his head. "No, I'll be back. I know I made a mistake, but I know just as well that...I need you."

"That's a sad, overused line, Malone. You don't need anyone. You never have."

"I need you to teach me how not to always see the worst in everything. To show me that better, brighter side of life you talked about." He moved slightly closer, bringing his body almost against hers.

"That would be like the blind leading the blind, wouldn't it?"

"No." His hand raked up her side, his thumb brushed against her ribs and his palm finally came to a stop and rested beneath her breast. "You have the brightest, most beautiful heart I have ever known. There's more hope here than I knew existed in the world."

She shook her head. "That's not true."

"It is." He lowered his head and barely brushed his mouth across hers. "So when this is over, I'll be back. I'm going to fight for us, Cleo."

Her eyes closed and her mouth instinctively searched for his. "Don't bother."

"I've never fought for anything before," he said against her lips. "Not once in my entire life. But you...Cleo, you're definitely worth fighting for."

She wanted to believe him, she wanted so much to believe that what they had almost found was worth fighting for. "It's too late."

"I'll be back," he said again, and then he turned and walked away.

Chapter 17

Luther laid everything before him, covering the top of his desk with manila folders and scribbled notes. It wasn't all that unusual for him to be working on a Sunday afternoon, not when a case was fresh. What was he supposed to do? Sit around his apartment and wait for Henry Copeland to change his story? Cleo's secret admirer confessed to sending roses to the club, but not to her home. He admitted to lusting after his favorite singer, but hotly denied killing anyone.

The kicker was, Luther believed him. So who had sent roses to Cleo's home? Who had killed Jack Tempest and Willie Lee Webb?

Cleo wanted to believe that Copeland was guilty, and she was not happy that Boone was still on duty. Tough. Luther wasn't about to let down his guard until he was absolutely positive the coast was clear. Either Henry would change his story, or someone would call Luther out onto the street and try to run him down.

The information from the lab in Birmingham was spread before him: the findings from both murder victims. They'd just gotten the reports on Webb. Everything in Birmingham moved too slowly to suit Luther. The fluids that had been taken from the bodies had been carefully analyzed, along with the clothing the victims had been wearing and the little evidence that had been collected at the scene. They had also discovered that Webb had gotten a phone call from the same pay phone as Tempest, the Sunday of his death.

As much as he wanted to, as easy as it would make things, Luther didn't buy Copeland as the killer. Whoever had killed Jack Tempest knew him. Tempest had been dragged to the roof while already unconscious, but it appeared that he had ingested the furniture polish willingly, along with a goodly amount of beer. Cleo's ex was much too suspicious a man to take a beer from a stranger.

Same for the heckler. No tainted beer had been spilled onto his shirt or his chin, so it hadn't been poured down his unwilling throat. Someone had poisoned the beers with commercial furniture polish, a now hard-to-find brand that contained GHP, a chemical that turned into GHB—gamma-hydroxy butyrate, better known as liquid Ecstasy—inside the body. A large enough dose would kill. Even a small dose was enough to knock a man out for a while.

Did that mean the heckler also knew the killer? Or was he simply a more trusting man than Tempest?

They had a partial print that had been found on the underside of a piece of tape, but it had taken them nowhere. The print had been smudged and too small to be of use. Something he didn't like niggled at the back of his brain.

"Russell," Luther said, spinning his desk chair slowly around. His partner was not happy about being in the office today, but since he had Luther's back, he was here. And he pored over his own notes, trying to spot a clue that he might have missed the first time around.

‘‘Find something?’’ Russell raised his eyebrows, young and hopeful.

‘‘Let’s say you’re Tempest. You have your fair share of enemies. You are not a particularly trusting man. It’s Sunday afternoon. Alcohol sales are limited. Unless you’re in a restaurant that serves beer, you’re not buying anything, and Randi swears they ate in. Where did he get the beer?’’

‘‘Out of his own refrigerator,’’ Russell offered. ‘‘If Randi is involved, she easily could have gotten into his stash and doped it up, then had her new boyfriend do the physical work of dragging Tempest up the stairs and tossing him over.’’

Luther shook his head. ‘‘The only beer in his refrigerator was half a six-pack of cans. A can would be tough to doctor, and it wasn’t the same brand as what was in his stomach.’’

‘‘Oh.’’ Russell leaned back and propped his feet on his desk.

The office was eerily quiet today, the phones silent.

‘‘Besides,’’ Luther added, ‘‘we have Webb to explain away. Why would Randi kill him? This comes back to Cleo. Someone did this for her. Someone who thought they were doing her a favor.’’ He disliked Palmer, but doubted the man had the guts for murder. Flinger wanted her to sing for his next CD, but he couldn’t see how killing Tempest and Webb would accomplish that. Eric had always been high on his list of suspects, even though he kind of liked the piano player. The kid adored Cleo. Enough to kill for her and think he was doing her a favor? Then there was Edgar, who was like an overprotective bulldog.

‘‘If a bartender offered you a drink, say, inside a closed nightclub, would you take it?’’

Russell dropped his feet from the table and sat up straight. ‘‘Edgar?’’

‘‘Makes sense, in a way. Let’s say he calls his victim

over to the club on a Sunday afternoon, when no one else is there, to discuss...whatever it takes to get them there. Something tempting. He might have offered to help Tempest run Cleo out of business, for the right price. He might have apologized to Webb for the shoddy treatment he received, and offered them both a beer on the house.'' Luther closed his eyes and shook his head. ''Edgar was outside the club when Webb gave me his name. The old man even put the drunk in a cab. Finding his number would have been as easy as picking up a phone book.''

''So, is he going to call you this afternoon and invite you over?''

Luther stood up, snatching Edgar's file from the top of his desk. ''I don't think I want to wait around and find out. Let's pay the old man a visit.''

Cleo usually loved Sundays. She slept late, took Rambo to the park if the weather was nice, watched old movies on television and hung out with Syd. It was her recovery day, her only day off.

But she didn't mind that Edgar had called. She hadn't been able to rest, not while sitting there wondering if Henry, a customer she had recognized when Luther showed her a photograph, was the man who'd killed Jack and the heckler, or if Luther was right in remaining cautious. If the killer was still loose, would he manage, despite all their plans, to run Luther down in the street? Luther, who wouldn't give up. Who wanted to fight for her. For *them.* Luther said he'd be back, and in spite of everything that had happened, she wanted that to happen.

She unlocked the door and stepped into the club. Boone was right behind her. Edgar stood at the bar, his hands on his head as he leaned over a sheaf of papers.

''This could have waited until tomorrow,'' Cleo said as she locked the door behind her. ''You need a day off, too.''

"I know," he said. "But I was sitting at home and I kept thinking about these numbers, and I didn't want them waiting on us tomorrow. But I just can't get things to add up right." Edgar lifted his head and frowned, as Cleo walked toward the bar with Boone at her back. "You look different."

"It's my day off, too," she teased. Of course she looked different. Her face was scrubbed clean, her hair was pulled up off her neck, and instead of a snug dress made for performing in, she had on well-worn jeans and a deep blue sweater, perfect for a cool February day.

"You're short," he said.

Cleo smiled as she glanced down at her rarely worn sneakers. "I know."

Edgar snarled at Boone. "Unless you're an accountant, back up, sit down and entertain yourself for a while."

Boone didn't move from her side.

"Okay," Edgar said when he saw that Boone was not going to move. "Have a beer and stay out of my way." He grabbed a glass and drew a beer from the tap, banging it onto the bar before Boone.

Boone looked at her. "We shouldn't be here," he said. "We should have, at the very least, called Malone."

She wrinkled her nose. "He doesn't need to know where I am twenty-four hours a day."

"I believe he thinks differently." Boone pulled his cell phone from his pocket. "I'll just give him a quick call and let him know—"

"No," Cleo said, reaching out and laying her hand on Boone's wrist. "By the time he gets here, we'll be finished. There's no need to waste his time with this." Besides, she didn't want to be the one to draw him out of his apartment. He was safe there. She had this horrible vision of him laying in the street outside her club, the third victim of the killer who was making a career of taking out the men who made her life miserable. Much as she wanted to believe the customer who'd sent her roses was the killer, she wasn't willing to gamble with Luther's life.

She shooed Boone down the bar. "Go. Drink your beer. By the time you're finished, we should be done, or close to it."

Edgar laid the papers on the bar, and as Cleo pulled herself up and onto one of the stools, Boone obediently moved to a nearby table, taking his drink with him.

Cleo checked Edgar's figures on the inventory, and found everything no more of a mess than usual. He had ordered too much Scotch and not enough vodka, but she checked and double-checked his figuring and found nothing wrong. He urged her to look again, telling her that he knew something wasn't right. She started at the top and went down each column.

"It looks fine, Edgar," she said, shuffling the papers into a neat pile and smiling. "I'm going to get out of here, and I want you to do the same. Go home and watch sports on television or take a nap." What he really needed was a lady friend, but since his wife had died, more than a year ago, he didn't seem interested. He was too young to give up on life, but at times it seemed that was just what had happened.

"I think your bodyguard is taking a nap right here," Edgar said, nodding his head.

Cleo swiveled around to see that Edgar was right. Boone had his head down on the table, an empty beer mug sitting beside the long strands of hair that hid most of the PI's face. Something grabbed at her heart. It wasn't right. Boone rarely slept, and she just couldn't see him falling asleep here and now.

"Boone?" she called. He didn't move.

Edgar walked around the bar and came up on Cleo as she slipped from the stool. She took a step toward Boone, and Edgar stopped her with a quick hand that closed aroun her wrist.

"He'll be all right," Edgar said calmly. "He'll just slee for a while, that's all."

She turned terrified eyes to the bartender, a man wh continued to look calm and friendly.

"He has no reason to fear, because he didn't hurt you."

"Oh, Edgar..."

Edgar dragged her to the table and made her sit dow across from an unconscious Boone. He snapped up Boone' cell phone and handed it to her. "Call him and tell him t come here. Now. Alone."

She shook her head. "No." She would not be respon sible for bringing Luther into danger, where Edgar coul finish his work. "You have it all wrong. Luther never hu me. There's no reason—"

"You're only saying that because you care for him, i spite of everything he did to you," Edgar snapped. "H treated you badly, and still you have feelings for him." H took a deep breath, as if trying to calm himself. "I sav you last night, letting him kiss you. Letting him hold you And all the while you wore *my* white rose in your hair. knew what you were trying to tell me by wearing that whit rose."

"I wasn't trying to tell you anything," she said softly.

"No, it was my cue to continue, my reassurance that yo wanted Malone dead."

"No!" she said. "I...I love him. If you care for me a all—"

"Care for you?" he said darkly. "You're my entire life You're the daughter I never had, my reason for living. was brought here to protect you, Cleo." He gave her small smile. "Sometimes, when you sing, I know in m heart that you're singing to me."

Cleo's world tilted and spun. Her vision narrowed. Sh

ad never fainted before, but right now she felt she might. he shook off her fear and did her best to regain control.

"Edgar, you're my friend," she said evenly. "Please on't do this."

He placed the cell phone on the table before her with ne hand and reached behind his back with the other, taking ut a revolver. He pointed the gun at Boone. "Make the all, or I shoot."

"No!" She picked up the phone and dialed Luther's umber, her hands shaking. The phone rang four times, and hen his answering machine picked up. "He's not there."

"Try his cell phone."

Her hands shook so hard she wasn't sure she could dial gain. "Edgar, I don't understand..."

He leaned down close, but the gun remained pointed at he head of an unconscious Boone Sinclair. "After my wife ied, I thought I should die, too. I kept waiting, to die in ny sleep, to walk in front of a bus, to just...die. But I idn't. Finally, one night about six months ago, I decided o end it myself. I had this gun in a safe under the bed. All had to do was go home, put it to my head and..." He wallowed hard. "It seemed like such a simple solution. ut that same night, you sang to me. I glanced up, and my yes fell on you and I knew you were singing to *me*." He eached out and touched her cheek. "You saved me that ight, because I suddenly knew why I was here. You sang o me, and I swore that I would watch over you forever, hat you would be the daughter Susan and I never had."

"Edgar," Cleo said, trying to remain calm. "You have lways been my friend. Please, please don't hurt anyone lse."

"But you were glad when I killed Jack. I could tell, even hough you didn't say you were glad. And then Malone ame along." His eyes flashed, then darted this way and hat. "He...he touched you and he kissed you, and you allowed him to take advantage of you. I wasn't pleased b that, Cleo. I was very disappointed. I thought when showed how much I loved you by killing that heckle you'd appreciate the sacrifice and realize that you're to good for the likes of Luther Malone."

"Edgar—"

"No more talking," Edgar said gruffly, pressing th muzzle of his revolver against Boone's head. "Call Ma lone. He's to come here, and he's to come alone. He'll b sorry if he doesn't follow my instructions."

Edgar rented an apartment not far from Cleo's club. Th ancient, yellow brick building had seen better years, bu wasn't exactly a rat trap. Some efforts had been made t make the place suitable.

There were six units in the long building. Edgar lived o the top floor. The closer they got to the door of Edgar' apartment, the antsier Luther got. Something wasn't righ His gut told him something was terribly wrong. He reache inside his jacket and retrieved his six-shooter. Behind him he heard the unmistakable scrape of metal on leather, a Russell unholstered his own weapon.

At the top of the stairs, he stood aside and banged o the door. "Edgar!" he shouted. "Police. Open up." Ther was no response. He banged again, standing to the side c the door, which needed painting. "Edgar, it's me. Luthe I just want to ask you a few questions." Still nothing.

"Hey!" a strident voice from the bottom of the stairwa shouted. "What are you doing?"

The overweight woman wore a housedress so brightl colored, it put his Valentine boxers to shame. And she wa annoyed.

"Who are you?" Russell asked.

"I manage this apartment building," she said sharply

"And you two are making entirely too much noise! This is a nice, quiet neighborhood."

Luther flashed his badge. "We need to get into this apartment."

"What for?" she shouted, unimpressed.

"I think something might be wrong with Edgar." That was the truth. No sane person would kill the way their perpetrator had. If Edgar had killed Tempest and Webb, there was definitely something wrong with him.

"Oh," she said, sounding deflated.

"Do you have a key?"

"Of course I have a key." She drew a key chain from a deep pocket in her housedress, and tossed it to Mikey. "The keys are labeled," she said. "I'm in 1A. Just drop the keys off when you're finished." She waddled off, apparently not concerned enough about Edgar to stick around and see what they found. Just as well.

If Edgar was here, he knew what was happening. The manager hadn't kept her voice down and neither had Luther. But the place was so quiet, he didn't think Edgar was in. He had to be sure, though, so he found the proper key and inserted it into the lock.

"Edgar?" he called, his voice somewhat friendly. "Are you here?"

The apartment smelled of week-old garbage and stale booze. And something else...some perfumy odor under it all, as if the old man had tried to cover his bad cleaning habits with a hint of perfume.

"Edgar?" Luther moved through the living room and glanced into the kitchen. The garbage can overflowed, the sink was piled high with dirty dishes.

Russell moved down the hallway and glanced into the first bedroom. Luther was right behind him. Unmade bed, clothes on the floor, half-empty bottle of Scotch on the bedside table. The bathroom was even worse.

Luther passed Russell and opened the last door off the hallway. The sweet scent hit him full in the face, the aroma of oft-burned scented candles and a spray of perfume. Cleo's perfume.

His heart almost stopped. It was spotless. No dust, no litter, no signs of neglect marred this room. Two walls were plastered with photographs of Cleo, some old and some new. A long table had been set against one wall, and on it sat a framed picture of Cleo flanked by two fat candles that had been burned more than halfway down. Red roses, half a dozen of them, sat in a crystal vase behind the photograph.

A pair of red spike-heel shoes—Cleo's, he was certain—sat on a shelf in a place of honor. She'd mentioned, once, losing her best pair of red shoes. A cassette player was placed just beneath it. A stack of cassettes sat beside the player. No doubt her single release was in there, along with recordings of nights at the club. Nights when Cleo had no idea she'd been recorded.

Luther uttered a foul word. Russell reacted in the same way. Since it was obvious Edgar was not home, Luther holstered his six-shooter and reached for his cell phone, dialing Boone's number from memory. Busy.

"You go to Cleo's and check on her," he said to Russell. "I'm—"

"No," his partner said crisply. "I've got your back. Where you go, I go. Where do you think he is?"

There was only one place he could think of. The club. "We'll swing by Cleo's house first, check in with Boone, get a patrol car on her place, and—" His cell phone rang, cutting him off in midsentence.

Boone's number came up on the caller ID. Thank God. "Listen," Luther said, in place of his usual "Malone."

"Luther?"

His gut clenched when he heard Cleo's voice.

"Where are you?" he snapped.

"I didn't want to call," she said, "but he held a gun to Boone's head. He wants you to come here, but don't, Luther. Don't—" There was a sharp intake of breath. When she said "Don't" the second time, Luther knew she wasn't talking to him.

"Are you all right?" He could *hear* her shaking.

"We're at the club. Edgar says come now, and come alone. If you don't, if he sees anyone else or hears any sirens, he'll kill me and then himself."

"I'm coming," he said. "Hang in there. Everything's going to be—"

The phone went dead.

"All right," he finished softly.

"What's up?" Russell asked.

Luther looked at his young, enthusiastic, never-say-die partner. It was no longer a matter of whether or not he trusted the kid. Cleo's life was on the line.

Chapter 18

Once she'd made the phone call, Edgar took Cleo's keys in case she should decide to run. He then dragged Boone' body out of the chair and to the rear door, and dumped unceremoniously in the alley. He maneuvered the big ma with no apparent effort. Of course Edgar was strong! H would have to be, to drag Jack all the way to the top c that building and toss him over. Cleo shuddered at th thought.

With Boone disposed of, Edgar sat in the PI's place an gave her a wide smile.

"Will he really be all right?" she asked.

"Sure. He might have a headache when he wakes up but he's a big guy. I don't think I gave him too much."

Cleo's insides quaked. "You don't *think?*"

Edgar shrugged, clearly unconcerned.

"Now what?" she asked.

"Malone shows up, alone as I requested. He drinks, an when he's unconscious, I'll lay him in the street, and yo and I will get in my car and run him over a dozen times."

"No," she said hoarsely.

"Yes," Edgar snapped, his smile gone. "That's the way it has to be, Cleo. You and I can't make things right as long as he's around."

She swallowed hard. "Edgar, you and I can't ever make things right."

His face tensed, and a muscle in his jaw twitched. "We're family, Cleo. We can't let a man like Malone come between us."

She prayed that Luther wouldn't come. She didn't want to see him die. Enough people had died, in her name. What had she done to make Edgar believe that there was anything between them aside from friendship? "I didn't mean to mislead you," she said, trying to remain calm. Inside she didn't feel calm at all. Her heart hammered, and she couldn't manage the deep breath she felt she needed.

"You didn't mislead me," Edgar said. "You just don't understand, yet. But you will. Once we're together, you will know that I'm right." His eyes went dreamy. "You sang to me. I looked at you and I could tell that you were looking right back at me. No one else mattered. Nothing else mattered. There was a connection in the air, an electricity. I know you felt it."

"I didn't," she said softly. "I just… You're my friend, Edgar. Let's end this now, before anyone else gets hurt."

He shook his head. "It's too late for that. We're going to get rid of Malone, and then you and I are going to keep on driving."

"Where will we go?" she asked hoarsely.

"I don't know." His lack of direction didn't seem to bother him. "I thought I'd let you decide."

How was she supposed to reason with a man who wasn't thinking rationally? The minutes ticked past. "He won't come, you know," she said. "Luther won't come. He

knows you plan to kill him. Why should he put himself i
that position?''

''I'm sure he thinks he can save you and himself. Hi
kind always does.''

''No. This place will be surrounded by cops before yo
know it,'' she said. ''You should go, now, before they ge
here.''

Confident, Edgar shook his head. ''No. He won't risk
your life like that. I told him what I would do.''

''Would you?'' she asked. ''Would you really shoo
me?''

''I don't want to,'' he said, ''but I will. If I must.''

More silent minutes ticked past. With each passing one
Edgar became tighter, more on edge. Cleo decided tha
maybe if she could keep him talking, he'd calm down. I
this agitated state he was likely to do anything.

''Did you plan it for a long time?'' she asked. ''Hav
you been planning to kill Jack for months?''

Edgar shook his head. ''No. That night was just…it wa
just the last straw. You tried not to let him bother you,
could see that, but you can't hide your feelings from me
Cleo. That man was ruining your life.''

She nodded gently.

''He needed to die.''

Cleo shivered. Edgar's words were so matter-of-fact. ''
know you meant well, but…I never wanted anyone to die.'
Her words faded into nothing.

With narrowed eyes, Edgar looked around the club. Usually it was so noisy, so full of life and people. Today it wa
just the two of them.

''That cop ruined everything,'' he said gruffly. ''Malone—'' he snorted ''—it was bad enough that he starte
hanging around here trying to smoke out the killer, bu
when he started manhandling you, looking at you like h
was the one who was supposed to take care of you, *touch*

ing you..." Edgar worked himself up, and then quickly calmed himself with a deep breath. "I tried to throw him off the scent by stealing your fan letters. I figured if he started searching for some smitten secret admirer, he wouldn't look too closely at your friends."

"You had Eric lie to support your alibi for the night Jack was killed."

Edgar grinned, just a little. "Yeah. After you insisted on telling Malone the truth about you not being here, I convinced Eric that if he didn't have an alibi he'd be suspect number one. Everyone knows he has a crush on you."

Cleo shook her head, trying to cast off the frustration and sadness. "Why didn't you just let it go? Henry Copeland is in custody. If no one else had been killed, no one ever would have known the truth."

The old man—her employee, her friend—reached out and stroked her cheek with one rough finger. "Malone made you cry. Am I supposed to ignore that? Am I supposed to just let him walk away after what he did?"

"Oh, Edgar," she whispered. "Please, please don't hurt anyone else. Don't...don't hurt Luther. He was only doing his job." She could tell he was not moved by her plea. "For me. Let him go—" She almost jumped out of her skin at the sound of insistent banging on the door.

"Cleo!" Luther shouted as he pounded. "Are you all right?"

Edgar stood, gun in hand, and dragged Cleo from her chair. He handed her the key and instructed her to unlock the door. With shaking hands, she did as he asked.

The door swung open, and Luther rushed inside. There was no one on the street, no police cars, no sign of Michael. Luther held his hands up to show that he was unarmed. His holster was empty, and he carried a portable cassette player, a boom box, in one hand.

Edgar pointed his weapon at Cleo's head. She actually

felt the metal of the muzzle press lightly against her scalp, as he instructed her to relock the door. Luther was shooed farther into the room with a silent nod of Edgar's head.

When the door was securely locked, Edgar, still holding the gun to Cleo's head, turned to face Luther. His face was harsh and solid, for a moment, and then something crumpled. "Hey!" he shouted. "That's my stereo."

Luther held the boom box up. "This old thing? I would hardly call it a stereo—"

"It's *mine,*" Edgar shouted.

Luther placed the cassette player on the nearest table. "Drop the gun," he said hoarsely. "I'm not going to rush you."

"I can't take that chance," Edgar said. "Why do you have my stereo? Were you in my home?"

"Drop the gun and I'll tell you."

"Did you come alone?"

"Drop the gun and I'll tell you."

Edgar sputtered, frustrated by Luther's calm responses. "You've been nothing but a pain in the ass since you walked through that door! Why don't you just walk on over to the bar and drink that shot I poured out for you. I didn't bother with the beer, this time. No need to hide what I'm doing."

"You want me to drink that?" Luther asked, pointing.

"Luther, don't," Cleo whispered.

"Then, drop the gun," he finished with clenched teeth.

Edgar sidled away from the door. His grip on Cleo was tight, the hand that held the revolver to her head was rock steady.

Luther didn't move, but stood in the middle of the room and stared at Edgar with cold, expressionless eyes. "Do you think you love her? Is that why you're doing this?"

"I do love her."

Luther shook his head. "No, you don't. If you loved her,

you wouldn't be able to point that gun at her head. I know, because just seeing it makes me hurt. Physically, sharply, *hurt.*"

"I have to be sure you'll do what I say."

"Then, point the damn gun at me," Luther growled. "You coward."

"Luther, no..." Cleo began. Edgar was much more likely to pull the trigger if Luther was in his sights.

"At me!" he insisted, pointing at his own chest and taking a single step forward.

Edgar finally complied. The weapon snapped around and pointed at Luther.

Luther visibly relaxed. "That's better."

"My stereo," Edgar prodded.

"I was in your apartment," Luther confessed. "I found your shrine."

Edgar shook with anger. "That special place was for me, and me alone. You had no right!"

Luther shrugged.

"Were you alone?" Edgar whispered.

"Yes."

"Did you come here alone?"

"Just as you instructed," Luther answered. "Yes. It's just you and me, now. Why don't you let Cleo go, while we settle this between us?"

Edgar shook his head. "I can't let her go. Once you're dead, she's coming with me."

"Running away together, huh?" Luther asked.

"Yes."

"The two of you are going to live happily ever after, is that it?"

Edgar shook his head. "You don't understand anything."

"What makes you think she'll stay with you," Luther asked, "after you've hurt her?"

"I would never hurt her!"

Luther nodded at them. "You're holding her too tight," he said. "She'll probably have bruises on her arms tomorrow."

Edgar loosened his grip. "I didn't mean to hurt her."

"I know you didn't," Luther said casually. "But scaring her is just as bad. Why did you scare her?" he asked, making it sound like Edgar had committed the greatest of sins in doing such a thing. "The note that said *Boom,* the white roses. How did you know the white roses would affect her that way? Did she confide something personal to you one night, something a woman might tell someone she trusts? She opened up her heart to you, and then you used it against her." Luther shook his head.

Edgar took a deep, ragged breath. "I wanted Cleo to know that *you* can't protect her. Only I can do that. Only me."

"Now what?" Luther asked, all business.

"You drink." Edgar nodded toward the bar.

"Don't I get a last wish?" Luther asked, without making a move toward the lone shot glass on the long bar.

"Why should I grant you a wish?" Edgar snapped.

"It'll make you look magnanimous in front of the lady," Luther said evenly. "Might go a long way toward making her forgive you for killing three people."

Three people. Jack. The heckler. *Luther.*

Edgar was silent for a moment as he considered this possibility. Luther looked at Cleo, hard and deep.

"He's right," she said, feeling a hint of calm. "It would be a generous thing to do, and you've always been such a generous person. It's one of the things I like best about you, Edgar."

"It is?"

She nodded, her eyes on Luther. She didn't know what he had planned, but she did know that he was not going to drink that poison and willingly die, leaving her in Edgar's hands.

"Yes," she said.

Edgar shook the gun at Luther. "What do you want?"

"One last dance with Cleo."

Cleo's heart skipped a beat, and Edgar's grip went tight again.

"No," her captor said. "I have to keep her away from men like you."

Luther smiled crookedly. "Come on, one last dance for a dying man. She's going to be yours for a very long time, right?"

"Right," the husky voice behind her said. "But you have it all wrong. Cleo is like a daughter to me. The child Susan and I never had. It's my mission in life to watch over her, to make sure no one hurts her ever again."

Luther nodded. "I understand that, Edgar, I really do. What will one last dance with me matter? A few weeks from now, she'll probably barely remember me, anyway."

"That's right enough, I reckon."

Luther lifted one hand and offered it to Cleo. Slowly, still not sure that this was the right thing to do, Edgar released his prisoner.

Cleo ran to Luther. He took her hand, pulled her close and glanced over her shoulder to snarl at Edgar. "Be careful where you point that gun. I'm not armed and neither is Cleo. Just...point it into the air or something. Even if I were to try something, and I won't, you'll still have the advantage."

Keeping one arm protectively around her, Luther reached down and hit the play button on the boom box. She recognized the way Eric played "Someone To Watch Over Me," the background noises of the club and her own too-loud, badly recorded voice.

"Turn it down!" Edgar shouted.

"What?" Luther gathered her close and began to dance, spinning around so his back was presented to Edgar. "I can't hear you."

"Turn around," she said. "Edgar won't shoot me but he very well might shoot you."

"That's not a chance I'm willing to take," he said.

They swayed gently, and Luther's arm drifted up her back. He glanced at his watch, hummed and leaned down to speak in her ear. "When I say 'now,' you hit the floor. Got it?"

"I didn't say you could talk to her!" Edgar shouted, moving closer.

"You shouldn't have come," Cleo hissed. "He's going to kill you!"

"Five, four, three..."

"That's enough dancing!" Edgar yelled.

"Now!"

Everything happened at once. She fell to the floor and Luther came with her, covering her body with his. The front door burst open, the lock breaking with an ear-splitting crack and the door banging against the wall as it flung inward. With the one eye that could see past Luther, she caught a glimpse of Michael Russell, bulletproof vest in place and weapon raised, rush in with a half-dozen uniformed officers behind him.

Edgar fired, the bullet from his poorly aimed weapon going high and wide to smack into the wall behind the advancing officers. When a separate contingent of officers came bursting through the back door, Edgar dropped his revolver and raised his hands above his head.

Luther came up off her slowly, his eyes remaining pinned to her face. The threat was over, and still it seemed he protected her with his body. He shielded her. Kept the rest of the world at bay, for a moment.

"Are you okay?"

Unable to speak, she simply nodded.

She turned her head to watch, as they led a handcuffed Edgar out the door. He glanced back at her, a sad longing in his eyes. He looked at her as if she had betrayed him.

"What will happen to him?" she asked, as Luther gently assisted her to her feet.

"He's going to jail for a very long time," Luther said as he drew her up against his side.

"He's sick," she whispered.

"I know."

She leaned into him, her knees shaking so hard she could not possibly stand on her own.

"Don't let them—hurt him." Her voice cracked, just a little. "It's not his fault. I must've—"

He grabbed her chin and forced her to look him in the eye. "Surely you don't blame yourself."

Tears filled her eyes. "He killed them for me. I must've done something to make him believe that I wanted them dead. Oh God, Luther, I didn't want it to be Edgar."

The place was overrun with uniformed cops and plain-clothes detectives. And still, Luther leaned down and gave her a quick, soft kiss. "I know, and I'm so sorry," he said. "But nothing about this is even remotely your fault. Edgar built his own fantasy world where he was king and you were his little princess. You can't hold yourself responsible for someone else's delusions."

"Edgar said he loved me, that he did what he did because—"

"No," Luther said angrily. "He was obsessed with you, and he took a little vacation from reality. That's not love."

"But..."

"I know that's not love, Cleo, because—"

"Hey, everybody in here okay?" Michael sauntered into the club with a crooked smile.

Cleo glared at Michael. What a time to interrupt! And

then she remembered what he'd done for her. She couldn't possibly stay mad. "Thank you," she said. "Great plan."

"The plan was all his," Michael said, nodding.

"How's Boone?" she asked, tightening her grip on Luther's jacket sleeve.

"He's awake, very unhappy and on his way to the hospital for observation."

"He'll be okay?"

Michael nodded. "Yeah. He's fine. What about you? We need a statement, but it can wait until you've had a chance to calm down, I guess. If you're not ready to be alone, we can get a female officer to drive you home and sit with you until you're feeling better."

"I need a ride," she said. "But I'll get Syd to come sit with me." She glanced at Luther. Had he been about to tell her that he loved her? The moment had passed. She might never know. "I guess you guys still have lots to do."

Luther nodded. "I'll drive you home first, though," he said.

"No." She shook her head. "You have work to do. I'll just… Anyone can drive me home."

Luther nodded, found an officer to do taxi duty, and put her in the car. The case was over, the bad guy was in custody, and she had no way of knowing if she would ever see Luther again.

"Thank you," she said, as he released her hand.

"Anytime." He gave her what might pass as a smile, and then closed the door. She looked back just once, and Luther was still there, standing on the sidewalk in front of her club and watching her ride away.

Edgar was in custody, and it hadn't taken much to get him to confess to killing Jack Tempest and Willie Lee Webb. Once he had no place to run, he seemed proud of his actions.

Luther sat back in a chair and stared at the empty stage. The club was empty. Silent. He didn't want to hang around the office any longer, he didn't want to go home; when he'd called Cleo's house, Syd had answered and told him Cleo had just gone to bed. After what she'd been through, she needed her sleep.

So he'd taken her keys and come here, and with half the lights on, he sat and went over every aspect of the case. He'd suspected Edgar and Eric all along, but like Cleo he hadn't wanted the killer to be one of her friends. She kept her circle of friends small. This was going to hurt for a long time, he knew.

But sooner or later he was going to have to tell her everything. Edgar might have said his love for Cleo was fatherly, but Luther had seen the man's home. A father figure didn't keep a shrine to his daughter: shoes, perfume, candles, a hundred or more pictures. Eventually his fatherly affection would have turned ugly, and he would have hurt Cleo, just as he'd hurt Tempest and Webb. Somehow Luther had to make her see that, so she could rest easy with the outcome. Edgar would never leave prison, and that was a right and just ending.

The case was over, but this thing with Cleo was not. At least, he hoped not. He loved her. Big whoop. Jack had loved her, and he'd done his best to ruin her life. He'd broken her heart and made her life hell. Men like Henry Copeland had said they loved her, sent her flowers and fell head over heels for the voice and the body and the face. But they didn't know the woman inside, they didn't care about what made her smile or laugh or sigh. Edgar had claimed he loved Cleo enough to kill for her, and he'd done just that.

So, if Luther showed up at Cleo's door and confessed that he loved her, would she slam the door in his face? Hell, maybe she should.

The key in the lock was loud, rattling through the cavernous, half-lit club. For a second Luther thought, *Cleo.* But of course, it wasn't her. She was home huddled beneath her quilt, warm and safe. Someone else was entering the club at well past midnight.

He wasn't surprised to see Eric come waltzing in. Of course the kid had his own keys. The piano player was surprised to see Luther, though. He all but jumped out of his skin.

"What are you doing here?" the kid asked as he recovered from the shock and locked the door behind him.

"What are *you* doing here?"

Eric headed for the stage. "Cleo's friend Syd called and said Cleo is going to close the club this week. I came by to collect some sheet music."

Luther nodded. Made perfect sense. "Have a seat."

Eric obviously didn't like the idea, but he did sit across from Luther and place his folded arms on the table. "So, what are you going to do? Arrest me for giving Edgar an alibi for the night Tempest was killed?"

"No," Luther said calmly. "He explained that. Said he convinced you that if you didn't have an alibi you'd be a suspect."

The kid, who seemed much more than eight years younger than Luther at the moment, blushed. "Yeah, well, I've never made a secret of the fact that I like Cleo."

"You like her," Luther repeated. Did the kid think himself in love?

"Very much."

Luther locked his eyes on the kid's baby blues. "Why?" he whispered.

The question confused Eric. "What do you mean, why?"

"I want to know what it is about Cleo that you…like so much."

Eric's nose actually twitched. "She's beautiful."

''Yep.''

''And she has perfect pitch.''

Luther shook his head. ''I don't even know what that means.'' Eric opened his mouth to explain, but Luther lifted a hand to silence him. ''And I don't care.''

''Well, it's extraordinary,'' Eric said.

''That's it?'' Luther said, when Eric went no further.

''She really *is* beautiful.''

Luther nodded. Eric was infatuated with Cleo, but the kid didn't love her. Not like Luther did. And yes, he had been fascinated by her beauty, in the beginning, but there was so much more. She had a lovable guard dog named Rambo, who wouldn't hurt a fly. She would give a friend the shirt off her back. She pushed hurt deep, where no one else could see it. But he had seen it. She had opened herself up to him and shown him her heart, and that made her his, in the way a hundred other little things made her his.

And he wanted that damn heart-shaped meat loaf.

He gave Eric a tight smile. ''You're going to have to find yourself another woman to moon after, kid.''

Eric muttered and shook his head. ''Yeah, I figured as much.''

Cleo padded toward the kitchen as the sun was coming up, but when she caught sight of Syd sleeping on the couch she changed directions. With a gentle hand, she shook Syd awake. ''What are you doing here? You should have gone home to sleep in your own bed.''

Syd came awake slowly. ''I couldn't leave you here alone.'' One eye opened, then the other. ''Are you okay?''

Cleo nodded.

''Sure?''

She sighed. ''Yeah. I'm still shocked that it was Edgar, but...I'll be all right.'' Rambo, frisky even at sunrise, bounded toward her. Cleo sat on the floor and gave the dog a big hug. "I guess I'm not a very good judge of character," she said. "I knew that years ago, when I found out what Jack was like, but...I was hoping my judgment had improved. I was completely fooled."

"Honey," Syd said huskily as she sat up. "He had everyone fooled, not just you."

Cleo nodded and buried her fingers in Rambo's fur. "He's not the only one I was wrong about," she said sadly. Something inside her wrenched painfully. "I kinda thought Malone might call last night, after—"

"Oh, he did!" Syd said brightly. "You had finally fallen asleep, and I didn't want to wake you. When I told him you'd gone to bed, he said not to disturb you. That you needed your sleep after what you'd been through."

In spite of her exhaustion, she wished she'd heard the phone ring, or that Syd had awakened her. She'd come awake more than once, in the night, wishing he was with her.

"I don't suppose he said...anything else?" *Tell Cleo I love her. I'll see her tomorrow. Tell her goodbye and good luck.*

"No."

Cleo nodded and rested her cheek on Rambo's head. Luther had said he'd fight for her, for them. Did he still want to? And if he didn't, did she have the strength to do the fighting herself?

Luther Malone didn't take chances, not ever. He expected the worst and usually got what he expected. So why was he doing this? He leaned on Cleo's doorbell for the second time. Where the hell was she? It was much too late for her still to be asleep, no matter how harrowing yesterday had been.

He knew she'd been able to sleep last night, since he'd talked to Syd. Tempted as he'd been to come here late, after he'd spoken to Eric, he'd decided to let Cleo rest. They had time. Lots of time. At least, he hoped they did.

Finally he heard her on the other side of the door. He knew she peered through the peephole, because he heard her laugh. There was a sleepy smile on her face when she opened the door. She wore that purple nightshirt with the cat on the front, her hair was wild, her cheeks were pink.

"I woke you up?" he asked. "It's almost noon!" Then he felt guilty. "I didn't mean to wake you."

"I was up at the crack of dawn," she explained, leaning against the doorjamb and looking him up and down. "Sent Syd home and went back to bed."

"Are you all right?" he asked solemnly.

She nodded. "Better. Yeah, I'm fine." She proved her statement to be true by giving him a wide smile. "Nice outfit. Joining the circus?"

He glanced down at the purple shirt and red tie. For a split second he thought he'd made a huge mistake. If she didn't understand… "I'm just trying to learn to color outside the lines."

Her gaze dropped to below his belt. "Hearts or six-shooters?"

"Hearts," he confessed.

Cleo hummed contentedly and nodded at the bag in his hand. "I almost hate to ask. What's in the bag?"

He held the plastic bag up and waved it before her. "Tim's bread pudding and lots of it. Since you said you'd walk over broken glass to get to a piece, I thought maybe you'd agree to talk to me for a couple of pans full."

"You're a rare man, Malone," she said. "I think you actually listened to everything I ever said to you."

"Every word."

Her smile faded. "Why are you here? Is this about Edgar?"

"No. This visit is strictly personal."

"What do you want?" she asked gently.

Here? On the porch? Hell, why not? "I've made a lot of mistakes in the past two weeks, one in particular that I'm not sure I'll ever be able to make amends for."

"Luther..."

"Let me finish. You said you couldn't forget, and I understand that. But you also said you could forgive me. I want that more than anything. And then I'd like to work on the forgetting part," he added.

He liked the expression on her face. It wasn't tough, it wasn't cynical. It was soft and wonderful.

"I'm taking a vacation next week," he continued.

"Florida," she said.

Luther nodded. "I want you to come with me."

"Why?"

He took a deep breath. Had he really thought she'd make this easy? "For one thing, my idea of the perfect vacation includes sun, sand and making love to you every night."

Cleo actually blushed. "Oh, it does? That sounds nice, but I'm sure there are women in Florida."

"I didn't say I wanted to make love to just anybody every night," he snapped. "I said *you.* No one else will do."

"I see," she said.

"Besides," he added with a sigh, "I want you to hold my hand when I make a stop in Georgia."

Her widening grin was fabulous. "Your grandmother?"

He nodded. "Yeah. And I want you there with me when I meet her. After all, you...gave her to me."

"I don't know," she said. "That's a family moment. You don't want—"

"I love you," he interrupted impatiently. "And I want you with me because that's the way it should be. If I have to dress like a clown every day and clean Tim's out of bread pudding to get that through your thick skull..."

Cleo reached out and grabbed his tie, tugging him gently forward. "Took you long enough, Malone," she said as she pulled him inside.

Luther kicked the door closed behind him, dropped the bag of bread pudding on the floor and pulled her close. She rose up on her toes, bringing her mouth to his.

"It's the truth," he said, whispering against her lips as he kissed her. "I do love you."

"I love you, too." She draped her arms around his neck and feathered her own small kisses on him.

He lifted her off her feet, and she wrapped her legs around his hips. "Maybe I should start my vacation now."

Cleo laid her head on his shoulder and sighed. "Sorry. There's no sand here, and no sun. Though we could turn all the lights on, and I have lots of candles."

"I think I could learn to live without the sand and the sun." He carried her toward the bedroom. "But there's no way I could ever learn to live without you."

"You won't ever need to."

Epilogue

Cleo lay back in the bed and stared at the faintly lit ceiling. The warm June air wafted through an open window bringing with it the scent of the ocean. The radio was on playing low, and she rested in Luther's arms where she so loved to be.

"On a honeymoon scale of one to ten, with one being a single, unsatisfying night at Flo and Mo's Dew Drop Inn and ten being two weeks of sex and sun in Hawaii, where would you rate ours, so far?"

"Fifteen," Luther answered without hesitation.

She smiled. "And it's just our first day."

She had never thought to be so happy. A new home awaited them, on their return to Huntsville. They'd picked the house out together, and it had everything she had ever dreamed of. A fenced backyard for Rambo, a large master bedroom with a walk-in closet and a deck, and three other smaller bedrooms she had great plans for. Syd had been a little perturbed about Cleo moving out of the duplex, but when she'd learned that Michael Russell was moving into Cleo's vacated half, she'd quickly offered forgiveness.

The wedding had been small but beautiful—a definite fifteen on the wedding scale—with Syd as maid of honor and Ray as best man, and Luther's grandmother, who had been delighted to discover the grandson she'd never known, in beaming attendance. Cleo's own family had been there, too, and even though her mother had been horrified at the notion of her daughter marrying a cop, Thea had been extremely supportive. Thea had also finally gotten wise and dumped Palmer, much to Mother's dismay.

Eric and Lizzy attended the wedding together and seemed quite chummy. They were a beautiful couple. Cleo sensed a great deal of potential there.

A notebook rested on the bedside table in their honeymoon suite, on Cleo's side. It contained scribbled notes that no one but she could decipher. She'd started writing songs again, happy songs. Maybe no one would ever see them but her, but that wasn't important. Her heart was open again. The songs were there.

"I brought you a present," Luther said, sitting up and reaching under the bed to grab a sloppily wrapped gift.

"You sneak!" she said, grinning as she shook the package.

"Open it."

She tore open the paper and opened the box, and drew out two scraps of black material. She screwed up her nose. "What is this?"

"It's a bikini."

"Luther Malone!" she said, trying to make sense of the bits of fabric. "I can't wear this!"

"My perfect honeymoon includes a beautiful woman in a bikini," he said, taking the top and showing her how it was supposed to go.

"But it's so...so *tiny*. Luther, I'd be horrified to wea this in public."

"I didn't say you were leaving the room in this thing,' Luther growled. "I didn't say I want anyone *else* to se you in it. It's just for me."

She laughed and threw her arms around his neck, just a a new song came on the radio. Since the movie had bee released, "Come Morning" got lots of airtime. Yo couldn't take a twenty-minute drive without hearing it! I had hurt, at first, but the more she loved Luther, the less i hurt.

And while Luther showed her how the bikini was sup posed to be worn, she sang along.

He arranged the sliver of fabric that was supposed to b the bikini bottom, his fingers brushing her skin familiarly

"Remember how you said you wanted kids right away?' she said, taking his hand in hers and laying his palm agains her belly.

He smiled. Oh, she did love his smile.

"I definitely remember."

"Well, I'd better wear this bikini now, because in a cou ple of months it's not going to fit."

"When?"

"February, I think. I haven't seen the doctor yet, but... think February."

"Maybe she'll be a Valentine's baby."

"She?" Cleo asked.

"Or he. I can't call our baby *it*, now, can I?"

"No."

Luther tossed the bikini aside and rolled her over, takin her face in his hands. "Do you know how much I lov you?"

She nodded, unable to speak without shedding an emo tional tear or two.

"You changed my life, Cleo Malone." He kissed her riefly, tenderly, his lips barely lingering.

"Loving you certainly changed mine," she said.

"On the happiness scale, you took me from a miserly ree to a really great fifteen," he teased.

She smiled. "I wonder what a twenty is like?"

"Let's find out."

* * * * *

The Sinclair boys will return!
But first look for Linda's next
emotional, romantic and wonderful
storytelling in April.

SECRET AGENT SHEIKH

is part of the Intimate Moments special
ROMANCING THE CROWN
You won't want to miss it!

HARLEQUIN MOTHER'S DAY CONTEST 2216
OFFICIAL RULES
NO PURCHASE NECESSARY TO ENTER

Two ways to enter:

• **Via The Internet:** Log on to the Harlequin romance website (www.eHarlequin.com) anytime beginning 12:01 a.m. E.S.T., January 1, 200 through 11:59 p.m. E.S.T., April 1, 2002 and follow the directions displayed on-line to enter your name, address (including zip code), e-mail address and in 100 words or fewer, describe how your mother helped with the romance in your life.

• **Via Mail:** Handprint (or type) on an 8 1/2" x 11" plain piece of paper, your name, address (including zip code) and e-mail address (if you one), and in 100 words or fewer, describe how your mother helped with the romance in your life. Mail your entry via first-class mail to: Harle Mother's Day Contest 2216, (in the U.S.) P.O. Box 9076, Buffalo, NY 14269-9076; (in Canada) P.O. Box 637, Fort Erie, Ontario, Canada L2A

For eligibility, entries must be submitted either through a completed Internet transmission or postmarked no later than 11:59 p.m. E.S.T., April 1, (mail-in entries must be received by April 9, 2002). Limit one entry per person, household address and e-mail address. On-line and/or mailed entries received from persons residing in geographic areas in which entry is not permissible will be disqualified.

Entries will be judged by a panel of judges, consisting of members of the Harlequin editorial, marketing and public relations staff using the following cri
- Originality - 50%
- Emotional Appeal - 25%
- Sincerity - 25%

In the event of a tie, duplicate prizes will be awarded. Decisions of the judges are final.

Prize: A 6-night/7-day stay for two at the Inter-Continental San Juan Resort & Casino, including round-trip coach air transportation from gatew airport nearest winner's home (approximate retail value: $4,000). Prize includes breakfast daily and a mother and daughter day of beauty at beachfront hotel's spa. Prize consists of only those items listed as part of the prize. Prize is valued in U.S. currency.

All entries become the property of Torstar Corp. and will not be returned. No responsibility is assumed for lost, late, illegible, incomplete, inaccu non-delivered or misdirected mail or misdirected e-mail, for technical, hardware or software failures of any kind, lost or unavailable network connections, or failed, incomplete, garbled or delayed computer transmission or any human error which may occur in the receipt or processing entries in this Contest.

Contest open only to residents of the U.S. (except Colorado) and Canada, who are 18 years of age or older and is void wherever prohibited b all applicable laws and regulations apply. Any litigation within the Province of Quebec respecting the conduct or organization of a publicity cont may be submitted to the Régie des alcools, des courses et des jeux for a ruling. Any litigation respecting the awarding of a prize may be submi to the Régie des alcools, des courses et des jeux only for the purpose of helping the parties reach a settlement. Employees and immediate fam members of Torstar Corp. and D.L. Blair, Inc., their affiliates, subsidiaries and all other agencies, entities and persons connected with the use, marketing or conduct of this Contest are not eligible to enter. Taxes on prize are the sole responsibility of winner. Acceptance of any prize offer constitutes permission to use winner's name, photograph or other likeness for the purposes of advertising, trade and promotion on behalf of To Corp., its affiliates and subsidiaries without further compensation to the winner, unless prohibited by law.

Winner will be determined no later than April 15, 2002 and be notified by mail. Winner will be required to sign and return an Affidavit of Eligi form within 15 days after winner notification. Non-compliance within that time period may result in disqualification and an alternate winner m selected. Winner of trip must execute a Release of Liability prior to ticketing and must possess required travel documents (e.g. Passport, photo where applicable. Travel must be completed within 12 months of selection and is subject to traveling companion completing and returning a Re of Liability prior to travel; and hotel and flight accommodations availability. Certain restrictions and blackout dates may apply. No substitution o permitted by winner. Torstar Corp. and D.L. Blair, Inc., their parents, affiliates, and subsidiaries are not responsible for errors in printing or elect presentation of Contest, or entries. In the event of printing or other errors which may result in unintended prize values or duplication of prizes, affected entries shall be null and void. If for any reason the Internet portion of the Contest is not capable of running as planned, including infec by computer virus, bugs, tampering, unauthorized intervention, fraud, technical failures, or any other causes beyond the control of Torstar Corp. which corrupt or affect the administration, secrecy, fairness, integrity or proper conduct of the Contest, Torstar Corp. reserves the right, at its sol discretion, to disqualify any individual who tampers with the entry process and to cancel, terminate, modify or suspend the Contest or the Inter portion thereof. In the event the Internet portion must be terminated a notice will be posted on the website and all entries received prior to termination will be judged in accordance with these rules. In the event of a dispute regarding an on-line entry, the entry will be deemed submit by the authorized holder of the e-mail account submitted at the time of entry. Authorized account holder is defined as the natural person who is assigned to an e-mail address by an Internet access provider, on-line service provider or other organization that is responsible for arranging e-m address for the domain associated with the submitted e-mail address. Torstar Corp. and/or D.L. Blair Inc. assumes no responsibility for any com injury or damage related to or resulting from accessing and/or downloading any sweepstakes material. Rules are subject to any requirements/ limitations imposed by the FCC. **Purchase or acceptance of a product offer does not improve your chances of winning.**

For winner's name (available after May 1, 2002), send a self-addressed, stamped envelope to: Harlequin Mother's Day Contest Winners 2216 P.O. Box 4200 Blair, NE 68009-4200 or you may access the www.eHarlequin.com Web site through June 3, 2002.

Contest sponsored by Torstar Corp., P.O. Box 9042, Buffalo, NY 14269-9042.

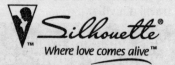